THE
FORGOTTEN
MEMORIES
OF
VERA
GLASS

THE
FORGOTTEN
MEMORIES
OF
VERA
GLASS

ANNA PRIEMAZA

AMULET BOOKS • NEW YORK

Cataloging-in-Publication Data has been applied for and may be obtained from the Library of Congress.

ISBN 978-1-4197-5259-9

Text copyright © 2021 Anna Priemaza
Book design by Hana Anouk Nakamura

Printed and bound in U.S.A.
10 9 8 7 6 5 4 3 2 1

Amulet Books are available at special discounts when purchased in quantity for premiums and promotions as well as fundraising or educational use. Special editions can also be created to specification. For details, contact specialsales@abramsbooks.com or the address below.

Amulet Books® is a registered trademark of Harry N. Abrams, Inc.

ABRAMS The Art of Books
195 Broadway, New York, NY 10007
abramsbooks.com

To Katelyn Larson.
And to Laura Geddes.
Without you, the emptiness in my heart
would weigh more than a thousand stars.

CHAPTER ONE

Sometimes I wonder how much better life would be without siblings. Well, maybe not better, but certainly quieter.

All four of us are in the dining room after school, plus Riven—who isn't my sibling, but who comes home with me after school so often that she might as well be.

"And so I told him that obviously the day structure in the creation story in the Bible is metaphorical because God didn't even make the sun until the fourth day, so how could days like we understand them now even exist before that, so believing in the Bible doesn't mean you can't also believe in the big bang theory and evolution and all that good stuff," says Al, who is standing at the head of the table, relating an argument he got in with his biology teacher.

"Just one game. Pwease," Isaac begs Riven as he climbs into her lap and reaches for her phone.

Around us all skips Gertie, who is singing some song about ghosts and pumpkins that ends each verse with an ear-splitting "Boo!"

As a particularly loud "Boo!" reverberates right in my ear and I stare down at my nowhere-near-done math homework, I wish for one brief moment that I was an only child. I wish the quiet house Riven and I walked into before Al got home with Gertie and Isaac—it was his turn to pick them up after school—could have stayed quiet for hours, and we could have gotten lost in our books, the ticking of the kitchen clock and the steady rhythm of our breathing the only noise.

But then Gertie skips over and throws her arms around me in a hug, and Al suggests we surprise Mom and Dad by making pasta for supper, and Riven compromises with Isaac by taking silly selfies of the two of them, and I swear that Isaac's giggles could cure cancer. And all my wishing flies out the window.

Riven offers to watch Gertie and Isaac while Al and I make pasta, so as she chases them around pretending to be an evil mutant rabbit from their favorite video game, *Legends of the Stone,* Al grabs two jars from the pantry and holds them up. "Alfredo or marinara?"

I choose marinara, since in my opinion it goes better with the zucchini, mushrooms, and peppers we're planning to chop up. From the dining room comes the sound of Gertie's and Isaac's giggles and screeches and Riven's roars.

I grab the zucchini and peppers—organic, of course—from the fridge, but before setting them down, I duck my head into the dining room. It's dark in there; Riven's flicked off the light to enhance the pseudo-scary atmosphere. "Hey, Riven," I say, "you're on the island, and you come across Bob and Fred. Bob says, 'We're both knaves.' Who's what?"

Riven stops chasing Gertie and Isaac around like a monster for a moment and throws her hand toward the ceiling to send all four bulbs of the rectangular, hanging light fixture to life. She looks at me in the now-illuminated room. "That's it? That's all I get for clues? Only one of them says something?"

Riven is used to me tossing these questions at her. I love logic problems, especially the knights and knaves problems. In them, you're on an island filled with knaves, who can only lie, and knights, who can only tell the truth. You come across groups of people, and based on what they say, you have to figure out who's a knight and/ or who's a knave. I love problems that rely only on logic and deduction to solve them.

"Bob's a knave and Fred's a knight!" Al calls from the kitchen behind me.

"Hey!" Riven calls back. "You didn't give me time to answer!"

"You want another one?" I ask her.

"Oh no. I'm much too busy being a monster to think about things like knights and knaves." She makes her fingers into claws and lunges at Gertie and Isaac, who squeal and dive under the table. Rather than chase after them, though, Riven pauses like she's still trying to think through the problem.

"If Bob was a knight, he'd say so," I explain. "Which means he has to be a knave. Which means the 'both' part of his statement has to be a lie. Which means—"

"That Fred's a knight. Yeah, yeah, I got it." She scrunches up her nose at me, grins, and says, "Hey, can you flick the lights back off on your way out?" Then she roars like a dinosaur and dives under the table.

I shake my head and return to the kitchen, flicking the light switch on the way and undoing Riven's small burst of magic. Riven thinks that the sort of one-way-ness of magic makes her light aptitude a pain in the butt, but I'd much rather have that than my mostly useless unlocking aptitude. (Useless unless you want to be a criminal, that is, which isn't exactly my life goal.)

Al has started chopping the mushrooms, so I pull out a second cutting board and settle in beside him, slicing open the peppers and putting the stems and innards in our compost bucket.

"How was your day?" Al asks as we chop. "How's your new science partner?" Al and I fight a lot—usually over whose turn it is to use the laptop we share—but we talk a lot, too. And my favorite thing about my big brother is that he always remembers the things that I tell him. He genuinely listens.

"She seems all right. Quiet. But she does what I tell her to. We got an A on our first lab assignment."

"That's a relief," Al says. We both know the fear of group projects, of slacker partners who threaten to bring down our straight-A averages, turning us into the underachievers of our family. Mom and Dad would understand if our grades dipped, of course; Al and I are harder on ourselves than they are. "Hey, I need the laptop later," he adds. "For a history project."

"No way! Al! I've been telling you all week that I need it tonight to write up my English paper! You can't—" I break off as I notice Al's grin. "You jerkface! Don't joke about things like that!"

"Sorry, Vera," Al says, though the smirk on his face says he's not actually sorry at all.

"You're such a jerk sometimes," I say, shaking my head. And then we go back to chopping vegetables.

Once the veggies are in the frying pan, Al asks, "Hey, can you keep a secret?"

"Of course."

He twists his hands together. "I'm . . . dating Cecily."

"Cecily Murphy?!"

A crook of a smile slips onto his face as if he's trying to hold it back but can't. He nods.

Cecily's in tenth grade with me, though that's not the shocking part, since Al's only a year older than me. "Mom and Dad are going to find out, you know."

His eyebrows furrow. "You swore—"

"Not from me! You're just not exactly invisible at school." Al's the kind of guy that everyone likes and everyone knows. "There's probably a dozen girls jealous of Cecily already."

Al's pale cheeks flush pink as he pushes around the veggies in the pan with a wooden spoon. "No way."

I raise a single eyebrow at him. "Well, you keep telling yourself that. Just know that one way or another it's going to get back to Mom and Dad that you're dating a girl who thinks she's a witch."

"She doesn't think she's a witch."

"They call themselves the Witches."

"It's facetious!"

I could say more. I could remind him that while some people call the single aptitude everyone has "magic," like my unlocking magic or Al's heat magic or Riven's light magic, all magic is explainable by science—or at least it will be once science expands far enough. Anyone who thinks magic is mystical is silly. I could remind him that there's only one God, and anyone who thinks magic comes from spirits or gods or dead souls is blaspheming. I could tell him she's not good enough for him.

Instead, I say, "Are you happy?"

The smile that's been flirting with his face blooms in full. "Very."

"Then I'm happy for you." I knock his shoulder with mine. "Congratulations, Einstein," I say, after his namesake.

He knocks my shoulder back. "Thanks, Rubin," he says, after mine.

When Mom and Dad get home, we're just pouring the finished spaghetti into a strainer. Abandoning Al, I pop into the hallway where they're taking off their coats and shoes. Mom leans against Dad's shoulder to steady herself as she pulls off her flats. "Good shoes mean happy feet means a happy body means a happy mind," she's told me numerous times.

They're both white with brown hair, but Mom's hair is big and messy, even when it's up in a bun, while Dad's is shaved as neatly as his goatee. Mom is short—shorter than both me and Al, who clearly got Dad's genes in that department—coming to just above Dad's shoulder. But that doesn't stop her from standing on her tip-toes, tugging his tie so he comes down to meet her, and kissing him right on the lips.

"Ew, gross!" I say loudly, though I don't truly mind. My parents have the type of relationship I can only hope for someday. I've never heard them yell at each other, and the only thing they fight about is science—and then it's less fighting, and more spirited, respectful debate.

Mom and Dad break apart, and Mom grins at me. She strides down the hallway in her stockinged feet and wraps me in a bear hug. "How's my favorite eldest daughter?" she asks. And then Dad's arms are around me, too, and as they smother me, I want to roll my eyes at how corny my parents are, but at the same time, it just feels happy and warm and nice.

As we start to pull away, a wail erupts from the living room and accompanies the Gertie-shaped blur that races into the hall and attaches itself to Mom's legs.

Riven appears in the doorway a moment later. "I don't know what happened. She was playing happily, and then suddenly she was crying."

Mom kneels down to comfort Gertie, whose sobs have quieted a little but who keeps glancing toward the kitchen in a way that makes my stomach inexplicably twist in knots.

"I made dinner. Pasta," I say, trying to ignore the tightness in my gut.

"You did?" Dad looks away from Gertie to me. "All by yourself?" I haven't been known to be the most capable cook in the past.

"No, I—" I break off as I turn back to the kitchen Gertie is still staring at. The empty kitchen.

Obviously it's an empty kitchen. I've been in there by myself making dinner for the past forty-five minutes, while Riven was watching Isaac and Gertie in the living room. Still, something about its quiet stillness doesn't feel right. Perhaps it's just the way the hall is shadowy with darkness before giving way to the kitchen light.

As if she's telepathic, Riven throws up her arm and magics on the hallway light.

When I turn back to Mom and Dad, Mom's grin is gone, and she's staring past me into the kitchen, mouth hanging open like she's seen a ghost. Dad looks unsettled, too, though he gives his head a bit of a shake and says, "That must be why you wanted to stop and get that fresh french bread, huh, Valerie?"

Mom has intuition magic, and she's always sensing when we need something.

"Hmm?" Mom is still staring into the kitchen behind me,

though her eyes are glazed, like she's not seeing anything in particular. Part of me wants to turn around and look again, but another part of me is afraid of what I won't see. Which makes no sense at all.

Gertie, at least, has given up staring and has buried her face in Mom's sweater.

Before I can think about it any further, though, Dad turns to Riven and says, "You're staying for dinner, I assume?"

Mom at last tears her gaze away from the kitchen and smiles gently at Riven. "Obviously she's staying, Frank. She has to try out Vera's cooking!"

Riven smiles back. "Thanks, Mr. Frank. Ms. Valerie." When we first became friends, Riven used to call my parents Mr. Phillips and Ms. Glass, using their last names, but then Dad told her to call him Frank, and she couldn't quite bring herself to do it, so Mr. Frank and Ms. Valerie were born. The names have confused more than one stranger who—despite Riven's golden, stick-straight hair and rounder face than the rest of us—thought she was a member of the family.

A short while later, we're all sitting around the table, a big bowl of pasta in the middle, the veggie-laden sauce in a big bowl beside it. And on the other side, the fresh french bread Mom's intuition magic told her to pick up on the way home.

"This looks delicious, Vera," Mom says.

"It really does. Thank you, Vera," Dad agrees, thanking me and me alone.

And I'm struck with a deep-in-my-gut feeling of having lost something. Of having lost someone.

But I look around the table, and we're all here: Mom, Dad, Isaac, Gertie, me, and Riven.

So I bow my head for grace like everyone else—even Riven, who's an atheist but who respects our family's traditions even if she doesn't believe in them.

"Vera, would you say grace, please?" Dad asks.

And I jerk my head up, because that's not right, either.

I'm not . . . it's not . . .

Mom must sense it, too, because her head has snapped up as well. "Frank," she says, "it's not Vera's job." There's a tenseness in her voice that I've never heard directed at my dad before.

"It *is* Vera's job," Dad says, and there's a tightness in his voice, too.

From her place across from me at the table, Riven raises her eyebrows. She's told me before that she thinks it's cute but creepy how well my parents get along, but apparently she's not a fan of when they're not getting along, either.

"Vera's the eldest," Dad continues. "She always says grace." He says this like it's obvious, and of course it's obvious. Of course I'm supposed to say grace. Dad always asks me. That's the way it's always been. Because I'm the eldest. I look around the table again. Mom. Dad. Isaac. Gertie. Me. Riven.

"It's fine, Mom," I say, before she can come up with some other weird protestation.

And I bury my feeling of loss so deep that it goes right down to my toes. Then I bow my head and say grace.

CHAPTER TWO

I can't find Gertie.

Mom and Dad have to leave early each morning for their research job at the Aptitude Research Institute, so after they get Isaac and Gertie up and ready and then rush out the door, it's my job to take my siblings to school.

Usually, Gertie has been standing patiently by the door with her coat and backpack on for a good five minutes by the time Isaac and I get our acts together and join her, but today she's not there. She's not in the basement, the living room, the kitchen, or her bedroom, either.

"Where's Gerts?" I ask Isaac. I've at least managed to get him bundled up and ready for the day care program we just call "school."

"In the woom," he says, pointing upstairs.

"The ... empty room?" An unexpected knot in my gut has me vaulting up the stairs two at a time and down the hallway to shove open the door of the bedroom across from my own. "Gertie?!"

Gertie looks up at me from where she sits cross-legged on the floor in the middle of the dark, shadowy room. The room is mostly empty aside from a few boxes piled in the corners, filled with clothes we've outgrown or things that never ended up getting unpacked when we moved in over a decade ago. I don't know why we've never turned this room into anything else. It would make a nice playroom, or a library—though just the thought of using it as anything other than this empty room makes the tangle in my stomach pull tighter.

For a moment, I expect the light to flick on of its own accord, but then I remember that Riven's not here right now to read my mind. "You're an awfully creepy six-year-old, sometimes," I tell my sister as I feel around for the light switch. "Come on, we've got to go. We're going to be late."

After I steer her out of the room, though, I stand in the doorway for a minute longer, breathing in the stale emptiness of a room that, for reasons I can't explain, feels like it has a matching space in my heart.

▲ ▲ ▲ ▲ ▲ ▲ ▲ ▲ ▲ ▲ ▲ ▲ ▲

Despite the delay, I still make it to school with a bit of time before the first bell. I use my unlocking aptitude to pop open my locker, as usual, just to feel like my power's got a use beyond criminal activity and those too-frequent times I lose my house keys. Then I toss my jacket in my locker and head to Riven's. The Davis twins are already there. They're identical twins, and with their matching buzz cuts, broad shoulders, and same uneven way of standing with their weight on their right foot, they're tough to tell apart—until they open their mouths. Or rather, until Pete opens his mouth and Simon doesn't.

"So it's settled," Pete is saying, as if to prove my point, "the two of us will marry the two of you." As I stride up, he looks at me and grins. "I'll marry Vera, and Simon can marry Riven."

Simon stares down at his feet, clearly embarrassed. He won't admit it, but he's definitely had a crush on Riven for as long as I can remember. I know Pete and Simon's parents wouldn't care if Simon dated a white girl; if he tried dating a non-Christian, though, their mom would ground him for life. The three of us—Pete and Simon and I—met at church and became friends through our youth group in junior high.

"Riven, are you selling our friend off into the mail-order bride industry again? I've told you a thousand times it's not a good idea." Bolu throws her arm around my shoulder as she joins our circle, her beautiful micro braids swaying as she does. Her flawless skin is so smooth and perfect that I'd think she had some sort of anti-zit magic if I didn't know otherwise.

"What, are you jealous?" Pete jokes. "You don't have to be. I'll marry you both. We'll have one of those poly families."

"That's illegal," Riven points out, though lawbreaking doesn't always stop her. She once convinced me to unlock the back door of the school late at night so she could trespass inside to retrieve the *Doctor Who* shirt she'd forgotten in her locker and desperately needed to wear even though she's got about five others. I made her throw on the outdoor light, so I at least didn't have to sit alone in darkness while I waited for her to re-emerge from the shadowy building.

"Oh, that sounds fun, though," Bolu says. "Let's forget about marriage and just buy a big old farmhouse in the country where we can all live together and raise goats and chickens and sell organic vegetables on the roadside." She puts her other arm around Riven's shoulders and holds tightly to both of us, like she's locking us into this fun, little family cult dream of a future. Bolu is the newest member of our friend group—her family moved to Canada from Nigeria when she was five, but they only moved to Edmonton this past year, when her dad took a position as a surgeon at the university hospital—but somehow she's almost more invested in our group than the rest of us.

"Why are we talking about getting married, anyway?" I ask.

"Because dating is garbage," Pete says.

"Hear, hear!" Bolu releases my shoulders and raises an imaginary champagne flute in her dainty fingers—rather than the imaginary pint I would have gone for. Bolu has more class than the rest of us combined.

Pete's face grows serious. "Annika shot me down," he says, referring to a girl in our youth group who goes to a different school. He says it casually, but his whole face droops, like he's just pulled off a mask we didn't know he was wearing. Like admitting it has made it real all over again.

"Oh, Petey, I'm sorry," I say. I know he's been crushing on her for a while.

Simon puts his hand on Pete's shoulder. "You're too good for her anyways," he says. Which makes Pete's sagging shoulders straighten just a little. When Simon does speak, his words feel like truth.

"And Bolu and I will marry you after all," I add. "Won't we, Bolu?"

"Most definitely."

With that, the first bell rings, which means we've only got five minutes to get to class.

The boys head off down the hall, and we're about to follow when Bolu turns to me. "Oh, Vera, here." She pulls a calculator out of her pocket and holds it out to me.

"What's this for?" I ask.

She shrugs. "Just thought you might need it."

"I don't—" I start, but then stop. I slide off my backpack and reach my hand into the front pocket, feeling nothing but air. "Crap!" An image comes flooding back to me of my calculator sitting on my desk, where I took it out to do homework and never put it back. I have a small tendency to forget things like that.

I take the calculator from Bolu. "Thanks, friend."

"The universe is looking out for you," Riven says.

"Or God is," I say, and Riven crinkles her nose at that, even though we basically both said the same thing. Riven loves to talk like there's a higher power; she just refuses to call it God.

"Or my magic is looking out for you," Bolu points out.

"A good point," I say.

"Dude, if I had a dollar for every time intuition magic saved your butt, I'd be rich," Riven says, laughing. Bolu, like my mom, has intuition magic.

"If you start making money off my forgetfulness, you'd better share it with me!"

"Obviously," says Riven. Then she turns to Bolu and mock whispers, "Fortunately, she'll forget this conversation."

"Hey!" I say, but I laugh. Then I loop my arms through Riven's and Bolu's, and we head off after the guys.

I love my friends. I don't know what I'd do without them.

There's a pop quiz in my math class first period, but thanks to Bolu's calculator and the fact that I've never once missed doing my math homework, I breeze through it.

Second period, I have science, so I say goodbye to Riven, who's in my math class, and head down the hall to the science lab. The second bell hasn't rung yet, so people are still milling around. A couple of guys goof around by the door, while in the front row, two girls have squashed their stools so close together they're practically sitting in each other's laps. If Ms. Larson wasn't here already, they'd probably be making out.

At the back of the room, three girls—two white, one Asian— hover together. The Witches. Cecily and Hayden and Rachel. They always wear flowing skirts and dresses in pinks and purples and pastel greens and blues, with glittery eye shadow and streaks of color in their hair. Turquoise in Cecily's auburn hair, purple in Hayden's wavy brown hair, blue in Rachel's rounded black bob.

They've been calling themselves the Witches since we studied Macbeth in eighth grade, though as Pete says, with their obsession with pastel colors, they should really wear wings and call themselves the Faeries. Someone should talk to them about their branding.

As I reach my seat near the front, Cecily looks up, our eyes meet, and a chill runs down my spine. I don't know why. Cecily and

I have nothing to do with each other. But looking at her stirs some deep sadness in the pit of my stomach that feels like it's reflected in her own green eyes. If I didn't think it was garbage, I'd think she was performing some witchcraft or faerie magic right now.

"You're staring," says a voice to my right. I break my gaze from Cecily's and turn to see Sarah, my lab partner, sitting on her bench stool in jeans and a knit sweater. She's white with reddish-brown hair almost to her shoulders, freckles dotted across her nose, and braces.

I look back at the Witches, but Cecily's turned to her friends. No more piercing green eyes staring at me. Still, the feeling in my stomach lingers.

"Are you okay?" Sarah asks.

"Hmm? Yeah. I'm fine." If thinking one of my classmates might actually be performing witchcraft is fine. I turn back to Sarah just as the second bell rings. Ms. Larson hands a pile of lab instructions to the first row, and they pass it back. I settle ours on the table between us and start reading through it, then pass it to Sarah, who reads it as I start getting out supplies.

None of my friends are in this class, which is how I ended up with Sarah as a partner. Sarah and I went to different junior highs, which in our area go up through ninth grade. So tenth grade is the first year we're in school together, and all I know about her is her name and that she likes knit sweaters. Which is fine with me. I don't need a bestie as a partner; I just need someone competent.

We work mostly in silence, which I like, but Sarah must find it awkward, because after a while she says, "I like your name. Vera. So much better than Sarah."

"Oh, thank you. My siblings and I were all named after

scientists. Isaac after Isaac Newton, Gertie after Gertrude B. Elion, me after Vera Rubin, and . . ." I trail off as I twirl one of my curls around my finger. "No, that's it. Just three of us." For some reason, I find myself glancing over my shoulder at Cecily again. She's bowed over the lab table, looking back and forth between the assignment sheet and the measuring cup she's holding.

"Are you mad at the Witches or something?" Sarah asks.

"What?" I turn back around in my seat. "Oh . . . no. I just . . ." I trail off again. I have no idea how to finish that sentence, because I have no idea why I keep looking at them, at Cecily. I shrug.

"Your name is nice, too, by the way," I say before she can ask any more questions.

It's her turn to shrug. "It's so plain. I'd rather be a Penelope or an Anastasia." As soon as she says it, her cheeks flush red, as if she's accidentally divulged a secret.

"Well, I think Sarah is nice," I say. And since apparently neither of us has anything further to say on the topic, for the rest of class we don't talk about anything except our assignment. And I don't look at Cecily again.

Dinner at our house is always full of constant interruptions and questions and random singing until Mom or Dad finally releases Isaac and Gertie to go play in the living room so the rest of us can finish our meal in relative silence.

Tonight is no different, with the added drama that Isaac spills his water all over the table, causing all of us to jump up and grab for towels.

"Oops," he says in his adorable little four-year-old voice that makes him near impossible to be mad at. "Sowwy." His regret seeps into the table around his fingers in various shades of blue. We still haven't been able to figure out what Gertie's aptitude is, but Isaac's has been obvious since he was a baby, with colors trailing him everywhere. Color magic. The colors aren't permanent, just temporary. But we've all gone to work or school with Isaac's handprints in places we didn't notice.

Dad sighs. "It's okay, buddy. Are you and Gertie done eating? Why don't you go play?"

Once my siblings disappear and the water has been mopped up, the table feels extra quiet with just the three of us. It's like the silence has its own place at the table.

Dad helps himself to another scoop of tuna casserole, while Mom appears to be just pushing hers around and around her plate, not actually eating any.

"How was your day?" I ask Mom.

When she looks up, it takes a moment for her eyes to focus on me. "Um, I guess it was good. We're getting into some really interesting research—can't talk about it, obviously."

It's my turn to sigh. Mom and Dad work for the ARI—the Aptitude Research Institute—and their logo is all over our house. On mugs, on papers, on their clothes. Dad's even wearing a golf shirt now with ARI in white stitching above his heart. And yet, this is their answer pretty much any time I ask about their job. *It's interesting. It's fascinating. Exciting things are happening. No, we can't talk about it.*

They can't talk about anything until it's been published publicly in a research paper.

"But I'm your kid," I say now, not for the first time. "You can trust me."

Mom gives me a tired but stern look. "Vera, our confidentiality contracts don't say, 'you can't tell anyone—except for your kids.'"

"Well, they should!"

"Next time our contracts come up for renewal, we'll try to negotiate that in there," Dad says. It's a joke, but neither Mom nor I laugh.

Mom goes back to pushing her casserole around on her plate. I scowl at Dad.

The silence takes its seat at the table again.

This is not what a normal family dinner is like. Normally, Mom peppers me with questions about my day. Dad rambles about newly published scientific findings, and Mom jumps in to correct him so many times that it has us all laughing.

"Oh, Lewis's paper about the light aptitude just came out, though," Dad says now, as if he's just remembered his dinnertime role. "Not exactly new findings, but they confirmed that—" And then he devolves into some scientific explanation about electricity and light waves and other things that go over my head. Mom doesn't jump in to correct him at all, but at least she looks up and nods along with what he's saying.

I stab a bit of tuna with my fork. At school, I feel like I know what I'm talking about most of the time; around my parents, I feel like I know nothing.

I remind myself that Dad has a master's and Mom has a PhD as I chew my casserole and try to follow along.

"And that's why they used to call it lightning magic," Dad finishes.

"That's really interesting, Dad," I say, and I'm not lying, not really. I did catch most of the end of the story, about how it should really be called electricity magic, not light magic, and how light bulbs just give the electricity somewhere to go. But I know that story already. We learn it in school—how the first light bulb inventors probably had light magic and were looking for a place to put the electricity that tingled their fingertips.

"Why don't people use it for other things, then?" I ask now. "Like heating houses or running a blow-dryer and stuff?"

"Well, I've only recently gotten into studying light aptitudes," Dad says, "but my understanding is it's hard to direct and control. Light bulbs are the perfect vessel."

I remind myself to ask Riven later if she can make a blow-dryer run. I've only ever seen her use her magic for light.

I wonder if my magic could do anything more useful than unlocking lockers and doors. I don't bother asking, though. Mom and Dad don't like to talk about unlocking magic, and since Mom seems to be in A Mood, I don't want to push it. Once, years ago, I joked that I was going to become a thief when I grew up, and Dad immediately pounced down my throat and told me that I shouldn't joke about things like that.

Since then, he and Mom have told me numerous times that I should never risk using my unlocking magic on things belonging to others. I've gotten the impression that Dad was falsely accused of something at some point while he was in school and that maybe that's why he didn't go on to do his PhD like Mom did, but they've never told me the details.

Under the table, I clench my hands into fists. Riven gets

electricity thrumming in her fingertips. I get magic that could make me an instant suspect in any local, unexplained break-in.

At least I've got access to light magic whenever Riven is around—which is most of the time.

"Oh, did you hear that the Russian government finally agreed to a payout to the family of that young boy . . . what was his name?" Dad asks.

Mom sits up at that. "Tomas Ivanovich Petrov. That poor boy."

Tomas was all over the news a while ago. At only eight years old, he had been seized from his family and taken in for testing, all because of his aptitude. There are only seventy-two known aptitudes, all divided into categories—from mental aptitudes, like Mom's intuition magic or perfect memory recall, to sensory aptitudes, like the ability to enhance smells or sounds. But Tomas had been born with a mutation that gave him a previously unknown aptitude. It's not entirely clear what that aptitude was, but the most common rumor is that it was the ability to make water out of nothing.

I say *was*, not *is*, because the testing they did on him eventually killed him.

"I just don't get what they were hoping to accomplish with the testing in the first place," I say.

Mom shakes her head. "No one knows for sure, but I suspect they were trying to figure out how to accomplish gene manipulation. Imagine if you had the ability to create any aptitude you wanted—even ones that don't even exist yet—in a fetus."

"Do you think that's possible?"

Mom shrugs. "So many more things are possible than we currently understand."

"Are you guys doing things like that at the ARI?"

Dad clears his throat. "Confidentiality, Vera. You know we can't talk about anything we're doing."

I sigh. "Well, I just want to put it out there: If you guys invent the ability to fly, I hereby volunteer myself as a guinea pig."

They both laugh at that, clearing the solemnity from the air. If there's nothing else positive about this family dinner, at least I made Mom smile.

CHAPTER THREE

"We have got to get serious about what we're doing for Halloween," Riven says as she slips onto the cafeteria table bench across from me and between Simon and Bolu.

"I thought we were doing the food drive thing again," I say. Last year, Mom deemed us too old for trick-or-treating and signed us up for a food drive. We're supposed to dress up and go door-to-door collecting canned goods instead of candy—though lots of people still offer candy anyway, and like Riven says, "If the universe offers us candy, we're not going to refuse!"

"I meant for our costumes!" Riven says as she snags a baby carrot from my small Tupperware container. "Halloween's only three-and-a-bit weeks away. We're running out of time!"

"Right." Ever since we became friends in fourth grade, Riven and I have coordinated our costumes. Or perhaps I should say, Riven has coordinated our costumes and I've worn whatever she's told me to. We've been Disney princesses, M&M's, Anne and

Diana from *Anne of Green Gables*, and chocolate bars. In eighth grade, the boys joined us, and we were characters from *The Adventure Zone* one year and an earthbender, firebender, airbender, and waterbender the next.

Pete slides into the seat beside me. "We could each just do our own thing this year."

Bolu and Simon both stare abruptly at him, aghast.

"What? No!" Bolu cries, sounding a little more desperate than she probably intends. "We have to do a group costume!"

When we first met, I asked her what she dressed up as for Halloween last year, and she scoffed and said she'd stopped dressing up a year or two ago. But I think that was before she saw our annual group Halloween photos all framed and lined up in a row at Riven's house.

"She's right," Simon says. "It's tradition." Then he returns to the book he'd been reading.

"You and your traditions," Pete says, and I'm not sure whether he's talking to Simon or Bolu. Either one works.

"Maybe we could be crayons this year," Bolu says as she pulls a few Tupperware containers out of her lunch bag. Even though she's the newest to the group, she was the first to get on board when I started lecturing them all about not using disposable plastics, like Ziploc bags or individual fruit cups, in their lunches. Now lunchtime at our table is generally waste free.

"Oh! We should be Transformers," Pete suggests, his face lighting up. "I could be Optimus Prime and—"

"How are you going to dress as a sentient robot who can transform into a truck?" Simon cuts him off.

"I don't know! Riven can figure it out!"

"Hey!" Riven waves a baby carrot in the air. "I'm not doing your work for you!"

"But you—" Pete starts, but a single raised eyebrow from Simon shuts him up.

"I don't know what we'd do without you, Simon," I say.

"Have to listen to a lot more of Pete's rants, for one thing," Riven says, and we all laugh except Simon, who stares down at his book, looking pleased but embarrassed.

Simon really is the perfect yin to Pete's yang, though. Whenever Pete gets an especially off-the-wall idea, Simon's usually the one to talk him out of it. Which is good, because about half of those ideas would probably get the guy killed.

It must be nice having a twin. I love Gertie and Isaac, but they're so young. I wish I had—I wish—

There it is again, that sick, empty feeling in my stomach. Like something is wrong. Like I'm forgetting something.

"You okay, Vera?" Riven asks.

I look up, and she's staring at me with concern. The sick feeling in my stomach must have made it onto my face as well. I consider telling her that I can't shake this feeling that I'm forgetting something. That I can't stop wondering if the Witches have cast some spell on me or something. Which is ridiculous. I know it's ridiculous.

The feeling is passing now anyway. And I don't believe in spells. Or witches.

People used to think our aptitudes were magic—bestowed by gods or brought about through charms or the position of the stars in the sky. There are still some temples to various aptitude-related gods around the world, even though it was proven by scientists decades ago that our aptitudes are in our genes. Just like everyone has a particular eye color, everyone also has a particular aptitude. Scientists have been working ever since to prove that every aptitude is explainable by science. So much of what Mom and Dad talk about goes over my head, but I do know that science has made a ton of progress.

If our aptitudes are explainable by science, then every other seemingly unexplainable thing in the world probably is, too. And yet, there are still people who believe in spells, in demons, in spirits, in curses.

"I'm fine," I tell Riven, even though my moment of thinking about curses and spells suggests that I'm not.

She narrows her eyes at me, but she must sense that I don't want to talk about it, at least not here, because she grabs her tea—in the reusable travel mug I gave her—and says, "Oh, Simon, would you be a dear?" And she passes her tea over to him.

Simon just nods, takes the tea, swirls the spoon in it around, then hands it back. Riven takes a sip. "Mmm, perfection. Thanks, Simon."

"Someday you're going to mix up me and Simon," Pete says, "and I'll get to watch your face as you gulp down a mouthful of pure salt." He winks at me when he says it, and I shake my head at him. Simon has sweetening magic. Pete has salt magic.

"Thanks for the warning, Petey boy," Riven says, cheerily. Then her whole face grows fierce and she points a finger at him. "But rest assured that if you ever pull a prank like that on me, I'm making you drink the entire thing!"

We argue about Halloween costumes for the rest of the week,

before we finally decide to go to Value Village to look at costumes for inspiration. Riven wants to go this weekend, but most of us have big family plans for Thanksgiving, which is in early October in Canada. And then next week, I have to babysit Gertie and Isaac every day after school, as always, and it can be hard to convince Pete and Simon's mom to let them go out after dinner on a school night, especially since their family eats so late. So we end up settling on the following Friday.

"Is that okay, Riven?"

"Sounds like it has to be." She shrugs nonchalantly, and though I can feel her eagerness to get started thrumming through her like an aptitude, she drops the subject.

🔺 🔺 🔺 🔺 🔺 🔺 🔺 🔺 🔺 🔺 🔺 🔺 🔺

Thanksgiving weekend feels like any other Thanksgiving weekend—with food and cousins and silliness and a lot of noise— except that it also doesn't. Mom zones out in the middle of conversations, we keep losing Gertie and then finding her sitting in the dark in the empty room, and my two teen cousins look at me weird when I ask them if they want to play euchre.

"There's only three of us," Beth points out. And apparently I momentarily lose my ability to count because I almost insist that there's four of us before realizing she's right. (We do find a three-person variant to play, though.)

When I magic open my locker on Tuesday morning, I'm so worn out after the weekend that I almost don't notice the orange paper leaf that floats down and out of my locker. I manage to snatch it up just before it hits the ground. When I read the words written across it in type and in pen, I clutch it to my heart, throw my coat in my locker, and hurry off to find Riven.

Unsurprisingly, Riven is studying an orange leaf of her own. "Simon?" she asks, holding it up as I approach.

"Simon," I agree, waving my own leaf in response. Although the leaves don't have Simon's name on them, they're so obviously his handiwork.

They're the sort of leaves you might get at a craft store before Thanksgiving, with "I am thankful for _____" typed on them in an oversize sans serif font. In the blank on mine, Simon has scrawled "the light and goodness Vera brings to this world," which is a level of hyperbolic mushiness that would make me roll my eyes if it came from anyone except Simon. It's also ironic, because sometimes I wonder if the only thing that keeps me on the straight and narrow path is having Simon around as my conscience. I'd definitely never have unlocked that school door for Riven if Simon had been there with his lovingly disappointed gaze.

Riven's leaf is less mushy—unsurprisingly, since Simon's unending crush on Riven makes him more guarded around her—but still perfectly apt. "I am thankful for Riven's endless patience with her friends, especially around Halloween," it says.

"So I'm not the only one who noticed your eye twitching when you were forced to wait until this coming Friday to shop for Halloween costumes," I tease her.

"Who leaves costume shopping until just two weeks before Halloween?!" she spits out, finally letting out the impatient angst she's been unsuccessfully hiding since last week.

"We do!" Bolu says as she waltzes up to us, orange leaf of her own in hand. The twins appear moments later, and Pete pulls a folded leaf out of his jeans pocket.

"I thought you left that at your locker," Simon mumbles.

"And miss putting you through this?" Pete grins, then signals for everyone to share their inscription.

On Pete's, Simon is thankful for "a brother who is also my best friend."

On Bolu's, he expresses gratitude for "new friends who you feel like you've known for as long as the old ones."

"This is so nice, Simon," Bolu coos, giving him a one-armed hug.

Simon shoves his hands in his pockets. "I didn't make the leaves," he says quietly. "My aunt had them on the table at Thanksgiving, and no one was using them, so . . ."

"So you made only the part that really matters, is what you're saying," Riven chimes in, and with the way Simon is staring at the floor, fingers knit together, I suddenly worry that he might die of attention and embarrassment.

Pete must also sense we've gone too far, because he steps into our little circle and says, "Look, I don't know what the big deal is. It's not like he's said anything profound. I mean, look at mine . . ." He waves his creased leaf in the air. "It's a rule of the universe that you've got to be best friends with your twin. Everyone knows that."

He turns and reads Bolu's again. "Yours just means he's as tired of you as he is of us." I worry for a moment that he's gone too far the other way, but Bolu simply laughs.

"And Vera's . . . Simon's obviously mixed you guys up. Riven makes the light, not Vera." He throws his hand up in the air, mimicking Riven's frequent light magic gesture.

"Well, what about mine?" Riven asks, holding up her leaf again.

Pete considers it. "No, he nailed yours. We all know it's killing your soul that we haven't gone Halloween shopping yet."

"I thought I was hiding it so well," Riven moans, and we all shake our heads, grinning.

Later, at lunchtime, while Simon is in the bathroom, I pull out a piece of paper and ask if anyone has scissors.

"I knew there had to be a reason I brought these today," Bolu says as she pulls small craft scissors out of her pencil case.

I mangle the leaf on my first try—it looks more like a star—so I pass the scissors to Riven, who manages to cut out a passable-looking new one. Bolu has the best handwriting, so she does the writing. "We are thankful for . . . Simon," says the lined paper maple leaf.

Then we slip it into Simon's bag for him to find later.

CHAPTER FOUR

"**Have you ever thought of putting Isaac and Gertie in** after-school day care?" I ask right after dinner on Friday, as Isaac and Gertie keep running at me with pillows, insisting on a pillow fight, despite the fact that I pillow fought with them for at least an hour after school. It's not like Mom and Dad act as if they birthed me just for the free labor; they do pay me a bit. But babysitting my siblings every single day after school is starting to feel exhausting.

Mom tilts her head to the side. "We haven't. I don't know why we haven't ever discussed it before."

"Maybe because we—" Dad starts, then stops as he looks around the room like he's confused.

"What is it, Frank?" Mom asks.

He shakes his head. "Nothing. Just been getting a lot of déjà vu lately."

Déjà vu. Maybe that's what all these weird feelings have been for me, too, lately. Though instead of feeling like I've been here before, I feel like something isn't here that should be. "Me, too," I admit.

"Maybe we all ate some bad chicken," Mom says. "I told you this family should have gone vegetarian years ago." Then she laughs at her own joke; Mom's the biggest meat lover in the family, and it's Dad and me who prefer vegetarian.

"We don't need after-school day care, though," Dad says after shaking his head at Mom's joke. "Because we have you, dear daughter." He's smiling, but there's a tone of finality to his voice.

Before I can argue, there's a knock on the door. Riven has arrived, and we're off to Value Village, and I'm still stuck watching my siblings every single day after school, all by myself.

▲ ▲ ▲ ▲ ▲ ▲ ▲ ▲ ▲ ▲ ▲ ▲ ▲

We meet Bolu and Pete and Simon in the parking lot. "I still think we'd dominate as Transformers," Pete is saying to Simon, though the way he glances at Riven makes me think he's doing it just to rile Riven up. Those two fight like brother and sister sometimes—as if Riven's three older brothers weren't enough.

"Is there a transformer that transforms into a minivan?" I say to Pete. "Because that's what you should be."

"A minivan? Uncalled for! What, are you going to stab me next?" He puts his hand over his heart in mock agony. "Come on, can't I at least be a station wagon?"

"Ooh, yes, one of those really old ones with wood paneling down the side. Fits you perfectly."

"Oh, shush you two, let's go inside," says Bolu. She's still wearing the skinny jeans, T-shirt, and cardigan she was wearing at school, but she's pulled half her braids up into a loose bun and added these classy turquoise teardrop earrings that make her look like she's going out for a night on the town, rather than trying on a few Halloween costumes with some friends. Makes me wish I'd worn something other than my trusty yoga pants that I've worn so often they're starting to pill.

"You look so glamorous, Bolu," I say, sidling up to her as we head toward the entrance.

She starts to laugh, then stops when she sees my face. "Oh, you're serious," she says.

"I think it's the earrings." They're outlined in an intricate golden edge that almost looks braided.

She reaches up to touch one of them, lightly. "I knew they were too much."

"It's a compliment, Bolu," Simon says, appearing on her other side.

She turns to me and cocks her head. "Is it?"

"Of course! Looking glamorous is a bad thing in your world?"

She shakes her head. "No. It's just . . ." She chews her lip for a moment as she considers. "My friends at my old school had this way of saying stuff that sounded like a compliment but really wasn't. Like, 'Those boots are so bold! You're so brave to wear them in public!'"

"Wow!" Simon says as Riven and I share a glance—the kind that says, *I'm so glad you've been my best friend all these years because you're so much better than the passive-aggressive jerks who apparently exist out there.* And my heart goes a little squishy.

"Well, like Simon said, it's a compliment," I reassure her, leaning my head against her shoulder.

"Thank you, then," she responds with a small smile.

"You guys coming in or what?" Pete yells at us from just inside the Value Village entrance. The rest of us have stopped outside.

"Give us a minute!" Riven yells back. "We're bonding!"

"Hey! Let me bond, too!" Pete shouts. And then he runs at us and somehow envelops the whole group in an enormous bear hug.

Inside, the place is busy. There's a line at every till—kids with their parents, university students, a few people our age I recognize from school, even an elderly woman holding a severed foot decoration. I do most of my clothes shopping at Value Village, since used clothing is not only cheaper but also better for the environment. It's not usually anywhere near as busy as it is now; for Halloween, they bring in a whole department of costumes—new, not used.

We weave our way through the crowd to the racks of costumes in the corner. Pete grabs a short-skirted sexy cat costume and suggests it for Simon, who rolls his eyes. Bolu finds a chef's costume and suggests we dress as contestants on the *Great British Baking Show,* and then Riven suggests that if we're going to do that, we should do the Canadian show instead, which Pete and Simon haven't seen yet, so they veto that idea.

"We could go as characters from *The Wizard of Oz* and I could be the dog," Bolu suggests, holding up a fuzzy brown adult-size onesie with puppy ears.

"That's adorable," Simon says.

"Hey, there are more of them." I reach behind Simon and pull out a light blue onesie with a fin down the back and sharp teeth around the face. "It's a shark!"

"Yes, please," Pete says, reaching out to take it from me.

"No way! I'm keeping the shark!" I snatch it out of his reach and hug it to myself. He sticks his tongue out at me and I stick mine out right back.

"Are there more?" Riven asks. "We could go as Beanie Babies!"

"What are Beanie Babies?" Bolu asks as she starts putting the dog onesie on over her clothes.

"You know . . . those old beanbag toys of all different animals. We could make big-size versions of the little heart tags that came with them and wear those around our necks!"

"Guess we need three more, then," Pete says, diving into the costume display. The whole thing is a mess, like a hundred monkeys went rummaging through it—which is pretty much exactly what happened. After throwing aside a couple of witch costumes, he emerges with a fuzzy black-and-white onesie. "A panda!"

"That's a good one for Riven," Simon says.

"For me? Why?" Riven asks, though she happily takes the onesie from Pete.

Simon only shrugs.

"He means you're *soooooo* huggable, like a panda," Pete teases.

Simon looks down at the ground like his cheeks are burning, as though he did indeed mean exactly that.

"Let's keep searching," I suggest, and we all dive back into the mess of costumes. After a few minutes, Bolu finds a dinosaur onesie that Pete immediately claims, and we start to argue about whether his dinosaur or my shark is better—my shark is, obviously—until Riven points out that we still need to find one more onesie for Simon.

We all glance over the wall of costumes as if we're expecting another onesie to jump right out at us. When it doesn't, we spread out along the display and start digging. I find five more shark onesies and a couple of dog onesies in one bin, but nothing new. As I look through a rack of Disney dresses, some girl I recognize from school practically elbows me in the face as she reaches across me to grab a Belle's blue provincial town dress. As I step backward, I bump into a woman who's standing with her back to me, looking at the opposite wall of costumes with her daughter. "Sorry," I say, then hurry over to where Riven is scrounging through a bin of miscellaneous costume parts. "You'd think there was a Boxing Day sale on or something, with how busy it is," I say.

"This is why I like to plan so far ahead!"

"So you don't get left battling over the scraps with the commoners, oh Halloween Queen?"

"Exactly!" She grins, then immediately frowns as she emerges from her bin. "I can't find anything. You?"

I shake my head.

The others have no luck, either. We gather at the end of the aisle of costumes, each of us clutching an animal onesie except for Simon.

"Sorry, Simon," Bolu says.

"That's okay. Maybe I could be . . . a zookeeper or something? And you guys the animals?" But there's a sadness in his voice.

My heart hurts. Simon's not the kind of person who would snatch up a shark costume or dinosaur costume and claim it as his own if someone else wanted it. I look down at the shark onesie in my arms, then hold it out to him. "Here, take my shark."

"Hey, you wouldn't give it up when I asked!" Pete protests.

"Yeah, well, you don't look like a sad, abandoned puppy," I point out.

"Okay, true."

"Guys, I'm okay. I don't need the shark." Simon crosses his arms, refusing to take the onesie from me. "I don't have to match all of you."

But we've always had matching costumes. It's tradition. And Simon loves tradition. Every year at Christmas, he hangs stockings in each of our lockers, puts a present in each one, and insists it's from Santa. At Easter, he brings us egg-shaped cookies that he decorates himself. On St. Patrick's Day, instead of pinching us if we don't wear green, he hugs us if we do. He'll probably give us Thanksgiving leaves again next year now that he started it this year.

"Let's both be sharks, then," I suggest. "We can be twin sharks."

"Or twin dogs," Bolu says from inside her onesie.

"Hey, don't steal my twin from me," Pete says. "We'll obviously be twin dinosaurs!"

"Thanks, you guys," Simon says, "but—"

"Wait!" Pete cuts him off. "I see . . ." Then he darts past us and across the aisle. His broad shoulders block the view of what he's doing, but I hear him say, "it's life or death!" to someone.

And then he's back with us, thrusting a onesie into Simon's arms.

"A unicorn!" Simon's voice is somewhere between amusement and delight.

Riven laughs. "That's perfect! Good job, Pete."

I look back across the aisle so I can give whoever Pete got the onesie from a thank-you wave. A pack of university students is ambling past, blocking the other aisle from view, and I start thinking that whoever it was will be long gone by now. But then the students clear out and a girl is still standing there. It's Sarah, from my science class.

I raise my hand to wave, then drop it. Sarah is staring at Pete, looking partly like she wants to murder him, partly like she wants to cry.

Pete did ask her for the onesie, right? He didn't just snatch it from her? I turn back to ask him, but my gaze stops on Simon. He's pulling on the unicorn onesie, and even though it's a little small for him and ends just above his ankles and wrists, the look on his face is pure delight. No more abandoned puppy.

I can't help but smile, but then the smile falls off my face and I glance over my shoulder again at Sarah. Who is gone.

Well, not gone. I spot her down the aisle a ways, searching through a rack of costumes. She's moved on, it seems. Thank goodness.

We finish up trying on our onesies and search through a couple more bins to make sure we're not missing any options. When we all come up empty-handed, Bolu says, "Five different onesies; five of us. It's like it's meant to be!"

And while I don't believe in fate, and I'm not as mushy as Bolu or Simon, as we all stand in a circle happily clutching our five different-but-the-same costumes, I have to agree.

CHAPTER FIVE

It's Saturday afternoon and Riven and I are sprawled out on my bed, arguing about *Doctor Who*. "It makes no sense," I say. "How does River Song even know to leave Amy her diary if the Doctor doesn't exist?"

"It's wibbly wobbly timey wimey stuff! You can't think about it too hard!" She throws a pillow at me.

"Hey!" I throw it right back.

Riven's been coming over on Saturday afternoons for years. Sometimes we bake, sometimes we play video games, sometimes we just sprawl on my bed and do nothing. For the last little while, we've been rewatching *Doctor Who*. Riven originally introduced the show to me. She binge-watched the first season and a half, with Eccleston and Tennant, while I was away on vacation a few years ago, then decided it was something we needed to watch together. She went back and watched every one of those first episodes again with me (though of course, we've watched those episodes together more than once since then). We've been obsessed ever since.

"Okay, here's one," I say. "You're on the island, and you meet Amy and the Doctor. Amy says, 'Either the Doctor is a knight or I'm a knight.' The Doctor tells you, 'Amy is a knave.' Who's what?"

Riven cocks an eyebrow at me. "If this puzzle ends up with the Doctor being anything but a knight, it's clearly wrong."

"Well, if the Doctor is a knight, that means he's telling the truth, which means Amy isn't. But that scenario makes Amy's statement true, which it can't be if she's a knave. Which means—"

"Hey, isn't that one of the Witches?" Riven cuts me off. She's looking out my window.

I get up on my knees and look out. Sure enough, Cecily is walking past, staring up at our house as she does.

"She looks like she wants to put a curse on you," Riven says.

"There's no such thing as curses," I say, even though I can't help thinking the same thing. She doesn't look angry, exactly, just determined. Like if she focuses hard enough, she could turn our house the same color as the dreary autumn sky.

Riven leans back against my headboard. "I don't understand how you cannot believe in magic when you have magic," she jokes.

"I don't have magic. I have a variation in my DNA, just like you, just like everyone. We only call it magic because it's a centuries-old word, from back when no one knew what they were talking about."

"Well, what about that girl who knew that her mom was going to die?"

"Obviously just an extreme version of intuition magic."

"Or that boy who accidentally blew up his house because he was angry!"

"He didn't blow it up, he set it on fire. And I'm pretty sure they discovered later that he was playing with matches and lied about it."

"What? No way!" Riven pulls out her phone and starts looking it up.

While she does, I peer out the window again. Cecily is gone.

"You're right!" Riven reports. "Matches! How disappointing."

I shake my head at her. "I don't understand how you can be so willing to believe in magic and karma and whatever else, and yet not believe in God."

She frowns. "Well, I don't understand how you can be so skeptical of everything *except* God," she teases.

"Touché," I say. I pull another episode of *Doctor Who* up on my laptop. It's nice having my own laptop that I don't have to share with anyone, though for some reason that thought fills me with a sort of melancholy. Maybe Cecily did curse me after all. Maybe it's a curse where I can't think of happy things without feeling sad. "Hey, if curses were real and you were to curse someone, what curse would you put on them?" I tell her my curse idea about happy things and sad thoughts.

"Oof, that's harsh," she says. "But I like it." She thinks for a moment. "I'd make it so food tasted bland no matter how much seasoning you added."

"What if it was Pete's salt magic?" I ask, and then there it is again, that melancholy feeling, though a little different this time. Like a poisoned orange instead of a poisoned apple.

Riven frowns as if she feels it, too. "That'd be the only thing that could save you from the curse," she says, solemnly.

"Pete'd be very popular."

"He'd love that."

I feel as if we should laugh at that, but neither of us does. Instead, we both turn to look out the window again, like we're expecting the Witch to reappear and throw this exact curse on us. But the street is still empty. The days are growing shorter and there's already a hint of darkness in the sky. Here and there, some yellow leaves still cling to their branches, but other trees on the street are already bare and gray. Like they've lost the pieces that make them alive, that make them real.

"So, should we watch another *Doctor Who*?" Riven asks, breaking into my thoughts.

I shiver as I nod.

"You cold?" She lifts the edge of the blanket laying over her legs and wriggles over a bit so there's room under it.

And even though I'm not cold, I take the blanket and curl up under it anyway.

●　●　●　●　●　●　●　●　●　●　●　●

Monday morning at Riven's locker, it's quiet. She and I are the only ones there. "Is everyone running late or something this morning?" I ask. Since I have to drop off Isaac and Gertie, I'm never the first to arrive.

She shrugs. She's wearing her TARDIS dress with a black cardigan over black leggings. She probably has enough *Doctor Who* clothing to wear a different thing every day for a month.

I lean against the locker next to hers, tap my fingers against the ugly forest-green metal. I stare down at my shoes, wondering how long I can wear these beat-up old cloth lace-ups I love before Mom forces me to get new ones—well, new used ones. Wondering how disastrous my curls look after this morning's walk in the windy

October air again. Wondering what it is about the school building that makes time move so slowly here.

Then I look up. "Pete!" My heart does a weird little skip in my chest, like I'm pleasantly surprised to see him. Like I wasn't expecting to see him at all. I guess maybe I wasn't. I didn't see him or his parents at church yesterday.

"You weren't that happy to see *me* this morning," Riven jokes.

"I'm always happy to see you, Riv. You're just surprised because I'm not usually happy to see this guy." I point my thumb at Pete.

"Ha. Ha," Pete says mirthlessly, and I wonder if I've gone too far with my joke.

But then I catch another look at his face. It's not just my joke that's bothering him. His eyebrows hang heavy with the weight of some unspoken sadness.

Riven must notice, too, because she says, "Why so glum, chum?"

Pete raises his heavy eyebrows in a *who, me?* kind of look, then lets them fall again as he says, "Dunno. I've just felt out of it the last couple days. Not sure why."

"Is that why you weren't at church yesterday?"

"Not really. Well, sort of. We all slept in. My parents couldn't manage to drag themselves out of bed, either."

I raise my own eyebrows. I've never known Pete or his parents to miss church just because they slept in. Pete has to be close to death before his parents let him stay home from church.

"I've been feeling out of sorts, too," Riven says. "I think it's the fact that it's supposed to snow this week."

Pete shrugs. "Maybe that's it."

Maybe that's why I've been feeling so melancholy, too. What's it called? Seasonal affective disorder? Maybe we all have that. I know my cousin Beth struggles with it. She's described it to me before as having winter's darkness tied to her ankles, dragging heavily behind her with every step.

"Hi, everyone," comes Bolu's voice from behind me. And then, "Pete, I brought this for you."

I look up, expecting to see Bolu holding a spare calculator again or something similar. But in her outstretched hand is a single white rose.

"What's this for?" Pete asks.

Bolu shakes her head. "I don't know. I pass a flower shop on my way to school every morning, and today that flower called me in, and I knew right away it was for you."

I expect Pete to make a joke or laugh or something, but instead he reaches out and gingerly lifts the stem from her hand, careful to avoid the thorns. He lifts it so the blooming white flower is in front of his face, like he expects to see his own face mirrored back at him. "Thank you, Bolu," he whispers.

And for some reason, I have to choke back a sob.

Beside me, Riven grabs my arm. Clings to it.

Bolu grabs Pete's arm.

And then we're all clinging to one another—me and Riven and Bolu and Pete. Holding on to one another like if any of us let go, we'd lose them. Like we've already lost something.

I think we've lost something.

But what, exactly, I couldn't tell you.

After school, Riven comes home with me, like she often does. We chase Gertie and Isaac around for literal hours until Mom and Dad finally get home and shoo us upstairs while they make supper and take over watching the gerblins.

Up in my room, we sprawl out on my bed, and I stare out the window at the nearly leafless trees. The wind makes the branches twitch and the window frame shudder. It whispers a ghostly refrain in a language I can't understand.

Which makes me realize: Neither of us is talking. I draw my gaze away from the window and study Riven. She's leaning against the wall, a notebook propped up against her knees as she sketches something with a pencil. Her hair is pulled back into her usual ponytail, her eyebrows are furrowed in concentration, and she's staring at the page with such intensity that for a moment I wonder if she even remembers I'm here.

I lean across the bed to peek, then let out a simple, "Oh!"

Sketched across the page is a single rose—or most of one. She's still filling in the petals.

She pauses her sketching but doesn't look up. "I'm not sure why I felt like drawing it."

"I'm not sure why it makes me want to cry," I admit.

Riven looks up. "Does it?" She bites her lip. "It makes me want to cry, too."

"I think it made all of us want to cry."

"Yeah, what the heck was with that?" Riven asks, straightening up. We haven't talked about the white rose Bolu brought for Pete all day. After the first bell rang this morning, we all stopped clinging to one another and went our separate ways. And when I saw the rose in Pete's locker later, I didn't say a thing. Neither did Pete. Neither did any of us.

It does feel a little like Beth's seasonal affective disorder, but sharper. Like winter's darkness keeps intermittently and unexpectedly stabbing me in the heart. "Maybe we're all PMSing," I say. "Maybe our periods are in sync."

"Even Pete?"

"Especially Pete."

She giggles at that, and for a moment, everything feels normal again. We're just two best friends hanging out, laughing, having a good time together. But then we both look down at Riven's sketchpad, and our laughter dies away. And the world feels wrong again, like it's a puzzle that's missing its final piece. Like winter has stabbed me once again.

So I lean against Riven's shoulder and watch her shade in the petals of the flower that represents I don't know what, until Dad calls us both down for dinner.

We leave the notebook on my bed and head downstairs, and I wonder if, like me, Riven feels both relieved and guilty to be leaving it behind.

In the kitchen, I stop short. "Oh!" I say for the second time this evening.

"What is it, sweetheart?" Mom asks as she sets a pot down on the table.

"Spaghetti," I say, as if that's an explanation.

"Ah, yes, I know you made us spaghetti just last week, Vera, but it was so good, I was craving it again." She says it with a tone of finality as she gives the tomato sauce in the pot a stir. The veggies—zucchini, mushrooms, peppers—float in red marinara sauce. "I hope that's okay," she adds, almost as an afterthought.

Of course it's okay. Why wouldn't spaghetti be okay?

Except things are not okay. Because I want to cry. I want to scream. I want to grab the pot and fling it at the wall. All because of spaghetti.

I turn to look at Riven's face, hopeful it'll be a mirror of my own, just like with the rose. But she just raises an eyebrow at me as if to say *What is it?* She's left her weird feelings upstairs on the bed, leaving me alone in mine. Leaving me alone.

I hug my arms to myself and shake my head. It's nothing. Just spaghetti causing me to lose my sanity.

"Well," I start to say, wanting to try to explain this inexplicable thing to my Mom and Riven.

But Mom cuts me off. "Honestly, Vera," she snaps, "it's just spaghetti. I'm not sure what the big deal is." Her eyes look teary, but it must just be the steam from the pot.

"Never mind. Forget I said anything," I snap back. Then I shove my feelings away and slide into my chair at the table.

* * *

Later that evening, after Riven has left, I head upstairs. I pause for a moment in the hall, placing my hand on the closed door of the empty room across from mine. If Gertie has continued to go in there since Thanksgiving weekend, she's been doing it when no one is around to see her. Funny little kid. Though at the moment, I feel a weird pull of my own to enter the room and sit cross-legged in the dark in the middle of the empty space. Instead, I return to my room and settle onto my bed. Riven has left her notepad behind. I flip it open, and on the very first page is that white rose.

The way Pete looked at that rose is the way I felt about the spaghetti tonight. The way I feel when I let myself look at that door across the hall. Winter's stab every time. Maybe it's something even more serious than seasonal affective disorder. Maybe I'm losing my grasp on reality, on my sanity.

I pull out my phone and text Pete. *How are you?*

A moment later, he sends back a GIF of a dog with a box on its head, running into a wall.

I think about sending back a "ha ha" or a laughing emoji. Instead, I write, *How are you really?*

When he doesn't respond right away, my stomach twists with nervousness. Maybe I've overstepped. Pete and I never talk about serious stuff. Our texting history is filled with gifs and emojis and ridiculous jokes.

But when my phone finally pings, he says, *Everything just feels like it sucks right now.*

I have a strange desire to hug him. *Do you want to talk about it?* I type instead.

When he responds, *Nah, not really. Thanks, though,* I'm not surprised. How do you talk about an inexplicable desire to curl up in a ball and cry when you see an inanimate object? You can't. You don't.

So instead, I send him back a GIF of a cat stealing a pancake off a table.

He LOLs at that and replies with a GIF of a cat eating watermelon.

A little while later, once Pete and I have tired of sending cat gifs to each other, I grab the book of logic problems beside my bed, hoping to lose myself for a while in something that actually makes sense. Logic and deduction and order. But when the act of drawing Xs and dots in a grid to narrow things down to the final resolution doesn't draw me in like it usually does, I instead pick up the notebook Riven left behind and flip through the pages. After the rose, the rest of the notepad is empty.

I pick up the pencil she's left behind, too, and take up her place at the foot of my bed—back against the wall, knees up.

I waffle for a moment, trying to choose between spaghetti and a plain door, and then I start to draw—a bowl, noodles, sauce.

It looks like garbage. I'm no artist. The noodles look more like worms, the sauce more like fudge on a sundae. It's not exactly appetizing.

I shake my head, laughing inwardly at myself. Tomorrow I'll ask Riven to fix it. And I'll tell her about the spaghetti, too—about how I seem to be losing it.

Except if I'm losing it, I'm not the only one. I flip back a page to the rose, remembering Riven, Bolu, Pete, and I clinging to one another in the hallway at school this morning. Thinking of Pete having "just one of those days" for no reason. They all felt it, too. I know they did.

It's not just in my head.

Mom and I don't fight like this. Pete doesn't get sad like this. Bolu doesn't bring random white flowers. Riven and I don't usually share an unexplained sorrow.

Something is wrong.

Something is wrong and there has to be a logical explanation.

Something is wrong and I'm going to figure out what it is.

CHAPTER SIX

I find Riven at her locker before school the next morning, just like always. I hand her the notepad she left at my house. "I tried to draw something but failed miserably. Can you fix it for me?"

"Sure, what's it of?" She sets her backpack down on the beige, concrete floor, flips open the notebook, and turns to my sketch of a pile of worms covered in fudge sauce. She looks up at me. "That spaghetti last night really did a number on you, huh?"

At least she recognized it. "Yeah, it's weird. It's like—"

"Morning, lovelies," Bolu's musical voice cuts in as she waltzes up to us. "What's the gossip this morning?"

I glance at Riven, who snaps the notebook shut as if she can read my mind, and I give her a small smile.

I like Bolu a lot, and I'd trust her with most things, but even though she was the one who brought the rose yesterday, I'm still not ready to tell her that I'm getting weepy over pasta.

So we chatter with Bolu about school gossip, our homework,

teachers—about anything except the notepad and what compelled us to start drawing in it.

At lunch, at our usual table in the cafeteria, Riven pulls a small pile of red cardstock and a pair of scissors from her backpack. "Okay, team, get to work."

"On what?" Bolu asks.

"Our costumes. I can't believe I let you slackers put it off this long."

She's got a point. Halloween's on Friday. I don't think we've ever been this close to Halloween without having our costumes 100 percent ready to go before. But the bright red of the cardstock looks so much cheerier than I feel. Our whole costume idea is so cheery. Four cuddly Beanie Babies. Four of them. The number hits me in the gut. I eye Riven's backpack, wondering if the notebook is in there. Perhaps I should ask her to draw a picture of the number four, too.

Pete reaches out and slides the cardstock and scissors toward himself. "What's this for, again?"

For a moment, Riven just stares at him. Then she says, incredulously, "You're voluntarily helping out? What's the catch?"

I expect Pete to snark something back at her, but he just shrugs. "No catch. Just tell me what to do."

"Cut them into big hearts. For the tags."

He nods, then searches in his backpack and pulls out a pencil. He's actually taking his job seriously.

Riven and I share a glance. We've never known Pete to take something seriously before.

"So what's the plan for Friday night?" Bolu asks, and we leave Pete to his task and explain to Bolu our normal Halloween traditions: how we head to Riven's house after school, get costumed up, have an early supper, then head out.

"Afterward, we usually watch *It's the Great Pumpkin, Charlie Brown*, because that's about the scariest Halloween movie that Vera can handle," Riven says.

"Hey, it's not my fault that scary movies give me nightmares," I protest. "And besides, I could probably handle something scarier now!"

"Well, maybe it's time we changed that part of the tradition," Riven suggests.

"No! We can't change the tradition!" Bolu protests, even though she's never been part of our Halloween tradition before. I'm glad she speaks up, though, because with Riven suggesting a change and Pete busy with his task, apparently there's no one else who will. It feels as if there should be someone else who would.

"How's this look?" Pete slides a heart across the table—not the happy heart symbol we were expecting, but a bloody, oversize organ, with an aorta sticking out the top. Like he pulled his own heart out of his chest and magnified it onto the page.

"I—uh—" Riven says. "That's not—"

I snatch it up. "This is perfect. Petey, you're a genius."

"Wait, what?" Riven asks.

"Did I screw it up?" Pete asks.

"I think they were supposed to be hearts," Bolu says. "You know . . ." She outlines a heart symbol on the table with her finger.

"Oh, hell." He looks genuinely crestfallen—though he's looked that way a lot the last day or so.

"No, everyone, look; Pete had the right idea." I hold the heart up near my neck, where the Beanie Baby tag would go. "We can go as Beanie Baby monsters. With our hearts pulled out of our chests." The idea fits better in the jumble of my mind than the happy, cuddly stuffed animals do.

The look of protest falls off Riven's face. "With our hearts pulled out of our chests," she repeats.

"Beanie Baby monsters . . . is that a thing?" Bolu asks.

"It is now," Riven says.

"We should do more to the onesies, though," I suggest. "Put blood on them or something."

"Oh, you finally got over your fear of blood and gore? Proud of you," Pete says.

"I'm not afraid of blood and gore. I just can't watch movies full of blood and gore!" I throw the blood-red heart back at Pete. It sort of flutters in the air, then floats down to the table.

Pete pulls it toward him. "But real-life gore is fine?"

"Real-life fake gore on fake costumes is fine," I say, fake-scowling at him.

"Wouldn't a fake costume not be a costume at all?" points out Bolu.

"Shut up. I hate you all," I say, but I can't help smiling. It feels good to be bantering after what's felt like too much awkward silence since the rose happened yesterday.

"I can bloody the onesies up tonight," Riven offers. All our costumes are already at Riven's. She's demanded it be that way since our second year of trick-or-treating together. Which is fair, since our first year, I forgot my tiara and our second year, I forgot my M&M gloves.

"Perfect," I say.

"Perfect," Bolu and Pete both echo at the same time.

Then we all get to work tracing Pete's masterpiece onto more red cardstock. By the end of lunch period, we each have a heart pulled out of our chest. All four of us.

Since Riven has to work on our Halloween costumes and I have to pick up Gertie and Isaac from school, Riven and I go our separate ways after school. After supper, though, she texts me pictures of the costumes, which look delightfully gory. They all have gashes on the left side of the chest, dripping blood, plus other random cuts and bloodstains. Her own panda costume has a bloody handprint near the heart-gash.

Awesome work, I text her. *I'm so impressed.* I've never been great at art. If I had tried to do it, I'd probably end up staining them all entirely red or something. Which reminds me: *Can you add the number four to your notepad?*

Instead of answering by text, she calls me a moment later. "The number four?" she says instead of hello when I answer.

"Yeah. You know . . ." I trail off. I suddenly feel silly saying it aloud. Who feels punched in the gut by a number? But this isn't just anyone I'd be saying it to; it's Riven. Riven who's been my best friend since fourth grade. Who I've never kept a secret from. Who I would trust with my life. Who I would trust with my sanity, which apparently I'm continuing to lose. "Yeah, four," I continue. "As in four costumes. Four friends. Four of us. Me, you, Pete, and Bolu."

For a moment, the line is quiet, and my stomach twists with

fear that she won't get it. That she'll interrupt the silence with something like, "Aw, that's so sweet," and miss the point entirely.

But then she says, slowly, "So we're making a book of things that feel weird. Is that it?"

"Yes!" I practically shout into the phone, so relieved that if she were here, I'd probably smother her in a hug. "Exactly!"

I hear a rustling of pages and wonder if she's pulling out the notebook right now. "Do you think we've slipped into a parallel universe?" she asks.

Of course that's the first place her brain would go. Riven loves parallel universes. Last time I saw a book that mentioned parallel universes in the description, I immediately bought it for Riven for her birthday.

"Wouldn't we find things different, then, not just weird?" I point out, trying to be rational. It's theoretically possible that parallel universes exist—like Mom says, so many more things are possible than we currently understand—but I'd think it would be more obvious if we slipped into one.

"I don't know. Who knows what shifting from one universe to the next did to our brains? I'm writing it down."

"Are we making a list, then, along with the pictures?"

"Obviously. Why, have you got something to add?"

I think of the Witches and the way Cecily looked at me in science. The way she walked past our house, staring up at it as if mumbling a spell under her breath. I don't believe in witches or curses or spells or any of that garbage. "No," I say. "No ideas at all."

"Well, I've got more," she says, and I can hear the faint scratch of her pencil as she writes them down. "Mind control. Psychoses. Artificial reality."

"You think we're in an artificial reality? Like this is all a computer simulation or something?" I try to keep the skepticism out of my voice but fail miserably.

"Look, anything's possible."

"But not everything's probable," I point out.

"Well, your face gets scrunched up all weird when you think about spaghetti," Riven counters. "I think we're way past probable."

I sigh. "Fine. Then add, 'a message from God.'"

"A message from God? Really?" It's her turn for her voice to be filled with skepticism.

"You just said, 'anything's possible.'"

"You're right," she concedes. "I did. I'll add it."

"And global warming," I suggest.

"Ooh, yes, maybe the change in the atmosphere is messing with our brains in thus-far undetected ways."

"That's the first thing you've said so far that makes sense," I say.

"For the record, I am now sticking my tongue out at you."

"So am I," I say, sticking my tongue out even though she can't see it to confirm.

"You're sticking your tongue out at yourself?"

"Oh, shush, you dork," I say, then add, "Send me a picture of the list so far. I've got to go so I can finish my math homework."

"I will. Tell me if you've got more ideas to add to the list."

"I will."

A little while later, as I'm doing my math homework, I look up and out the window. And there she is again! Cecily! One of the

Witches! She's looking up at our house with intensity as she ambles past.

Maybe I should have told Riven to add the Witches to the list after all.

I hop to my feet, knocking my math textbook to the floor but not even caring. I rush downstairs, grab my coat out of the front closet, and shout into the living room at my parents that I'm going out for a bit and will be right back.

By the time I get outside, Cecily is already at the end of our block, turning right. Where is she going? Is she meeting up with the other Witches? Is she going to the witchcraft store to collect . . . I don't know what. Herbs? Gems? Body parts? How do witches cast spells, anyway? Is there even such a thing as a witchcraft store?

I've definitely lost it. The wind howls through the trees and between the houses. It's already dark out, and the moon is obscured by clouds. The shadowy branches of a nearby tree shake angrily at me.

I run to the end of the block, then look down the road to the right. Cecily is gone. As if she's disappeared.

I pull out my phone and Google a list of aptitudes, and then search through the list for something that might explain it. Disappearing magic isn't a thing, of course. That's something that would definitely be in the news if it was. And I can't see anything else on the list that explains her disappearance.

I squint down the street once more, then walk to the end of that block, looking up and down the next street. She's definitely not there. So I turn around and trudge toward home.

When I get back inside, Mom is standing in the hallway with

her hands on her hips. She may be short, but the fierceness of her glare turns her formidable.

"What's wrong?" I ask.

"Vera, you don't get to go running out the door without telling us where you're going."

I stare at her, confused. She's never had a problem with me going out for a walk before. "But it's not even late yet," I point out.

Mom's face softens. "What if something had happened to you and we didn't even know where you were?"

My parents have never been particularly protective. I've never had a curfew, and they've always wanted me to experience as much of life as I can, even if it means experiencing the hurt, too. But now, Mom is looking at me like if I sneezed too hard, she might lose me.

Dad appears in the hallway and puts his hand on her shoulder. "Val, I think—"

"Don't patronize me," she snaps at him. And then they're fighting with each other.

Which is weird. Mom and Dad don't fight. They wrote the book on love. Literally. They teach marriage prep courses at our church, and together they wrote a little book of exercises to accompany their class.

Part of me wants to intervene, but another, bigger part of me recognizes this as the perfect chance to slip away. Which I do.

By the time I'm back in my room, my phone is blinking with a notification. It's the pictures from Riven. The first is of our list.

> Parallel universe
> Mind control
> Psychoses
> Artificial reality

Climate change
Message from God
Message from the universe

I shake my head at that last one. Her refusal to believe in God would be much more convincing if she didn't refer so often to a higher power. Still, it makes me feel better, like this is all some silly game we're playing.

But then I switch to the next picture. It's her fixed-up drawing of my spaghetti. It looks so much better. The noodles are thinner. The sauce actually looks like marinara sauce, and she's added little chunks of veggies to it.

My stomach twists. It's just like the pasta we had the other day. The one that makes me want to cry for no good reason when I think of it.

I flip to the next picture, and my stomach twists even tighter. Instead of just writing the number four, she's drawn the four of us. Me and Riven on the left, Pete and Bolu on the right. In the middle is a gap. A space. A hole. It's probably not intentional, and it probably means nothing, but I find my finger drawn to it. I tap the spot where nothing is.

And suddenly, I'm crying.

Tears stream down my face, inexplicably, uncontrollably.

I switch back to the picture of the pasta, and my tears come faster.

I don't know why I'm crying.

But I do know: This is anything but a game.

CHAPTER SEVEN

Riven and I are sprawled out on my bed, watching *Doctor Who* on my laptop, when Isaac throws open my bedroom door and comes running in. As he races toward the bed, he bumps into the chair holding my laptop, and I have to throw out my hand to stop the laptop from tumbling to the floor.

"Isaac!" I snap. "What the heck! Get out of here!"

Mom must be passing through the hall right at that moment, because she pops her head in. "Vera! Don't speak to your brother that way!"

It doesn't seem to have bothered Isaac, because he's climbed onto my bed and is jumping on it—sometimes avoiding our arms and legs, sometimes not.

Riven and I watched Isaac and Gertie after school until Mom and Dad got home—as always—and it's as if their teachers fed them buckets of sugar before they left school. They're still going like Energizer Bunnies, and I'm wiped out. I stare longingly at the now-open door of my room. If only I had locking magic instead of unlocking magic.

"Fine," I say to Mom. Then I turn to my brother. "Isaac, would you please go play in the living room downstairs?" I give him my cheesiest grin.

"No!" he shouts, then bounces directly on my shin.

"Ow! Mom, can you take him, please?"

She sighs and leans against my doorframe. "I'm busy cooking dinner, Vera."

I narrow my eyes at her. She might be cooking dinner in theory, but in practice, she's just standing there watching my brother cover my legs with bruises. "Just take him with you on the way back downstairs."

"Vera," Mom says with a sigh. And then that's it; she just disappears down the hallway. Leaving me with a bouncing ball that plops his butt down right on my knee.

Which is apparently Gertie's cue to come running into the room. "I want to play, too!"

I slam down the lid of my laptop. "Sorry, we're going for a walk."

"We are?" Riven asks, but then she must catch the exhaustion in my face. I need a break from these two whirlwinds. "Right. Yes. We're going on a walk."

"Ew," Isaac says, scrunching up his face. He can run around the house like Road Runner, but ask him to walk somewhere and he's begging to be carried after two seconds.

"Ew," Gertie agrees. Even though she's the older sibling, she copies Isaac more often than he copies her.

I extricate myself from Isaac, who's bundled himself into my lap, and we head downstairs.

"We're going on a walk," I call to Mom as we pass the kitchen.

She appears in the doorway as we pull on our shoes. "But dinner will be ready soon."

"Then it'll be a short walk."

"Vera!"

"Mom!"

We stare each other down. It's a strange feeling.

Mom gives in first. Her shoulders sag and the corners of her mouth droop. "All right. But be back in twenty minutes."

We don't argue—just pull on our coats and shoes and head outside. It's not exactly picturesque out. The sky is gray, and the tree in front of our house is almost bare. The ground around it is littered with small yellow leaves. As soon as we step off the porch, a biting wind grabs my curls and throws them into my face.

"Brr," Riven says as I pull hair out of my mouth.

"Yeah." I pull my hair into a loose ponytail, and then we head down the street. The sun is going down, and without its bright rays warming up the dry air, it's chilly. I wish I could throw my hand up and light the sky back up, but I suppose even Riven doesn't have that power. I jam my hands into my pockets, wishing I'd put on a scarf or even my winter coat instead of my fall one.

As we walk, I notice that Riven and I are both adjusting our stride so we don't step on any of the cracks in the sidewalk. "Step on a crack . . ." I say.

"Break your mother's back," Riven finishes. We grin at the childhood rhyme we've both been obeying for as long as we've known each other.

Avoiding stepping on the cracks isn't enough distraction from the cold, though. By the time we've gone half a block, I'm shivering. My teeth chatter with every gust of wind.

"Hey, let's go in here." Riven grabs my arm and pulls me toward a nearby bus shelter. It's one of the small, boxy ones, with a blue roof, four walls, and an open door. We duck inside and collapse onto the bench.

The difference in temperature is immediately noticeable. "Okay, apparently it was just the wind that was being a jerk," I say.

"Apparently," Riven agrees.

We sit in silence for a moment or two, giving our goose bumps time to recede back into our arms. One of the walls boasts an advertisement, but the other three are clear, and through them I can see the trees on the street swaying back and forth with the wind.

"Well, I guess we live here now," I say.

"I guess so. It's not so bad as far as homes go. It's basically like being in the TARDIS," she says, referring to the time-traveling spaceship in *Doctor Who* that looks like an old, British emergency telephone box from the outside.

"That's a phone box, not a bus shelter," I point out. "Plus, it's supposed to be bigger on the inside. It doesn't look anything like a TARDIS from in here."

"Not yet." Riven pulls a bobby pin out of her hair and snaps it in half. Using the broken tip, she starts to carve into the wooden bench between us.

"Riven! We'll get in trouble!"

"From who?" Riven looks pointedly up and down the street. Aside from the occasional car that zips past, no one is around.

"Okay, no one. But . . . shouldn't we . . ." My protestations die off. We wouldn't be the first ones to carve into the bench. It already boasts dozens of proclamations of love and of hate and of simply being here. And anyone who *might* stop us isn't here, which feels like such an obvious statement but it gives me a little of the winter's stab again.

She either takes my silence for agreement or doesn't care, as she starts her carving again. When she finishes and straightens up a couple of minutes later, I laugh. She's simply carved the word "TARDIS" into the wood.

"Now you can't say it doesn't look like a TARDIS in here," she says with a grin.

"You're such a dork," I tell her.

"Takes one to know one." She leans back against the clear wall behind us. "So, if you had to choose whether to travel to the past or the future in the TARDIS, which would you choose?"

"Hmm." I take my time to consider the options.

When I don't answer right away, she says, "I'd pick the future for sure."

"Aren't you afraid of what you'd see? If the whole world devolves into chaos in the next fifty years because of global warming, I'm not sure I want to know that. Too depressing."

"Where would you go in the past?"

"It would be cool to go back and see how the pyramids were made. No explanation I've read makes perfect logical sense. It seems so impossible that they were made without any present-day technology."

"Maybe they were made by aliens."

"Yes, I'm sure aliens came to earth just to help some pharaohs make their tombs, then left."

"Maybe they never left. Maybe they're still here. Maybe you're an alien, and you're acting like aliens don't exist just to throw me off the scent." She narrows her eyes at me.

"If your theory was true, why would I have brought up the apparently-alien-made pyramids in the first place?" I point out. "That makes no sense."

"Hmm, a good point."

We talk like that for a while longer, debating where we'd travel in time, until we realize it's probably been longer than twenty minutes. So we rush back to the house, still careful to avoid stepping on any cracks, leaving our TARDIS behind.

It rains Halloween morning. Not just a light drizzle, but the kind of rain where it feels like the clouds have opened up hatches and are pouring their entire insides out. Mom and Dad leave late for work so they can drive us kids to school, and I put up the hood on my coat, but even so, by the time I get to school, my hair is coated in droplets of rain. Which means once it dries, it's a frizzy mess.

I duck into the bathroom after first period to pat the frizzier parts of my curls down with a bit of the gel I keep in my backpack, which means I'm almost late for second period science. I step through the doorway just as the second bell rings.

"Close call, Vera," Ms. Larson says. "Take your seat quickly, please."

I slide onto my stool beside Sarah. She gives me a half smile but says nothing until Ms. Larson finishes her lesson and releases us to do our lab work with our partner.

"What are you supposed to be dressed as?" Sarah asks as we start to set up our Bunsen burner. "A grape?"

I shake my head. "Just the color purple." Riven was worried we were going to make a mess of our costumes before tonight, so she insisted we wear simple costumes during the day and save the big guns for our evening festivities. Riven, Bolu, Pete, and I decided last minute to dress as colors for the school day, and since I was the only one with a purple skirt and leggings, that's the color I ended up with.

"That's kind of boring," Sarah says.

"Says the person not wearing a costume at all," I counter. Sarah's wearing jeans and a knit sweater—a burgundy and orange one this time—like usual.

Her freckled cheeks turn pink. "Um, yeah, I was going to wear a costume, but I chickened out at the last minute," she says quietly so only I can hear. "I wasn't sure if that's something kids still did in high school."

"Oh!" I say, suddenly looking around to see how many of our classmates are in costume. (Answer: significantly less than half.) "I didn't even think of that."

"Well, you and your friends dressed up, right? I saw you all this morning. So even if you were the only ones dressed up, at least you wouldn't be alone."

Does that mean she doesn't have any friends at all or just none that dress up for Halloween? It feels rude to ask, so instead I say, "What were you going to dress up as?"

She shrugs. "A unicorn."

I gasp. I don't mean to, but I do.

"What?" A crinkle of worry appears between her eyebrows. "Is that weird?"

"No. Not at all. I—" I break off. Because I don't know why I feel like I've just been punched in the gut. Why the world feels unwound. I blink away the tears that have suddenly pricked my eyes and force a smile onto my face. "I think a unicorn costume would be awesome."

"Would you like a caramel?" comes a voice from the right. I turn and it's Cecily, though her usual pastel colors have been replaced with a flowing black dress and a pointy black hat. I blink a few times, wondering if my imagination has conjured the outfit onto her. But no, she's really dressed as a witch.

I glance back to her usual lab table. Rachel and Hayden, the other two Witches, are dressed the same way.

Is it her fault I'm suddenly feeling this way?

"Nice costume," I say.

"Thanks. Caramel?" she holds out a bag of them. I eye them warily as Sarah declines, pointing to her braces. Are the caramels hexed in some way? Is that a thing you can do—cast a spell on food?

I quickly shake the nonsense thought out of my head. Of course you can't cast a spell on food. Spells don't exist. I take a caramel. "Thanks," I mumble.

"Oh, don't thank me. Ms. Larson asked me to hand them out."

Of course they're not even hers. My mind is slipping away to ridiculous places.

Still, as she moves to the next table, I can't shake the thought that the terrible feeling in my gut arrived just as she did. But maybe there's a perfectly reasonable, scientific explanation for that. Maybe it *is* magic but not the kind my mind keeps freaking out about.

I glance at Ms. Larson, who seems fully engaged in unwrapping a caramel of her own. "Can you give me a minute?" I say to Sarah. "I just need to look something up." Then I sneak my phone out of my backpack and, holding it below the table ledge so it's hidden from Ms. Larson's sight, do a search and pull up a list of aptitudes.

I scan through the seventy-two of them, searching for an explanation as to how Cecily could make me feel these unpleasant feelings. An explanation as to how she managed to disappear the other night.

I glance through the sensory aptitudes. Smell enhancement: no. Sound enhancement: no. Sweet magic: no . . . but—I move on quickly to shove away the sudden rock in my gut. Salt magic: no. No, nope, no, no, nope.

I jump to the body structure aptitudes, where things like muscle growth or minor height fluctuation are no help, either.

Physical science aptitudes, such as Riven's light magic or my unlocking magic, are useless. Same with mental aptitudes, biological aptitudes, and the few miscellaneous, uncategorized ones.

Nothing jumps out at me as an explanation, but maybe I'm missing something. After all, I don't know how every single aptitude works. I slip my phone into my pocket and turn to Sarah, who's idly reading over our lab instructions. "Hey, do you know what type of magic Cecily has?"

Sarah shakes her head. "No idea."

"Darn."

"Have you asked James?" She points to the table behind us, where two guys look like they're about halfway through the lab already. They're both Filipino, like a lot of kids at our school.

"Asked me what?" inquires the shorter of the two. He's got

bright-green glasses and a contagious smile. James Pangilinan. I know his name because he ran for student council at the beginning of the school year and lost to this white girl with perfect teeth and flat-ironed blond hair. I voted for him because I liked his posters, which said "Free drinks on me" and then were hung over all the water fountains. But that's about all I know about him. He didn't go to my junior high.

"What sort of magic Cecily has," Sarah says, turning around in her seat. I glance at Ms. Larson, worried we're going to get in trouble. But judging by the fact that the chatter in the classroom is getting louder and louder and she's doing nothing about it except sitting back in her chair chewing a caramel, I think she's just accepted that it's Friday and it's Halloween and we're all jacked up on sugar and probably not going to be getting a ton of work done anyway. Though I still want to get our lab done, because every mark counts.

Still, if James has answers, I want them. I turn around in my seat, too. "Why would you know? You dating Cecily or something?" The words slip easily out of my mouth, but the thought sends an inexplicable roar of anger through me.

Fortunately, James shakes his head. "Barely know her." He glances back at the Witches, then adds with a cheery grin, "Besides, if I was going to date one of the Witches, it'd be Rachel."

I roll my eyes. "Then how—"

"James has telling magic," Sarah cuts in abruptly. "He can tell what type of magic people have."

"Oh!" I've heard of people with that aptitude, but I've never met anyone with it. My heart leaps in anticipation. "So do you know Cecily's?"

He looks back at the Witches' table and shakes his head. "No, sorry. If I ever knew, I've forgotten."

His lab partner looks back, too. His face is narrow and bony, and a single pimple on the side of his nose looks ready to pop. He didn't go to my junior high, either, so I don't know his name.

"Well, sense it, then," Sarah says, speaking the demand that pops into my head.

"I can't. Not without touching her."

"So go . . ." I start to say, then fade off, unsure of how to finish my sentence.

"Yes, go up to a girl I barely know and lightly rest my hand on her shoulder. That sounds like a great plan!" James laughs.

I study the Witches myself. They've pulled their stools into a little circle, and they're just chatting, not even bothering to work on their lab. The bag of caramels is on their lab table. Cecily reaches into the bag to grab one, and it twists her body so she's looking my way. Our eyes meet for a split second before I hurry my gaze away.

I have an idea. But first I need to know if James's magic really works.

I put my hand out toward him. "Can you sense what magic I have?"

"What do you think I am? A cheap parlor trick?" James swats my hand away.

"I—um—sorry." My cheeks flush hot.

James laughs. "I'm kidding. I rarely get to use my magic except as a parlor trick."

"Oh. Right. Okay."

I start to reach my hand out again, but he waves it away. "Got it already. You have unlocking magic."

"That's rare," James's lab partner says. It sounds sort of like an accusation.

"But still common enough that people want security systems," James says with a grin before I can wonder what his buddy has against rare aptitudes. "Thanks for keeping my family in business."

Thanks to some notorious criminals throughout history with unlocking magic, once security systems were invented, they became immediately popular. Unlocking magic might open a door, but it can't stop an alarm from going off or the police from being called.

"My pleasure," I say. "Hey, so what if there was a way for you to touch Cecily without seeming like a creep? Would you figure out her magic for me?"

James shrugs. "Sure. But you'd owe me."

I crinkle my nose. "I'm not kissing you or anything like that."

James crinkles his own nose in return. "Ew, no, I told you, I'm not a creep. I just meant you could buy me a bag of chips from the vending machine or something."

I laugh. "Okay. Deal." Then I explain to him my idea. His lab partner just shakes his head, mumbling something under his breath, but James agrees right away to give it a try.

A few minutes later, James and I are both heading toward the back of the room to get a caramel from the bag on the Witches' table. James gets one first, and he does a brilliant job of moving the bag right to the edge of the table, so when I reach for one, it's an easy flick of the wrist, and the bag is on the floor, caramels scattered everywhere.

"Oops!" I say, perhaps a wee bit too theatrically.

James and I both lean down to start collecting the caramels strewn across the floor, and for a moment, as we crouch down on the floor and our classmates just stare at us, I think the plan won't work.

But then Cecily hops down off her stool and gathers up caramels, too.

Which means James can time it so that they both reach for the bag at the same time. I don't catch the moment it happens—the moment their hands touch—but I hear James's polite, "Oops, sorry, go ahead," and when I catch his eye, he grins at me, and I know he's got it.

Speed magic. That's got to be what he'll report to me. Or some kind of emotional manipulation magic. I don't remember seeing either of those on the list, and I've never heard of them before, but if they did exist, they'd explain everything.

Well, speed magic would only explain why she disappeared, and emotional manipulation magic would only explain these strange feelings in my gut, so I guess one or the other wouldn't explain everything. It would need to be something that explains both. Something that would allow me to rule out this silly idea my brain has that she's an actual witch once and for all.

When we get back to our respective tables, I look at James expectantly. But he just gives me an impish grin. "Where's my bag of chips?"

I scowl at him. "What, you think I have some sort of chip magic and can conjure chips out of nothing? Even if that was a thing, you already read my aptitude and know I don't. I'll owe you."

"Fine." He sighs dramatically. "She has . . . drumroll please . . ." He waits for us to drum our fingers against the table. "Light magic."

"Light magic? Are you sure?" That's what Riven has. And Riven certainly can't disappear.

"I'm sure," James says. "Why? Were you expecting something else?"

At the back of the room, Cecily chats with her fellow Witches, oblivious to the fact that we're talking about her. I shrug. "I don't know what I was expecting." Something that would explain everything. But this explains nothing.

"Why did you want to know, anyways?" James asks.

I shrug again. "Personal reasons," I say, because I can't exactly say that I'm starting to wonder if she's cast some sort of spell on me that makes me cry at the thought of spaghetti or the mention of a unicorn costume.

"Oh, come on," James's lab partner says to me with a scowl. "You owe us a better explanation than that!"

I scowl right back at him. "What's your name again?"

The lines in his forehead deepen into rivets. "I've been sitting behind you for two months."

That doesn't magically make me know your name, I want to spit out at him, but I hold my tongue instead. "Yeah, sorry, I'm really bad with names."

We stare at each other for a moment before James jumps in, uncomfortable with the tension. "His name's Vincent."

"Well, Vincent," I say, "I owe you guys nothing. Except you, of course." I look at James. "I owe *you* a bag of chips." And then I whirl around in my seat and dive back into the lab assignment so Sarah and I can finish it before the period is over.

CHAPTER EIGHT

By the time the school day is over, the rain has stopped, though the pavement still glistens, reflecting the red and green of the stoplights.

"Weather looks good," Pete reports as he checks his phone.

"Good thing our costumes don't involve flowing dresses with long trains," Riven says as she steps over a big puddle.

"Aw, man, now I wish we were going to be wearing flowing dresses with long trains." Bolu hops over the same puddle.

"Me, too," Pete says.

Riven stops in her tracks and looks Pete up and down. "I think you'd look fabulous in yellow. Like Belle."

"That's it. Next year, we're doing Disney princesses again," I chime in.

When we get to Riven's house, we *ooh* and *aah* over Riven's exceptional fake blood work, then order pizza.

As we finish dinner, Bolu wanders over to the row of photos on a side table in the dining room that I've seen her eyeing before. "These are from past Halloweens, right?" she asks. "I love them."

She lifts them up one at a time. I grin as she picks up the first few of me and Riven, arm in arm, all dolled up in our various costumes. But then she picks up the photos from eighth and ninth grade, and the smile falls off my face.

"You're missing an earthbender," Bolu says, holding up the one from last year, and though I'm impressed she managed to figure out our costumes right away, there's a hole in my gut, as though a bullet has just shot clean through me.

"Yeah, well, that's the most boring type of bender, anyways," Pete says, though his voice sounds about an octave lower than his usual jokey self's.

Bolu sets the photo down and turns around. She studies all three of us, and I realize we've stopped moving, as if the photo has frozen us in place. "What's wrong?" she asks. "Was that a really bad year for trick-or-treating or something?"

Riven shakes her head. "No. It was great."

And it was. It snowed, but we bundled up in our costumes—especially easy for me to do in my waterbender parka—and when we finished doing our food drive duties, we decided to keep going and do some trick-or-treating and just not tell my mom. And we collected a crap-ton of candy, then gorged ourselves on it as we watched *It's the Great Pumpkin, Charlie Brown*, and then laughed ourselves silly doing Halloween-themed Mad Libs.

It was a laughter-filled evening of fun and silliness, and yet, when I think of it, it's like there's a hole where my happiness should be. And judging by Riven's and Pete's stricken faces, they feel the same way.

What is going on?!

"Well, this year will be even better!" Bolu declares, and something about that idea stings.

"Come on, let's costume up," Pete says, changing the subject.

"Yeah, good idea," Riven says.

Bolu's face droops as she looks from Pete to Riven to me, perhaps disappointed that we didn't agree that this year would be the best year ever. So I walk up to her, put the photo down, and throw my arm around her shoulders, turning us away from the inexplicably gut-wrenching picture. "You're right, Bolu. This year will definitely be the best year yet!"

She grins at that.

Half an hour later, we're in our onesies, with fake blood spattered on our faces, heading out to the food drive starting location, where we'll get the map of our assigned streets. Then we're going from house to house, explaining that we're collecting for the food drive and happily accepting any bonus candy that's offered to us.

On one street, as we pass a dark, sinister-looking graveyard, we run into a group of classmates from school. One of the girls is dressed as a sexy cat, with cat ears on her head and a short black skirt and black tank top under her open coat, while the other is in jeans with the word "Paprika" taped to her fitted orange shirt. *How unoriginal*, I think, though I can't help but glance down at the full-on onesie I'm wearing.

"You going to Morgan's party?" one of the guys—who doesn't seem to be wearing a costume at all—shouts at us as they pass by.

"Yeah, maybe," Pete calls back, noncommittally, though we all know our real answer is no. Pete and I don't drink, and Riven says that if she wanted the experience of going to a party, she could just blast crappy music and get her cat to vomit on her foot without having to step out of her own house. And Bolu—well, I don't know. I know she's not religious, though she insists that both she and Riven attend our youth group, since "we have to keep the group together." Maybe she'd want to go to that type of party if she could convince the rest of us to join her. Maybe she'd dress as the prime minister or something, if we hadn't forced her into a dog onesie.

I turn to her now. "Hey, Bolu, do you ever wish we were the kind of people who went to those sorts of parties?"

Bolu crinkles her nose. "What? No. I hang around with you guys for a reason."

I loop my fluffy shark arm through her fluffy dog arm. "And we're glad you do."

"Well, good, because—"

But I don't catch the rest of what she says because I spot something in the graveyard, and I release her arm and twist to see better.

Dark figures pass like shadows between the gravestones. It's too dark and they're too far away to make out their faces, but the shapes are clear. They're in black, with flowing dresses and pointy hats. Three of them.

"Vera, are you coming?" Riven calls to me. She and Pete are almost at the next door. Bolu is a few steps ahead of me, looking back, as though she wants to catch up with the others but doesn't want to leave me behind.

I return my gaze to the graveyard. It's all shadow and barren trees and moonlight bouncing off white gravestones. And those three figures, still winding slowly between the graves.

Witches in a graveyard. Holes in my happiness. Questions that need answering.

"I'll be right back," I call to my friends, and I set down my bag of canned goods and take off in a run down the graveyard path.

I regret my decision almost immediately. It's dark, and fog that I swear wasn't there before begins to rise around my feet. The moon disappears behind a cloud, and the gravestones all around me turn from shadowy to shrouded in darkness. A leafless tree reaches its arms menacingly out toward me. The *thud-thudding* of my shoes against the gravel path is almost as loud as my heart. I slow to a walk, afraid the Witches will hear me coming. Which is when I realize I've lost them. I spin around in a circle and don't see them in any direction.

I'm standing in the middle of a graveyard, all alone, in the dark, on Halloween. I'm an idiot. I'm that girl who hears a noise outside in a horror movie and goes alone to check on it instead of calling for the police.

A hand grabs my shoulder, and I try to scream, but nothing comes out except a high-pitched squeak.

I whirl around.

A creature stands on the path, blood-covered and fuzzy and . . . "Bolu?"

She puts her hands on her knees and leans over, panting. "You . . . run . . . fast . . ."

"Sorry, I didn't know you were following me!"

"I wasn't . . . about to let . . . you go into a graveyard . . . by yourself . . ."

"Hey, I could handle it!"

She straightens up. "Is that why you screamed when I touched your shoulder?"

"Well, you shouldn't sneak up on someone in a graveyard like that!"

She laughs, and I grin sheepishly, then take her arm. "Come on, let's head back. I lost—" I suddenly break off and duck to the ground, pulling Bolu with me.

"What the he—"

"Shhhhhh, they'll hear us," I whisper, though they're probably too far away to hear.

"Who will?" Bolu whispers back.

I just shake my head. "Stay here. I'll be right back." Before she can protest, I head off the path between the graves, staying as crouched and low to the ground as I can. I weave between the stones, right, then straight, then right again.

And then there they are. The Witches. Standing around a gravestone, holding hands. The clouds drift away from the moon at that moment, and the moonlight that pours down turns them into silhouettes. I'm not close enough to hear, but I can imagine them in my head—chanting, moaning, reciting the words of some spell, calling on some demon to help them.

It's wrong. It's blasphemous.

It's also ridiculous.

I almost stand up straight and laugh. It's illogical to be afraid of three girls from school who've never done anything the least bit frightening. I come up with a logic problem to calm my breaths. If Cecily said, "None of us are knaves," and Hayden said, "Cecily is a knight," and Rachel said, "Either Cecily or Hayden is lying, but not both," that would mean that all three Witches were knaves.

In front of me, the three knaves release one another's hands, and the one in the middle—Hayden, I think, though it's hard to tell from here—waves her hands around in the air.

And then something rises out of the grave.

The ground doesn't open. It's just a dark shape that starts at the ground and rises upward in a swell. Darkness. Blackness with sweeping arms and a swaying head.

My almost-laugh catches in my throat. I've found my fear again. It holds me in place for one long, breathless moment. And then it turns me on my heels and makes me run as fast as my sneakered feet can carry me.

"Bolu, run!" I hiss at her, grabbing her hand as I pass.

She doesn't ask questions, just takes off with me. Our feet pound up the path, past the tree, out the gate, where Riven and Pete are waiting.

"Are you guys okay?" Riven asks as soon as the graveyard spits us back out onto the sidewalk.

Bolu folds over to catch her breath again.

I look back into the graveyard, searching for a glimpse of the Witches, of the monster of darkness that surely must be chasing after us. But the graveyard is empty and quiet. I glance over at the stones where I remember the Witches being, but there's nothing there.

"We're okay," Bolu says once she's caught her breath. "At least, I think we are. Either we just almost got robbed or this is a really good episode of *Prank'd* or this chick is even more spooked by graveyards than I realized." She points her thumb at me, then turns to face me. "What was that about, anyway?"

And then all three of them are looking at me and waiting for an explanation. And I don't know what to say. Because I'm not sure they'd believe *I just saw some sort of monster rise out of a grave, summoned by the Witches*. In fact, now that I'm back out on the streetlight-illuminated sidewalk, with little kids and their parents walking past, I'm not sure I believe it.

I think of them making fun of me earlier for being a wimp. Somehow, I don't think saying, *I was running from a monster* would support my cause. So instead, I punch Bolu lightly in the arm. "Got you, Bolu!" I say. It comes out all false and loud, but only Riven narrows her eyes at me.

Pete starts to laugh and Bolu says, "You made me run for nothing?!"

"Halloween pranks," I say. "It's our brand-new Halloween tradition. Starting now." Which makes Bolu's face shift abruptly from annoyance to a grin.

"Good one, Vera," she says, still panting. "You really got me."

And then we're all laughing and Bolu's warning me to watch my back next year, and I'm convinced, suddenly, that my brain just made everything up, that I was running from nothing.

I look back at the graveyard as we head to the next house. It's quiet and empty. No sign of Witches. No sign of monsters. Whatever I saw was just a figment of my imagination.

Wasn't it?

That night, I end up staying over at Riven's after Pete and Bolu leave. It's almost midnight, and we should be in bed, but we're both still so jacked up on candy that we end up watching a *Doctor Who* episode instead.

"Hey, Riv," I ask when the episode finishes, "if I told you that I was time traveling with a man in a box, would you believe me or would you tell my parents that you thought I needed to see a therapist?"

Riven rolls over and looks at me. "Obviously I'd believe you. I know you'd never lie about something as brilliant as that." She props herself up on her elbows. "Why? Did the TARDIS show up?"

I shake my head. "No." I'm not sure how to tell her that I'm starting to wonder if magic—the dark kind, the non-aptitude kind—really exists. "I've thought of something else to add to our list, though."

Riven knows immediately what list I'm talking about. She sits up and grabs her notepad off her side table and flips open to the correct page, then grabs a pencil and raises it, poised to write.

"It's silly, though," I say.

"There's no such thing as a silly idea," Riven says.

I raise my eyebrows at her. "Artificial reality?" I say.

"Hey!" She puts her hand on her hip. "That's a brilliant idea!"

"I don't think technology has advanced enough for us to be in an artificial reality."

"Well, maybe it's not *our* technology. Maybe it's aliens." She straightens abruptly. "Aliens! I'm adding that to the list!"

"Aliens? Really?"

"What? You believe in aliens," she says as she writes it down.

"I don't believe aliens exist. I *want* to believe they exist. There's a difference."

"Stop being such a skeptic. What's your idea?"

I decide to just rip off the Band-Aid. "Witchcraft," I say. Then I wait for Riven to laugh at me.

Instead, she grins. "Witchcraft! Yes!" Then she adds it to the list. "What type of witchcraft?"

"Um, whatever kind the Witches do?"

She looks up from her notepad. "The Witches? You think they have something to do with this?"

"I don't know. No. Yes. Maybe."

She narrows her eyes at me and adds teasingly, "You know that witchcraft is completely unrelated to satanism or whatever, right? Wiccans commune with goddesses and gods, not the devil—and I get the impression the Witches are more of the naturalist, 'the power exists in all of us' type witches than goddess-communing Wiccans."

"Of course I knew that," I say, matching her teasing tone. Did I actually know that? I'm not sure. At the very least, I know that now.

"Okay, good. Just wanted to make sure this wasn't some gut feeling based on believing they're making deals with Christianity's devil or something."

I shake my head. "No. Nothing to do with the devil. And it's not just a feeling. I have—" But I break off, because what *do* I have? The fact that Cecily and I keep looking at each other funny in science class. The fact that I've caught her walking past my house, staring up at it intently. The fact that Cecily disappeared. The fact that I saw all the Witches in a graveyard conjure up some shadowy monster that definitely maybe didn't actually exist. Well, that last one is more than nothing, but I can't tell Riven about it. She says she'll believe me, but I know she won't—I don't even believe myself. "Okay, you're right, I don't have anything. But we don't have evidence for any of these theories."

Riven taps her pencil against her knee as she looks over her list. "Yeah, I guess that's true. Only one way to fix that, though."

She flips to a blank page and holds up her pencil again. "All right, what evidence have we got?"

I open my mouth, then just let it hang open. I pull at my bottom lip. "I don't know. I'm not even sure what we're trying to solve. It's like we've been called to the scene of a crime but aren't being told what the crime is."

Riven frowns. "We know what it is. It's—" But then she breaks off, too.

"Harder to describe than it feels, isn't it?"

"Yeah, I guess it is." She nibbles at her thumbnail. "So what do we do?"

I reach for the notepad and take it and the pencil from her. "Like you said. We make a list. Or multiple lists." I write at the top of the page, *The Problem*, then flip to the next page and write, *Clues*.

"Yes, I like it." She reaches over and takes the pad back from me, flipping back to *The Problem*. "Okay, tell me something— anything—about what's going on."

"Spaghetti makes me feel weird," I joke, and Riven laughs, but writes it down anyway. "It's more than just feeling weird, though," I say, growing serious. "There are these completely out-of-the-blue moments when something—like spaghetti—punches me in the gut and leaves me winded and gasping for breath. And I can't explain it, but I go from feeling fine to feeling anything but."

Riven lets out a sigh and slumps so her back hits the wall. "Yeah. Yeah, I know exactly what you mean."

We sit there in silence for a few minutes, before I finally say, so quietly it's almost a whisper, "Riven, do you think there's something wrong with us?"

She shrugs. "I don't know. Maybe." She taps her pencil against her knee again. "But if there was something wrong, what are the chances that we'd both be experiencing it? It's got to be pretty dang rare to have multiple people develop some sort of psychosis at the same time for no reason."

She's right. The decreasing daylight and incoming winter do trigger depression in many people around the same time, but this feels different than the symptoms of seasonal affective disorder that the Internet and my cousin Beth have described. It feels more acute, more fluctuating, more reality-altering. And I've never heard of a mental illness like that affecting multiple unrelated people at once.

I lean over and tap her book. "Multiple people," I say. "Write that down."

"As a clue or a problem?"

"Both."

And then we're writing down all sorts of things.

Under *The Problem*:

> spaghetti makes V feel weird
> multiple people
> different triggers for R and V
> some shared triggers for R and V
> Pete seems to experience it, too
> Bolu maybe does too, maybe not
> sad for no reason
> started recently
> kind of like déjà vu

And then under *Clues*:

*multiple people
get "the feeling" when look at Cecily or when
she's near*

Riven looks up at that. "You do?"

"Sometimes. At least I think so. You don't?"

She shrugs. "I don't know. I don't think I've tried looking at her."

"Well, what about the other night when she was passing my house? Did you get the feeling then?"

Riven shakes her head and my shoulders droop. Maybe it *is* all in my head.

But then Riven says, "That was kind of weird how intensely she was looking at your house, though. Like she was casting a spell or something."

"Right!" I say much too loudly, considering that Riven's mom is already in bed. "That's exactly what I thought."

Riven narrows her eyes at me. "You did? That doesn't seem like you. In fact, now that I think about it, this whole witchcraft theory doesn't seem like you at all."

"Yeah, well, it wasn't. But tonight . . ." I trail off. I wasn't going to tell her anything about tonight.

Riven grabs my sleeve and tugs it with a burst of excitement. "What happened tonight? I knew there was something more going on than you playing a joke on Bolu."

"Well, that's all it was. Just playing a joke. You know me— Jokey McJokerson."

"Dude. You're a terrible liar."

"I'm not."

She takes my hand in hers and puts on a serious face, like she's about to deliver bad news. "You are. You're an absolutely horrendous liar."

"Fine," I say with a sigh. And then I tell her everything. About seeing the Witches. About creeping up on them. About seeing the shadowy darkness that rose from the grave.

When I finish, Riven swears. "Wow. How big was it?"

I shrug. "I don't know. Person-size? I'm sure I only imagined it though and—" I break off as Riven grabs her phone and starts typing something into it. "What are you doing?" I ask, leaning over to look.

She's typed "Shadow Monster Edmonton" into the search bar. "Checking to see if there have been any reports of sightings or maulings or people with their souls sucked out of them."

I blink at her a few times. "We are very different people."

She looks up from her phone. "What? Why do you say that?"

"Because if you told me this, I'd be sure you were pulling my leg."

She furrows her eyebrows. "*Are* you pulling my leg?"

I bite my lip. There's still time for an out. Still time to not look like a fool. "No," I say. "I'm not."

"I didn't think so." She leans over and wraps her arms around my shoulders. "And I like my little different-than-me skeptic who doesn't even believe her own story."

I reach my hand up, awkwardly threading it through her arms, and pat her on the head. "I like you too, Riv."

She releases me. "Of course you do. I'm pretty great." Then she picks up the notebook again and flips back a couple of pages to our list of theories. Then she puts a little star beside "Witchcraft."

"Well, I think we know what we're investigating next."

"How are we supposed to investigate?"

"We can check out the graveyard to start." She moves forward on the bed as if she's planning to head there now.

"No way. I'm not going to a graveyard in the middle of the night on Halloween."

"I didn't mean now, you dork. We can go tomorrow."

"Okay. But if the shadow monster eats us, don't blame me."

"If I get eaten, I won't be capable of blaming anyone."

"A good point. Maybe we shouldn't go at all."

"Scaredy-cat," she teases.

"Reckless," I tease back, though I'm glad we've decided to go. I want answers. I'm not sure what I believe anymore, but there's one thing I do know: I'm glad I told Riven.

CHAPTER NINE

The graveyard looks so different in the morning. The grass is dotted with dew, and the drops glisten as the long rays of the morning sun scatter across the yard. In some places, the gravestones are cracked and mossy green, while in others they're new and glossy; none of them appear shadowy or foreboding like they did last night.

And it's big. Bigger than I realized last night, when the darkness faded away its far-flung edges. It's disorienting. "How far do you think I ran? This far?" I ask Riven as we walk along the gravel path.

"Oh, gosh, I don't know. You ran far enough that we couldn't really see you anymore. But it was really dark."

I spin in a circle, trying to get my bearings. "Well, I didn't get as far as when the path splits off," I say, pointing a ways ahead. "At least, I don't think I did. So maybe . . . around here? And then I crouched and walked through the graves for a bit." I lead Riven off the path to the left.

We wind through the gravestones, shoes soaking up the dew.

"Aw, this one's for a kid," Riven says, stopping beside a grave.

I draw up beside her, and we both bow our heads for a moment in respect for the seven-year-old girl and the family that mourns her.

"What are we looking for, anyways?" I ask as we move on.

"I don't know. A split-open grave, maybe? Or some bones on the ground in a circle?"

I shudder. "Creepy. You really think we'll find something that morbid?"

She shrugs. "You were the one who saw a shadowy monster rise out of a grave."

She's right, though in the brightness of morning, it seems near impossible that's what I really saw. "I don't know that I really did. It was probably just the shadow of a grave. Or maybe it was all a prank and they had someone rise from the ground dressed all in black."

"Yeah, because they totally anticipated that you'd pass at just the right time and stalk them into a graveyard," Riven says sarcastically.

"Maybe I wasn't the target," I suggest, though she's right. It seems unlikely that it was a prank. I don't think they even knew anyone was there.

So regardless of how silly it feels in the daylight, we wander through the graves, searching for signs of witchcraft.

After forty-five minutes, we've found . . . absolutely nothing. No split-open graves. No bones arranged in any shapes. No monsters made of shadow. No monsters at all except lingering mists of grief.

"Are you sure we're on the right side of the path?" Riven asks as we come together again after splitting up down two separate rows.

I nod. "I'm pretty certain."

"But not one hundred percent certain?"

"I don't know, Riv. I don't really feel certain of anything anymore."

"Fair," she says, and then we just stand there, looking around.

And as I study all the graves—all the monuments to lost ones who were loved, where their friends and family can come to remember them—I suddenly feel like I've been robbed. The anger swirls through me like a hurricane. I want to throw something. I want to kick up a chunk of grass and send it hurtling. I want to summon down asteroids to destroy the whole place.

Then just as quickly, the feeling is gone, and I'm left with an emptiness inside me where the anger used to be.

"Let's give it up," I say. "I don't think we're going to find anything."

"Give up the whole investigation?" Riven asks.

"No!" The word pops out of my mouth unbidden.

Riven laughs. "Okay, so give up on the graveyard but not the investigation. Got it."

I'm struck with a sudden fear that she's just humoring me about all of this. "You . . . you do think there's something worth investigating, right?"

"Dude. You saw the Witches conjure up a monster in a graveyard!"

"That I probably imagined! Besides, that's not really the part I mean needs investigating . . ." I trail off. I'm talking about the weird feelings—the crying for no reason, the anger that flares up in the middle of a graveyard, the pocket of emptiness that sits right behind my heart. But if Riven doesn't feel those things, too, then maybe there's nothing to investigate at all. Maybe it's simply time to see a psychiatrist.

But Riven grows quiet. "We should definitely keep investigating," she says, her voice coming out as barely a whisper. Then she reaches out and takes my hand. And we stand there together in the graveyard, mourning answers we have yet to find.

▲ ▲ ▲ ▲ ▲ ▲ ▲ ▲ ▲ ▲ ▲ ▲ ▲

Pete is back at church on Sunday. He slips into the seat beside me just as worship starts. We sit in the front left section of the church, where all the youth usually congregate—though it was sparse last Sunday and this one, since our youth pastor took a group of the older kids on a mission trip. Just sitting in this section makes me feel sort of sad, though I can't explain why.

I give Pete a nod and then stand to sing with the rest of the congregation. The words are on the screen at the front of the church, but I know this song by heart, so I close my eyes, let everything that's been going on all week wash away, and lose myself to the music. I love worship. It's the one time in the week where my brain lets me have a rest.

Once worship finishes, we sit down as our pastor starts his long-winded announcements. I wait for Pete to lean in and whisper a joke to me about something or other, like he usually does, but nothing comes. I glance at him out of the corner of my eye. His eyes are glazed over as he stares forward at the screen. His shoulders are slumped and his hands sit limp at his sides. He looks as worn out as I feel. Even more so, probably.

I lean toward him. "You feeling okay?" I whisper.

He blinks a few times before his gaze moves in my direction. "Yeah, just tired."

I have a weird desire to hug him, or just let him rest his head on my shoulder. Which makes me realize how close we're sitting. Only four or five inches apart. Closer than two unrelated teens of the opposite sex should be sitting in church. I slide away from Pete a little, then glance at him again.

If I had Riven's notebook with me, I'd add *Pete looks like he was run over by a bus* to one of our lists. I suddenly feel bad that we haven't included him in our investigation talk. He's obviously going through some weird crap, too. Well, I can include him now. Maybe he knows something about the Witches.

Onstage, our pastor flips to a new slide and tells us all in excruciating detail about the seniors' group that we've been hearing about every Sunday for my entire life. Our pastor's sermons are great—interesting and succinct—but he hasn't figured out how to use that same skill during announcements.

I lean toward Pete again. "Hey, do you think witchcraft really exists?" I whisper.

That wakes him up. He looks at me and frowns. "Witchcraft?"

"Yeah, like spells and curses and stuff?"

A laugh pops out of him, loud enough that one of the girls in the row ahead of us turns around and glares at him. He covers his mouth with his hand. He waits until she turns back around, her perfect curling-iron curls bobbing as she does. My natural curls never look like that. Then he whispers to me, "Obviously not."

My disappointment must show in my face because his eyebrows fly up. "Wait, do you?"

"No," I say automatically, but it's too late. He's read me.

"You do," he whispers, amusement spreading across his face. "You think there are witches with voodoo dolls and all sorts of magical crap who go around cursing people."

"I mean, those people definitely exist," I point out.

"Yeah, but you think their spells actually work." He's laughing at me. Not cruelly, just the way I would have laughed at myself a couple of weeks ago. Disbelievingly.

"Never mind. I shouldn't have said anything."

"Don't worry," he whispers. "Your secret's safe with me."

"I don't have a secret," I spit back. But I do. I have lots of secrets. I'm just not going to share any of them with him. Not anymore. Our investigation will continue without Pete's help. "Forget I said anything."

▲ ● ▲ ▲ ▲ ▲ ▲ ▲ ▲ ▲ ▲ ▲

On Monday at school, I half expect Pete to make fun of me as soon as he sees me, but I guess he was serious about the whole keeping it a secret thing, because he doesn't say anything. Though actually, he doesn't say anything at all, just ambles up to us and leans against a nearby locker with a sigh.

"You okay, Pete?" Riven asks.

"Hmm? Yeah."

Later, I'm adding *Pete not talking* to Riven's notebook, too.

Bolu glances at Pete and then says to us all, like she knows we need a change of topic, "Hey, did you guys notice all those try-hard girls wearing those sweaters this morning? Like the ones on student council and the newspaper and stuff? Apparently they're having an ugly sweater contest today."

Now that she mentions it, I did notice a higher-than-usual number of weird sweaters this morning, but I assumed there was some new fall fashion trend I wasn't aware of.

"Oh man, I wish I'd known," Riven says. "My dad has this absolutely hideous puke-green monstrosity—I totally could have won."

Her voice drops to a whisper. "Like them," she says. "I totally could have beaten them." As if we had just given them their cue in the ugly sweater fashion show, two girls stride down the hall in matching fitted pink sweaters with a pair of pom-poms hanging from their collars.

Bolu watches them stroll past, and I wonder if it bothers her that her new friends knew nothing about this seemingly popular event.

"We could have an ugly sweater contest of our own at Christmas time," I suggest.

Bolu's face lights up. "Ooh, that'd be fun. Another group tradition, like Halloween!" I should have known that she'd be more excited about being included in our group than about whatever wider school fads are happening. I need to stop doubting her. "By the way," she adds, "what did you all get up to for the rest of the weekend?"

Which makes me fidget with the strap of my backpack. She'd probably want to know the whole shadow monster story, except Pete laughed at me for hinting at a part of it. I don't feel ready to be laughed at all over again. And it should be okay to have some things that are just mine and Riven's, right? Like *Doctor Who*?

But I don't exactly want to lie to her open, smiling face, either.

"I . . . really have to pee," I blurt out. Which isn't actually a lie because now that I say that, I do.

Riven quirks an eyebrow at me. "There are places in this building where you can deal with that particular little issue, you know."

"A good point. I should go do that." When I turn, though, Bolu shifts her feet in my direction like she's planning to join me. And if she does, I'll have to answer her question. "Oh, uh, you guys don't have to come with me," I add awkwardly.

"Well good, 'cuz I don't think they'll let me," Pete says.

That starts Riven off on a rant about how the school really needs to set up some gender-neutral bathrooms, and while they're distracted, I speed off toward the nearest bathroom alone, narrowly avoiding being either a knight or a knave.

The girls' bathroom on the bottom floor is not exactly an attractive place. It looks like it was designed in the seventies—which it probably was. The walls and floor are covered in seafoam-green tile, and opaque green glass windows along the top of one wall let in a shimmering light that makes the whole place feel as if it's underwater. With the terrible lighting, it's not my bathroom of choice if I want to fix my hair or makeup, but it's fine if I just want to use the facilities.

The nice thing is since it's the least popular bathroom, it's usually quiet. Today, though, as I finish in my stall, I hear the bathroom door open, and then there's the sound of running feet, a sniffling nose, and . . . crying?

As I step out of my stall and head to the sink, I try not to look at the figure in the corner of the bathroom, behind the stalls. But I can't help but catch a glimpse of her in the mirror as I wash my hands.

"Sarah?" I turn around so I'm facing her. Yep, it's definitely my science lab partner who's crouching in the corner of the bathroom like a scared rabbit, tears streaming down her face. "Are you okay?"

She wipes a sleeve across her face, which is when I realize she's holding a piece of paper. The corners are torn off, like it was taped somewhere and she ripped it down.

"Sorry," she says. "Just having a bad day."

"That's a depressing thing to say, considering that the day hasn't really even started yet," I point out.

She sniffles. "Yeah. Well. This was taped to my locker when I got here."

I head over and sit beside her on the cold floor, and while she doesn't thrust the paper at me, she doesn't object when I reach out and take it from her, either.

"UGLY SWEATER CONTEST," it says in bold letters across the top. And then, below that, "Can you find and show off an uglier sweater than the ones Sarah Farrow wears every day?" Under that is today's date and a not-particularly-flattering picture of Sarah in a knitted, flower-patterned sweater that I've seen her in before and actually quite like. "The Ugly Sweater Queen" is scrawled across the bottom, and an enormous crown is doodled on her head.

I wrinkle my nose. "I take it this isn't some loving ribbing from your very best friends?"

I already know what her answer will be. A prankster friend might make up an "Ugly Sweater Queen" poster. But the picture would be flattering, the teasing would be admiring and love-filled, and it would be a private joke, not something that the whole school laughs at.

Sarah shakes her head sadly.

So much for the ugly sweater contest seeming like a fun idea. Why are people the worst?

I quickly fold the poster in half so the picture is no longer visible. "Have you shown this to the principal? Or a teacher? Or anyone?"

She reaches out to take the sheet back from me and shakes her head. "Things like that don't help."

My heart aches as I wonder if she knows that from experience. I'm reluctant to hand the paper back. She doesn't need it around, reminding her of its awfulness. But that's not my decision to make, so I hand it over.

"If it makes you feel any better, my friends and I heard about the ugly sweater contest, but we didn't hear anything about it being associated with you. So I'm guessing that's true for most people involved." I desperately hope that's true. "Still sucks royally, though. Do you want to talk about it?"

She shakes her head, wipes her face with her knitted sleeve again, then rises from where she's been crouched on the floor. She folds the paper again and slides it into her pocket. "No. I think I'll just go home."

I rise, too. "That sounds like a good idea."

I want to press Sarah for more details. I want to ask her if she knows who the ringleader is and why they'd do this, report them to the principal, and then maybe ask Riven to blind them with light magic or something. But Sarah looks like all she wants to do is escape. And with the school halls full of girls who may or may not realize that Sarah is the butt of the joke they're wearing, I don't blame her.

Sarah heads toward the bathroom door, stopping for a minute

at the mirror to rub at her face. She's fortunate she's not wearing makeup, or it'd be a runny mess.

"Hey, Sarah?" I call after her, and she pauses and looks at me. "If there's anything I can do for you, let me know, okay?"

She just nods, and then she's gone.

CHAPTER TEN

Sarah isn't at school the next day. In science class, Ms. Larson assigns me a temporary new partner. "Rachel, can you come up and work with Vera on this lab assignment, please?" she says to one of the Witches, since they are a group of three anyway.

As Rachel slides into the seat beside me, I expect to feel a thunderous sense of foreboding. The last time I saw her was in the graveyard on Friday night, when I watched her and her fellow Witches conjure a shadow monster out of a grave. She should be shimmering evil or at the very least she should give me that same feeling of discomfort I get when my eyes meet Cecily's.

But I feel none of that.

"Hi!" Rachel says with a big, friendly grin. "Sorry your normal lab partner's sick and you're stuck with me."

"Oh, I'm not—it's not—I don't feel stuck," I stammer out. Does she mean I wouldn't want to partner with her because she's a Witch? Does she know what I saw?

She tilts her head to the right. "It's okay; I hate group work, too. It's not fair when they make our grades depend on other people's competence or lack thereof, don't you think? I mean, that sounds kind of terrible, I guess. Now I'm just babbling. What I mean is that I like grouping with Cecily and Hayden because I know they won't bring my grades down, but I know in this case you're the one probably worried about me, because didn't you get the highest grades in your whole junior high last year or something?"

"Oh, um, I don't know," I say, though the heat flushing over my face probably gives away that I'm lying.

"It's okay," she says. "I'm not jealous or anything." Then she leans toward me with a conspiratorial grin that partly makes me want to smack her and partly makes me want to hug her. "Okay, I guess I'm a tiny bit jealous, but I'm sure you work really hard at it, and I have other things going on that take up my time, you know?"

My ears perk up at that. Does she mean her witchcraft? And it occurs to me, suddenly, that with one of the Witches as my lab partner, this is the perfect time to continue my and Riven's investigation. Except I can't figure out what to say or to ask until we're partway through our lab. Then, as I'm passing Rachel a test tube, I say, casually, "So, do you believe in monsters?"

I expect either dawning fear or laughter at the ridiculousness of my question to spread over her face, but she simply tilts her head again and considers. "Do you mean do I believe in the existence of creatures that aren't scientifically classified but that exist in myths and legends? Or do you mean do I believe that people can become so corrupt that they lose their humanity and become monsters? Or something else?"

"Uh . . . the former, I guess."

"Hmm . . ." She pauses, apparently giving it serious thought. "Well, scientists are still regularly discovering new species, especially in the ocean. So I think there are probably lots of creatures existing that haven't been classified yet. And I suppose it's theoretically possible that some creatures from myths and legends did actually exist at some point but have gone extinct or become so rare that we almost never see them."

I stare at her.

"What?" she asks.

"Nothing. That's just not what I expected you to say."

"No? Why not?" She looks straight into my eyes when she asks. It's disarming.

"I—um—" What am I supposed to say? Because I didn't realize how smart you are? Because you're pretty quiet in class usually, and I've never heard you talk this much? Because I thought you'd be all witchy and mystical? Because I saw you and your friends conjure a monster out of a grave Friday night? "I don't know. That's just an interesting way of thinking about it," I say pathetically.

"I have a hard time shutting off my brain sometimes," she says.

"You and me both."

"Yeah?"

"Yeah."

"Probably why we do so well in school. Always thinking."

I'm not used to talking so candidly about grades. Pete and Bolu and Riven and I almost never talk about our grades, unless something is particularly monumental or devastating. "Yeah, maybe," I say. "So, should we finish our lab?"

"Let's do it," she says. And for the rest of the class, we focus on our work, and I don't ask her about monsters again.

After school at my house, I tell Riven about my conversation with Rachel. We've taken Gertie and Isaac out to the backyard, where they're making restaurant food out of leaves and sticks. Riven and I are sitting on the steps of the back porch, notepad and pencil at our feet, all the "pizzas" we've "eaten" behind us on the porch.

"Rachel talked about monsters like they're something that could theoretically but probably not exist. Not like she and her witch friends just conjured one out of a grave." Riven listens intently, chin in her hand. "And I didn't get any kind of weird feeling when I looked at her, either," I add as an afterthought.

"Hmm. So what do you think it means?" Riven asks me just as Isaac runs up to her with a leaf on a stick. "For me? Delicious!" And then she pretends to gobble it down.

"I don't know what it means," I say once Isaac runs off again. "I don't know what anything means." I take Riven's notepad and write in some of the things I've been thinking about lately. How Pete has been strangely quiet. How Rachel didn't flinch at the mention of monsters. How my usual pew at church makes me sad. "Can you draw a church pew?" I ask Riven as I hand the notepad back to her.

"A church pew? I don't know how to draw a church pew."

"Of course you do. It's not like you've never been to church with me before." When we were younger, Riven used to come with us once in a while on Sunday if she slept over Saturday night, though now she just goes home when we leave for church. She's started coming to Friday night youth group, though, mostly because Bolu insists.

"Fine," she says. She takes off her mittens, even though it's only a little above freezing and her fingers will be cold, and then she proceeds to draw a perfect rendition of the front of our church, with a couple of rows of pews off to the left—exactly where I usually sit. And exactly the place that stirs up what I'm beginning to think of as "The Feeling."

"Maybe Rachel is just a really good liar," Riven suggests as she finishes up the sketch.

"Yeah, maybe." I chew on my lip. "How would we figure that out, though?"

A small grin sneaks across Riven's face. "We follow them."

"Hey! Don't actually eat the leaves!" I shout at my siblings, then turn back to Riven, who's leaned back on her elbows. "Follow them? Really?"

"Hey, you're the one who followed them through the graveyard!"

I laugh. "Touché. And I suppose I did try to follow Cecily when she passed our house once."

Riven sits up. "You did? What happened?"

"She disappeared."

"Disappeared? Like poof?" She waves her hand in the air.

"Like poof!" I mimic her gesture, then shrug. "Well, not quite like poof. I turned the corner and she was gone."

Riven taps her fingers against her leg. "So she could have gone into a house or something?"

"Who's the skeptic now?"

Before she can answer, Gertie starts to cry, and Riven and I both hop up off the porch and rush toward her and Isaac.

It turns out that Isaac used his color magic to turn Gertie's favorite purple shoes a splotchy green.

"Oh, Gertie, you know they'll just fade back to purple in a few hours," I tell her.

"B-But I don't w-want them to be g-green," she sobs.

I wish we knew what Gertie's magic was so in times like this I could just counsel her to use her own magic as revenge. Admittedly, that's perhaps not the best advice.

Riven leans down and wraps her in a big hug.

"Isaac, can you just change them back again, please?"

Isaac crosses his arms. "I'm not 'upposed to."

"I don't mean undo it," I say. He once got carried away and covered an entire wall of our house with a psychedelic rainbow of colors, then felt so guilty about it that he tried to undo the whole thing in one go and passed out right there on our living room floor. "Just change it to another color." I'd suggest he just layer on purple again, but that would probably just lead to Gertie sobbing that he didn't get the shade of purple quite right, so perhaps best not to risk that route. "Gertie, you can have your shoes be any color you want for the next few hours. Isn't that lucky? What color do you want?"

It takes Riven chiming in, too, about how cool and lucky it is, but we finally convince Gertie to choose a new color—sunshine yellow—and Isaac to make the change, and the next thing we know, they're back to playing together again like not a single tear was shed or shoe discolored.

"What were we talking about, again?" Riven asks as we stand there in the middle of the yard.

"Following the Witches and what a ridiculous plan that is."

Riven puts her hand on her hip. "It's not ridiculous."

"It is. What are we supposed to do? Stalk them out of school, always staying one block behind them, and somehow never be seen? I don't think that actually works in real life, especially when they know who we are."

"Hmm," Riven says, as she chews on her lip. "Do you know where they live? Whichever house they all go to has to be where they do their witchcraft, right?"

I shrug. "You'd think."

"Then we hang outside their houses in a car, like a stakeout. Wait and see where they all show up."

"We don't know where they live," I point out.

Riven walks across the yard to grab the notebook off the deck. She flips to a new page and writes:

> Plan
> Step 1: find out where the witches live
> Step 2: stakeout
> Step 3:

"What's step three?" she asks.

"I'm not even convinced we can accomplish step one."

"Sure we can. Who do we know who's friends with them?"

I scan my brain. "Maybe Larissa? From youth group? She knows everyone."

"There you go. Larissa from youth group. When's the next youth group thing?"

"Friday."

"This Friday? Perfect. We'll ask her there."

"You mean you're voluntarily coming to youth group?" Even though she always comes, it's not usually without complaint.

"If that's what we've got to do to catch some witches, that's what we've got to do."

Sarah is back at school for our next science class. She pulls herself onto her stool without even acknowledging me.

"Are you okay?" I ask.

She turns toward me and smiles. "Sure. Why do you ask?"

I hesitate, suddenly unsure what to say. I can't think why I feel so worried about her. It's not like anything's happened. I haven't seen her since her last science class. And she looks fine. She's wearing a pale pink knit sweater today, and it gives her freckled cheeks a rosy glow. "Well, you missed last class," I say, though that doesn't really feel like the whole story.

"Oh, yeah." She frowns and her gaze floats off toward the ceiling for a moment, as the smile starts to slip off her face. But then it's like she catches it before it hits the ground. "I'm fine. Onward and upward, right?"

"Right," I say.

Ms. Larson quiets the class then and lets us know that someone from student council would like to make an announcement.

And then James Pangilinan hops off his stool from behind us, approaches the front of the class, and starts to talk about an upcoming fundraiser.

There's a tug on my sleeve. "When did James join student council?" Sarah whispers.

When I turn to her, she looks spooked—like she's seen a ghost.

When I glance at James again, I've caught her confusion. Because yeah, there does feel like there's something weird about James being on student council that I can't quite put my finger on. I whisper back, "Didn't he . . . wasn't he . . ." I give my head a shake and the memory comes flooding back to me. "He ran unopposed at the start of the year, didn't he?"

Her eyebrows relax. "Yes. Yes, that's right." She chews her lip as she considers this. "What'd his posters say? It was something funny."

It takes me a moment, but then I remember. "'Vote for me. Because there isn't anyone else to vote for.'"

She lets out a snort-giggle that prompts Ms. Larson to glare in our direction, but it feels good to make Sarah laugh. Whatever strange feeling had washed over both of us has passed, and we both give James a thumbs-up as he returns to his seat and Ms. Larson starts her lecture.

At the end of class, as we're packing up our books, I turn to Sarah abruptly. "Hey, Sarah, do you want to come to my youth group with me and my friends on Friday evening? I'm not trying to convert you or anything. It's just a fun games night. My friends Riven and Bolu will both be coming, and they're not religious."

I'm not sure what compels me to invite her. As soon as the words are out of my mouth, I wish I could take them back. She probably has her own friends and her own Friday night plans. Though now that I think about it, I don't know that I've ever seen her hanging out with anyone in particular.

"This Friday night?" She takes only a moment to consider. "Sure. That sounds like fun."

"Oh, okay, great!" I tell her where to meet us and when. I hope the others don't mind that I've invited her along. I'll just tell them that I had my reasons, and hopefully they won't ask what those reasons were, because honestly, I'm not sure.

CHAPTER ELEVEN

Sarah meets us all at the church on Friday evening.

"Everyone, this is Sarah," I introduce her. Today her knit sweater is beige, with cute little horses prancing across her chest. I wonder how much of her closet is devoted to her sweaters. I'm not sure I've seen her wear the same one twice.

"Hi Sarah, you're in my English class, with Ms. Teter," Bolu says. "I liked your poem about looking on the bright side."

Sarah's freckled cheeks flush a faint red. "Thanks," she says.

"It's good you're here," Pete chimes in. "You look speedy, and we've gotta kick butt tonight at mega-size Dutch Blitz!"

"What's mega-size Dutch Blitz?" Sarah asks.

"Have you played normal Dutch Blitz? Where you have to play cards super quick?"

Sarah nods.

"Okay, well, like that, but the cards are enormous, and you have to sprint them to the center." Pete and I share a grin. We've been playing mega-size Dutch Blitz with our youth group for years; we even helped make the original cards. In fact, that's how we became friends in the first place.

I worry for a moment that Sarah will think the idea is childish and boring. That she'll wonder why she didn't go to some party where our classmates do drugs and make out and hang around doing nothing. A party like that sounds boring to me, but I can't help but watch her face for signs that she thinks this game we've been playing since we were kids is boring.

Thankfully, Sarah smiles. "That sounds like fun," she says, and she seems genuine. Though her face grows serious as she glances around nervously at the small crowd of teens milling about our church basement. "I can be on your team, right?" she says quietly to me.

Bolu puts her arm around my shoulder like she's afraid Sarah will steal me away and threaten the cohesion of our sacred group. "We'll all be on the same team," she says with a smile.

Riven puts her own arm around Sarah's shoulders. "And tonight, we're going to win!" she declares.

And we do end up winning! Our youth leaders—these two white guys in their twenties, Mike and Tony—fortunately do let us all be on a team together, and we win two of the three games. Probably because my and Pete's competitiveness is contagious, and the more we scream and cheer and sprint ourselves, the more invested the rest of our team gets. By the time we're finished, we're all panting, Sarah's discarded her sweater, Pete has pit stains, and I can feel sweat dripping down between my breasts—the most uncomfortable place to sweat.

The team that won the remaining one game suggests we play a fourth to see if they can tie it up, but we all shake our heads vehemently. "We're exhausted," Riven protests on behalf of all of us.

Mike takes pity on us and declares it snack time.

I glance at Sarah to see what she thinks about the fact that we have snack time like we're all in kindergarten, but she's eyeing the pitchers of punch thirstily. Bolu is already marching straight to the table to pour herself a drink.

As the others head to join her, Riven grabs my arm. "I'm going to talk to Larissa." She gestures her head in the direction of a curvy Black girl with curls past her shoulders.

I had completely forgotten that we were going to ask Larissa about the Witches and if she knows where they live. "Should I go with you?"

Riven shakes her head. "We don't want to overwhelm her." She glances at our friends who are clustering by the drink station as Bolu hands out cups of punch. "Or make them suspicious," she adds.

We have an unspoken understanding that if we tell Pete or Bolu, we risk being hysterically laughed at. Because thinking the Witches have conjured some sort of monster and are somehow manipulating our minds or the world or something is admittedly a weird thing to believe.

It suddenly all feels like a silly game. I try to remind myself of the stakes, but my brow furrows with the thought. The fact is that if I tried to explain all this to a stranger, I'm not sure I could. But there are these holes deep down inside me that, for this evening, I'd almost forgotten were there. Playing Dutch Blitz, laughing with friends—for a little while, these things eclipsed the emptiness. The minute I think of the holes, though, it's as if they expand and threaten to envelop me.

I want to fall to the floor and start keening and wailing, even though I couldn't explain to anyone why. I couldn't even explain it to myself.

"Go," I say to Riven. "Talk to Larissa." We need answers before the hole—the emptiness—takes over everything inside me.

As Riven heads off to speak to Larissa, I join our friends and accept a cup of punch. I sip at it quietly, smiling and nodding, but not really listening to Bolu and Pete and Sarah chatter away.

When Riven finishes talking to Larissa and starts to head back our way, I break off from the group and stand alone a ways away.

Riven slides up to me. "Larissa doesn't know where the Witches live," she says in a whisper.

"Darn," I say. My heart starts to sink into one of the holes in my gut.

"Are you allowed to swear in a church?" Sarah's voice comes from right behind me, and I jump.

"Sarah, I didn't realize you were there." She's smirking like she doesn't actually think *darn* is a swear word, though if I said it around my parents, I'd get a fierce glare.

"Why do you guys want to know where the Witches live?" she asks.

"Shhh, not so loud," I say, thinking again of how much Pete would make fun of us if he knew we were trying to investigate if the Witches were doing real witchcraft.

"Sorry," she says, lowering her voice to a whisper. "Does this have anything to do with science class?"

Riven's eyebrows knit together. "What about science class?"

"She and Cecily are always giving each other weird looks."

"No, we're not," I say, but then Sarah stares me down until I admit, "Okay, so maybe we are. And yeah, it's kind of about that. But we've hit a dead end."

"Well, I can tell you where Cecily lives. She lives by me."

Riven and I share a glance as our eyes both light up. My heart stops its slow descent. "That's amazing," Riven says. "Thank you."

Sarah frowns. "You guys aren't going to egg their house or anything, are you?"

I shake my head. "Nothing like that. I swear it."

Sarah stares at me for another minute, and I wonder if she has some sort of truth magic that she's using to read me. I haven't heard of truth magic before, but that doesn't mean it doesn't exist. It's not like I have the entire list of seventy-two aptitudes memorized.

"All right," Sarah says at last. And then she gives us her own address—which I put into my phone—and explains that Cecily's house is directly across from hers. "It has blue siding and white shutters. I'm not sure what the exact street number is."

"Thanks, Sarah," I say. "You're the best."

"Hey, do the other Witches ever meet at Cecily's house?" Riven thinks to ask.

Sarah nods. "All the time."

My heart rises right back up into its usual place and does a little skip-dance of relief. This has all been too easy.

"They usually come over right after school and leave at around dinnertime." Sarah's face suddenly goes pink. "Not that I'm watching them or anything."

I frown at that. After school until dinnertime is when I watch Isaac and Gertie. And there's no way I'm bringing them along on some kind of secret mission. Unless they're sneaking cookies off the counter, they don't understand the meaning of stealth.

"What are you guys talking about?" Bolu asks as she walks up to us.

"Nothing," Riven and I say at the same time.

Bolu narrows her eyes and looks from Riven to Sarah to me. It appears we're not exactly masters of stealth, either, but at least Bolu is unlikely to guess that we're talking about stalking the Witches.

"Let's go see what snacks there are," I say, grabbing Bolu's arm and leading her off to the snack table. I'll have to figure out what to do about babysitting my siblings another day.

▲ ▲ ▲ ▲ ▲ ▲ ▲ ▲ ▲ ▲ ▲ ▲ ▲

The next day, I ask my parents again about putting the kids in day care. "Can't you do it even just a couple of days a week?"

"What's this about, Vera?" Dad asks. "Are we not paying you enough?"

"I don't think it's about the money, Frank," Mom jumps in. She puts an arm around my shoulders. "She's just tired." She says it with confidence, like she's sensing it with her intuition magic and not just guessing.

And suddenly it feels very true. Watching my siblings every day after school, getting all my homework done, keeping my grades up, hanging out with Riven, trying to figure out a mystery I don't understand—it's all overwhelming. My shoulders sag.

Mom leans over and kisses me on the top of the head. "All right, sweetheart. Your dad and I will talk about it."

There are things about Mom's intuition magic that are frustrating. Her ability to tell which of us kids had knocked over a lamp, for example. Or her ability to sense that one of us is up too late—in bed but lost in a book.

But there are other things about it that I'm grateful for. Her ability to sense when I need to talk. The fact that she always gets me the perfect thing for my birthday. And now, when she sensed even before I did how tired I am.

It feels like forever since I last felt the benefit of her intuition magic. Since she last gave me just what I needed, exactly when I needed it. I rest my head on her shoulder, breathe in the scent of her coconut hair conditioner. Her hair is all frizz and curls like mine, though she wears it up in a ponytail or bun most of the time, while I usually wear mine down. "Thanks, Mom," I say, and she rests her own head against mine, and we stay like that for a while.

Isaac's day care has limited space in their extended hours program, but Mom's intuition magic helps her call just the right place at the right time for Gertie. When Mom announces that Isaac and Gertie will start in their respective after-school care on Tuesdays and Fridays, I give her the biggest bear hug I've ever given. "Thanks, Mom."

During the couple of days before they can start, Riven and I add more to her notebook, as if it might get us somewhere. With every day that passes, I feel like we're another day further from answers and another day closer to disaster.

"I feel like something else bad is going to happen," I tell Riven one afternoon.

"We don't even know what bad things have happened in the first place," Riven points out.

"I know. Doesn't that make it even worse, though? It's like we're aliens who've never seen cars before, so when we got hit by one, we had no idea what happened. No idea that it's our own faults for walking down the middle of the street."

"Don't we have aliens on our list already?"

I nod. "Not the fact that we're aliens, though. Maybe you should put that down."

When she picks up her pencil, I say, "I'm joking. We're not aliens."

"You don't know that," she says, writing it down. "Maybe we're aliens but our minds have been wiped so we can properly integrate."

"That would explain why we don't like the stuff that normal teens are supposed to like, such as partying and drinking and that sort of thing."

"What's there to like about that stuff? Maybe other teens are the aliens and we're the humans."

"Yeah, that's probably it. Write that down."

Joking helps a little, but underneath every joke is the fear that runs through me that we're never going to find any answers, and whatever's happening will keep happening until . . . until I don't know what. The world ends? We both die? I don't know.

What I do know is it's time to start stalking the Witches. It's time to start getting some answers.

CHAPTER TWELVE

Riven pulls a thermos and a Tupperware of chocolate chip cookies out of her backpack, which is in the back seat of the car. "If we're going to do a stakeout, we've got to do it right," she says.

"Hear, hear," I say, uncapping the thermos and releasing the bittersweet scent of piping-hot hot chocolate. The steam rises from it in visible puffs of white. "How'd you keep this so hot all day?" I ask as I pour us each some into the ceramic mugs Riven brought.

"I didn't. I put the cocoa powder in this morning, then begged the cafeteria ladies for some boiling water before I met you at the car after school."

"Smart."

We're parked on the road in front of Sarah's house. Riven convinced Blake, one of her older brothers, to loan her his car, and we drove straight here after school. I don't love that we're in a car, since walking or public transport are so much better for the environment—not to mention that Riven only has her learner's permit and is supposed to have an adult in the car—but it seemed weird to do a stakeout without a car.

Plus, Riven got her learner's permit as soon as she turned fourteen, which means she's been driving for almost two years already, and she's a more careful driver than anyone else I know. Plus *plus*, she swears to me that she'd be the only one who'd get in trouble if we got caught. "Besides," she pointed out, "what else are we going to do? Have Blake come along on our stakeout with us?" Which is a good point.

Just as Sarah said, there's a blue house with white shutters right across the road. It's a fairly nice neighborhood. The houses aren't especially fancy, but they're mostly two-story houses, which feels fancier than my neighborhood of all bungalows.

We settle into our stakeout groove, drinking hot chocolate, working through some knights and knaves problems I pull up on my phone, and listening to some mellow folk music Riven has on her phone, turning the car on to heat it a bit whenever we get cold.

I suggest we listen to something more upbeat, but Riven points out that if the music is too loud, people walking by will notice us.

"They're going to notice us anyways," I say, feeling suddenly conspicuous sitting right in front of the house we're trying to stake out. "Maybe we should park a little ways down the street, not right in front of their house."

So we move the car back, finding a spot a few houses down that still gives us a good view of the two-story blue house with white trim and shutters.

In the end, it doesn't matter. We stay in the car for two whole hours, solve a dozen or so pretty difficult knights and knaves problems, and drink all the hot chocolate and eat all the cookies, and no one shows up—not Cecily, not the other Witches, not even any of Cecily's family members.

"Darn," I say when we have to pack up and leave so we can both get home in time for supper.

"We'll try again on Friday," Riven says as she drops me off a block from my house so my parents won't see that Blake isn't supervising her.

"Okay," I agree. "Friday."

But on Friday, Riven's brother won't lend her his car again (which, honestly, is probably for the best considering the whole learner's permit thing), so we're stuck taking the bus and walking down Cecily's street, then around the block, then down the street again, over and over. Much better for the environment, but not exactly an optimal stakeout.

It's full-blown winter already. The streets and trees are coated with a layer of snow, and our winter coats don't do as good of a job as the car did at keeping out the chill. Since there's no youth group tonight, we have the whole evening for our stakeout, but within an hour of walking in circles and seeing no one enter that blue house, we're ready to hop on a bus and head home again.

"Do you think Sarah was lying to us?" Riven asks as we pass Sarah's house on our final loop around.

"I don't know. Maybe. Though I can't think why she'd lie."

"Maybe she's a knave, and all she can do is lie."

I shake my head. Maybe I'm judging a book by her knit-sweatered, freckle-faced cover, but I don't think Sarah is anything close to a knave. "I don't think—" I start to say, then break off, grab Riven's arm, and pull her down behind a nearby car.

"What in the—"

"Look!" I whisper and point down the street, where the three Witches have just turned the corner and are walking down the sidewalk across the road.

Oh! Riven mouths without making a sound.

From our hiding spot crouched behind a puke-green SUV, we watch them glide along, chattering to one another about things we can't hear.

Then, they turn up the walkway to Cecily's house—except instead of going in the front door, they follow the sidewalk around to the side of the house and out of view.

"Where are they going?" Riven asks at the same time I whisper, "What now?"

"I guess we follow them?" Riven says, though it comes out as a question.

"That's what we're here for, right?" I question in response.

So we do.

We step out from behind the SUV, then cross the road toward Cecily's.

"If we're caught, we'll just say we're looking for Sarah's house," Riven suggests.

"Good idea." I glance back toward Sarah's house, half expecting her to be standing in a window, peering down at us and giving us a thumbs-up. But the windows to her red-brick house are all covered in curtains and blinds.

We make it up the front walkway of Cecily's house without incident. I look up at the white-shuttered windows of the house, and thankfully, no one looks down from them, either. There are no cars in the driveway, and we haven't seen anyone other than the

Witches come or go, so it's likely no one else is home. Though our walk around the block strategy left a distressing amount of time when we didn't have the house in view.

My heart races as we reach the corner of the house and prepare to peek around it. I'm just ahead of Riven, so I signal for her to stop, then I slowly, carefully peer around the edge of the house.

There's nothing there. It's just an empty side yard, maybe ten feet across, with a sidewalk stretching down the length of the house. There's no side door or anything. The Witches must have continued into the backyard.

Sure enough, when I listen for it, I hear a few female voices talking away, though I still can't make out the words.

I wave to Riven to follow me, and the two of us creep along the side of the house. All my feelings of being cold are gone, replaced by the rushing, thumping heat of blood pumping through my body.

We stop short at the next corner of the house, pressing ourselves against the wall so we hopefully can't be seen from the backyard.

This time, when voices reach us, I can actually make them out.

"Yeah, but that's why we need to keep trying," says a voice that I'm pretty sure is Rachel's. "We can't half-ass it."

"I mean, we *could* half-ass it," Cecily says. "But then what would be the point of everything we've done already?"

"Okay, okay," says a voice I don't know as well, which must be Hayden's. "I'm just tired."

"We're all tired," Cecily says. "But if we—" And then a door clicks shut, and the voices are muffled and unintelligible again.

Riven must have been listening to the voices, too, because as soon as the door clicks, she pokes her head around me, all the way around the corner. "They've gone into the garage," she whispers.

"The garage?" I poke my own head around the corner, and sure enough, there in the garage door window is the silhouette of a girl.

Like many garages in Edmonton, it's detached from the house and set at the end of the backyard, with the big car doors around the other side, pointed into the alley. On this side is a door and two small, square windows.

Hayden appears in one window, and Riven lets out a quiet little squawk and grabs my hand. But Hayden's back is to us.

"Come on," I say, then tug Riven into the backyard. We sprint across the open area to the side of the garage, where there's only one window—a long, thin one, just above our heads. At least we're out of view for now, but I half expect to hear the garage door open, to hear Cecily shout, "What the heck are you guys doing here?"

But there's nothing. Just the quiet of our breathing, the rising and falling hum of cars driving past three streets over, and the muted, garbled sounds of the three Witches talking on the other side of this wall.

When I turn back to Riven, though, her brown eyes are wide with horror. She looks into the backyard, then back at me. I study the backyard. It's a simple square backyard, snow covered and quiet. The house has a lot of windows, and I do a quick scan of them, but I don't see anyone in any of them.

What is it? I mouth at her.

"We—" she starts to whisper, but I put a finger to my lips. The Witches are basically one wall away from us. I'm not risking anything.

Riven frowns, but then her eyebrows fly up as if they're ready to jump off her face. She reaches into her pocket and pulls out her phone, then starts typing something in it.

I realize what she's doing just in time and yank out my own phone and turn off the sound just before her text comes in.

Riven: We left footprints in the snow!!!!

I glance back into the yard. She's right. It's so obvious, I can't believe I missed it. We started out running on the sidewalk, but when it turned to go to the garage door, we kept going straight, our footsteps tracing our stalker route across several feet of white, to the side of the garage.

I chew my lip for a moment, then write back: It's okay. We'll be out of here before they see us. If they see the footsteps later, they'll just think it was someone scavenging for bottles. Right?

I mostly believe my own words.

Riven: What if they use their witchcraft to figure out who was here, though?

Me: I don't believe in witchcraft

Riven: Right. That's why we're spending our afternoon stalking three witches.

I roll my eyes at her even though she's right. Or at least sort of right. Maybe right? I don't even know anymore.

Before I can type out a reply, a banging noise comes from inside the garage. Riven and I glance at each other, and then Riven points at the window just above our heads. I nod. We need to see what they're doing in there.

We simultaneously rise up on our tiptoes to try to look in the window, but we're both too short and the window's too high, and we can't quite make it—though Riven's hood and my beanie are peeking over the edge, visible, and who knows whether they're looking in our direction. I gesture at Riven to get back down, then hold my breath, waiting again for the sound of the garage door banging open.

But again, there is nothing. Just the sound of muted voices and something being dragged across a cement floor.

I text Riven: We need something to stand on. She nods her agreement.

I look around. There are some snow-covered chairs on the back porch of the house, but we'd have to go across the yard to get them, making us fully visible through the bigger garage windows.

I peek into the alley behind the garage. The big, white garage door is closed, and there are no windows in the door or the wall. Perfect.

I head down the short driveway into the alley, with Riven at my heels. We stand at the end of the driveway, looking up and down the alleyway. It's a typical back alley. A few houses have garages; the other yards end in fences, with trees towering over them. Every house has a little wooden cubby or shed where they put their garbage for collection.

I'm not sure what I was hoping for—an abandoned chair or a box or something?—but the alleyway is tidy and clear. Maybe in one of the garbage cubbies . . .

I march over to Cecily's family's garbage shed, but it's empty. Must not be garbage collection for a few more days.

Riven copies me and goes to check out one of the neighbors'. She peers inside, then shakes her head. Then I head in one direction down the alley and she heads in the other, searching for something we can use for a boost.

I come back empty-handed, but Riven is carrying a large plastic trash can. I hurry over, expecting to see something inside, but there's nothing. But she's grinning like she's found something.

She wants to use the trash can itself, apparently. "I don't think that's going to work," I whisper.

"It's pretty sturdy," she whispers back. And I have to admit that it does look like a fairly hefty garbage can.

So I follow her back around to the side of the garage, where together we carefully and quietly tip the trash can over so it's upside down.

Riven gestures at me to go ahead, and I want to tell her that there's no way I'm testing out this death trap first. But then there's a scraping noise and a chatter of muted voices from the garage, and curiosity gets the better of me.

With Riven's help, I clamber on top of the trash can, then kneel on top of it. I expect the thing to teeter or give way, but Riven's right: It's pretty sturdy.

I've been kneeling so my butt is resting on my feet, but I rise, still kneeling, and the lift gets me just high enough to see in the window.

I'm ready to duck back down immediately if I'm in any of the girls' fields of view, but as Riven would say, the universe must be on our side, because their backs are all to me.

They're all in a little half circle around a white wooden backdrop that's maybe six feet high and painted with different-colored horizontal lines every six inches or so. Cecily is sprawled in a patio chair, with her legs over one arm and her back resting against the other. She has a notebook open on her knees. Rachel is sitting on a dresser, her feet dangling over the edge, holding some papers.

Hayden stands between them, looking from one to the other. They're talking about something—their muffled voices still reach us—but with their backs to me, I can't even hope to lip-read.

I watch them for a minute or two, and then Riven tugs at my coat. She mouths something at me that I can't understand but that I guess is a question about what's going on.

Unsure how to explain that they're just in a half circle, doing nothing, I carefully ease myself down and off the trash can, then gesture for her to take her turn.

Riven's a bit shorter than I am, so it takes a bit more hoisting and lifting, but soon she's situated on top of the trash can, peering in through the garage window, just like I was.

While Riven takes her turn, I look around. There's a fence behind us separating Cecily's house from their neighbor's. Cecily's family's side of the fence is lined with big bushes, all dusted with a light snow. I shiver as if they're reminding me of how cold it is.

"What the heck!" comes Riven's whisper from behind me.

I whirl around. Riven's mouth is hanging open and she stares wide-eyed into the garage.

"What is it?" I whisper, unable to stop myself.

Riven just shakes her head like she can't explain. I expect her to hop down off the trash can and let me see, but instead she leans in and presses her forehead against the windowpane, trying to get a better look.

When I tug at her coat, she just ignores me.

I have to see what's happening.

Riven isn't taking up the entire garbage can; there's about a third of it left—enough room for at least one of my knees. So I put my hands on top and give a hop, propelling myself upward.

It takes three tries, but on my third, I land with my knee on top, though my body pushes into Riven's and shoves her to the right. I grab her around her waist, and she grabs me, and for one long moment, we're teetering on top of the garbage can, threatening to fall. But then we both put one of our mittened hands out to the wall to steady ourselves, and we've done it. We're both together on top of the trash can. Both able to stare inside Cecily's garage to see what sort of witchly things are going on there.

Which—one arm still around each other's waists—we do.

The three girls are still in the half circle I saw them in, though Cecily is sitting up a bit straighter in her chair and Hayden is leaning against the dresser. Aside from that, though, nothing has changed. There's nothing to explain Riven's exclamation.

I study Riven's face now in the window reflection. Her look of shock is gone, replaced by fierce but puzzled concentration. Whatever she saw must be gone now.

We watch them that way for a few minutes. They talk. Cecily writes some things in her notebook. Nothing happens.

But then Hayden stops leaning on the dresser, takes her place in the middle of the half circle, and raises her hands.

And then, it starts rising out of the cement floor—a shadow monster, just like I saw in the graveyard. It's smaller this time, only up to her knees, and it's more of a wispy, tubular form rather than a person. But it's most definitely there.

"Whoa!" Riven whispers. "There it is again!"

And then it abruptly disappears.

Just as it does, the garbage bin holding us up collapses under our weight, tipping to the side and knocking Riven to the ground and me on top of her with a *thud*, a *bang*, and a much-too-loud *oof*!

CHAPTER THIRTEEN

As Riven and I pick ourselves up off the ground, there's the sound of hurried footsteps in the garage, and then the creaking sound of a door opening.

"Run," I breathe at Riven, and then it's like we're in a *Doctor Who* episode, as we both book it down the side of the garage and into the alley, where our feet pound against the snow-covered gravel. We don't stop until we've made it out onto the street and have run one full street over. Then we lean over, gasping for breath.

Riven swears.

"Do you . . . think they . . . saw us?" I say between breaths.

Riven looks back down the street and shakes her head. Once she catches her breath, she says, "If they did, they're not following us."

We head down the street toward the bus stop, looking over our shoulders every ten seconds, afraid that they're behind us. But no one appears on the sidewalk except an elderly man walking his small, elderly dog. They come out of their house and shuffle along in the opposite direction from us, moving so slowly that it must take them half an hour just to go around the block.

We, on the other hand, are still speed walking along, so we're out of view of the man and his dog within minutes. It's only once we're at the empty bus stop that we talk again.

"What *was* that thing?" Riven asks.

"A shadow monster. Just like I saw at the graveyard."

"So you actually saw something at the graveyard? Like, really?"

"Of course I did. You didn't believe me?"

Riven tugs at the drawstring of her hood. "I mean, I wanted to believe you. I told myself I believed you. But I don't think I actually really truly did until I saw that thing."

My brow furrows. Part of me feels mad at her for not taking me at my word, but the other part realizes that if she had told me about a shadow monster in a graveyard, I probably would have reacted the exact same way.

"Well, we've both seen it now," I say. "It was bigger in the grave-yard, though."

"How big?"

"Like, the size of a person."

Riven opens her mouth to say more, but someone else joins us at the bus stop, and we can't exactly talk about shadow monsters while other people are around. And then we're on the bus and there are even more people.

When we get back to my house, Mom and Dad are already home with the kids, and when Riven gets permission to stay for supper, Mom ends up recruiting us to help her chop veggies for dinner.

So we're not able to talk about it again until after supper when we're both up in my room, sprawled on my bed, finally alone.

"So . . ." I say.

"So . . ." Riven echoes.

"They're trying to conjure some sort of shadow monster."

"Or maybe it's not actually made of shadow. Maybe they just haven't been successful yet at drawing out anything more than shadow."

"Oh, I didn't think of that." I chew on my thumbnail. For some reason, the thought that they're actually trying to conjure up a zombie or a demon or some other flesh-based creature is creepier than just a monster made of shadow.

"Or maybe it's not a monster at all," Riven continues. "Maybe it's a portal. Or a ghost. Or someone from an alternate universe."

"I think we need to make another list," I suggest.

"Good idea." Riven goes fishing in her backpack for our notebook.

While she does that, I open up my laptop and do a search for "shadow monster." There are tons of hits, but they're all fictional. The villain from *Stranger Things*. A creature in Dungeons & Dragons.

I try another search for "real shadow monster" and find an article talking about depression, which is a great analogy but not exactly helpful.

There's another blog, though, that refers to "shadow people," so I do a search for that. "Hey, there's a Wikipedia entry for shadow people," I tell Riven. She slides over to me as I click on it, and we both read the thing in silence.

It turns out it's a snark-filled entry about people who believe in shadowy figures that they see in their peripheral vision. The article suggests that it might be from sleep deprivation, hallucinations, or heightened emotions.

"Whoever wrote this would laugh at us if we told them what we saw," Riven says.

"Yeah." I close the laptop.

"So . . . we're not telling anyone, right?"

"Agreed," I say. "At least not until we figure out what is going on."

Riven leaves shortly after that, but I stay up late, researching shadow people and shadow monsters. When I finally go to bed, my dreams are filled with shadows.

I forget things all the time, but I've never before forgotten to do my homework. But all the research I did all weekend, between church and family time, apparently wiped it from my mind, and I completely forgot to do my calculus homework.

Before school starts, I sit on the floor by Riven's locker, frantically scrawling down answers. Mr. Hlibichuk is the type of teacher to give detention if you don't have your homework done.

"What are you doing?" Bolu asks when she arrives.

"Our math homework. I was busy most of the weekend and completely forgot," I say.

"What were you busy doing?"

Riven and I share a look. If Riven didn't truly believe me about the shadow monster, Bolu certainly isn't going to. "Mostly just got caught up in playing *Legends of the Stone*," I say.

"That game's so addictive," Riven chimes in.

Bolu looks from Riven to me, as if she can tell there's something we're not revealing. As if she doesn't really believe I spent the entire weekend playing a video game—though that should be believable, because I've definitely done that before. But she says nothing further, just leaves me to keep scrawling answers. They don't have to be right; they just have to be done—though I'd prefer for them to be right.

"Want to copy mine?" Riven asks, and I wonder if she's offering more to change the subject than to truly offer. We've never copied off each other's answers before. I guess we're too goody-goody—aside from the whole stalking-our-classmates thing, that is.

"No, I'm almost done." I only have a few more questions to go, and there's still a few minutes before the first bell.

When I arrive at science class later that morning, the Witches are standing in a little huddle in the hallway. All three of them—Cecily, Hayden, and Isla. I wait for them to glare at me or even march up to me and accuse me of spying on them, but they don't even look my way as I walk past.

My own gaze, though, keeps sliding back to Isla, though I have no idea why. It's not like a couple of years ago, when she first transitioned, and I couldn't help but sneak the occasional glance at her as she switched from jeans and hoodies to flowing skirts and dresses.

This feels different. Then, it was just curiosity. Now, something feels wrong.

"Are you okay?" Sarah asks as I slip into my seat. "You look kind of pale."

"Hmm? Yeah, I'm fine."

The Witches enter the room soon after. Well, two of them do.

THE FORGOTTEN MEMORIES OF VERA GLASS

Cecily and Hayden glide into the room, flowy skirts swishing, not looking at all like they had conjured up some sort of shadow demon this weekend. Isla doesn't follow them. I give my head a little shake. That makes sense, of course. Isla's not in this class, has never been in this class.

"So what's the deal with you and the Witches, anyways?" Sarah asks, breaking into my thoughts. "Do you have a crush on one of them or something?"

"What? No." At least, I don't think so. I glance over my shoulder to where they're settling in at their lab bench. There's no fluttering of my heart or burning of my loins that books and media have taught me I should feel if I have a crush.

My interest in the Witches has nothing to do with romance and everything to do with the fact that I saw them conjure a shadowy person out of a grave and a wisp of shadow out of a garage floor.

"Well, what about that guy you hang around with? Pete?"

I frown. "What about him?"

She brings her voice down to a whisper. "Do you have a crush on him?"

"What? No! Of course not!" I don't know why my voice sounds so shrill.

Sarah raises an eyebrow, but before she can say anything further, the second bell rings, and Ms. Larson starts class. It's a lecture class, so we don't have time to talk again until the period is over and we've packed up our books and are heading out into the hall.

"Did you manage to find Cecily's house okay?" Sarah asks me once we're out in the hallway.

I'm not sure how to answer that. If I admit we were there, am I placing us at the scene of a crime? Is it a crime to accidentally break someone's garbage can while standing on it and spying on them through a window? Yeah, probably.

"Vera, Sarah, wait up!"

I look over my shoulder to see Bolu speed walking up behind us. Saving me from answering. "I'll tell you later," I tell Sarah as Bolu catches up to us.

Sarah glances between me and Bolu, her eyebrows raised like she's surprised I haven't told Bolu. But she has no idea what an unbelievable thing it would be to tell. She shrugs. "All right, I'll see you around," Sarah says, and then she heads off down the hall.

"What were you and Sarah talking about?" Bolu asks once Sarah's gone.

"Just science lab stuff." My stomach twists with the lie, but if I tried to be a knight, she'd think I was a knave. It's better not to tell her.

Bolu narrows her eyes and glances from me to Sarah's retreating back, and I'm reminded of Riven's comments about what a terrible liar I am. But Bolu doesn't say anything else, and I don't say anything, either, and we walk to lunch in silence.

CHAPTER FOURTEEN

The next week or so is quiet. Riven and I don't want to risk going back to the Witches' hideout so soon, because they might be on the lookout for intruders after our last debacle. Even my research time is limited, because I have a major paper due in English plus a big test in calculus, and especially after my scare with my math homework, I've decided I'm not flunking out of school just because of some witches.

Our next youth group is another activity night, so I invite Sarah along once again. She grins when I ask her. "I wasn't sure if that was just a one-time invite."

My snarky side has an urge to say that I don't own the youth group and she could come every time and there's nothing I could do to stop her. But I'm guessing that's not what she needs to hear right now, so instead I say, "We'd love to have you come along every time. Consider this an open invitation."

On Friday night, I end up being the first of our friends to arrive at the church. "Hi, Vera," Annika says when I arrive. She's the kind of person who's friendly to everyone. Her big smile lights up her warm brown face and makes it impossible to hate her, even though she broke Pete's heart by turning him down. "I love your pants."

I'm wearing my favorite pair of pants—brown ones scattered with quilted patches.

Before I can thank her, a slightly nasally voice comes from behind me. "You come to this youth group?"

I turn around. It's Vincent, the guy from science class who thought I owed him an explanation about why I wanted to know Cecily's aptitude.

"Hi!" Annika gives him a big grin. "You're new here, right? I'm Annika." She reaches out her hand to shake his.

His eyebrow twitches up in amusement, but he shakes her hand anyway. Then he turns to me, like he expects me to offer my hand, too.

"This is Vincent," I tell Annika, doing my best to keep the annoyance out of my voice. "He's in my science class."

Just then, arms are thrown around me from behind. "Vera! I've missed you!"

I disentangle myself and turn around. "Riven, you just saw me at school like two hours ago!"

"I know, and those two hours felt like an eternity. We should never be parted again!" She throws her arms around my shoulders. And even though she's just being silly, it makes my heart all squishy.

"Deal," I say. "We're going to need to get a second toilet installed in our bathrooms so we can be together even when we're going number two."

"Yes, definitely," Riven says with mock seriousness.

Vincent crinkles his nose. "You guys are weird."

"You're weird," Riven says. Then, "Who are you?"

Vincent frowns. "I'm in your English class."

"Right! I knew you looked familiar," Riven says, though I'm pretty sure she has no idea who he is.

Then the whole scene is repeated—minus the talk of duo-toilets—three more times as Bolu, Sarah, and then Pete arrive. Thankfully, by the time Pete arrives, Annika has gone off to chat with other people, which is good, because I don't want him to think I'm not firmly on Team Pete.

Before we have much time to chat, things are called to order by our youth leaders, Mike and Tony, who basically live for puns.

As if he's read my mind, Mike flicks the light off and on to get everyone's attention and then says, "Okay, everyone, let's get started! We need two teams for tonight's game. First two people to come up with an awesome pun are the team captains."

"Awesome pun's an oxymoron!" Pete shouts out, and people laugh.

Tony gasps in mock horror. "You, sir, are officially disqualified from being a captain."

"Hey, no Googling," Mike says, pointing at a guy who's got his phone out.

"How does Moses make coffee?" Annika calls out.

"How?" Tony asks.

"He brews it." About a quarter of the room chuckles. Tony guffaws. I roll my eyes.

Riven leans in to me. "I don't get it."

"Hebrews. It's a book of the Bible."

"Oh, good old biblical humor," she says under her breath.

"Oh, good old puns," I say under mine.

"Hey, Mike," Bolu shouts out from behind us.

"What?"

"These puns are giving me a Mike-graine!"

This time almost everyone laughs.

"Good one, Bolu," I tell her.

She smiles, though for some reason, it doesn't reach her eyes. Before I have time to question her about it, Mike declares, "We've got our two team captains! Annika and Bolu! Why don't you both come stand over here?" Bolu goes off to stand on the other side of the room, looking back at us.

And then they're picking their teams. Bolu picks Pete first, then Riven, then me. Annika picks her friends from her school. None of it is surprising.

Riven and Pete and I chat away as Bolu keeps picking.

"Pick Sarah," Riven abruptly says in the middle of our conversation. I turn around and realize with horror that there are only two people left to be chosen—Vincent and Sarah. Vincent is grinning, like it's a real laugh that he's one of the last two, while Sarah's staring down at her feet, as if her shoes are the most interesting thing in the room.

Thank goodness Bolu's our team captain. At least Sarah won't be the very last one standing. Though I'm not sure why Bolu's left her to the end. Except when Bolu opens her mouth, it's not Sarah's name that comes out; it's Vincent's.

Vincent grins obnoxiously at Sarah, and then marches to our half of the room.

"That means we get—sorry, what's your name again?" Annika says, all cheery. "Sarah? Awesome. Come on over, Sarah!"

"Bolu!" I hiss. "What the heck?! Why didn't you pick Sarah?!"

"Vincent looks fast," she says, though she doesn't meet my eye.

"Okay, let me explain how this game works," Mike bellows as Tony hands out kerchiefs to the other team to wear to mark that they're on the same team. "We're going to play chair basketball. Everyone gets a chair and has to put it somewhere in the room. Once everyone's chairs are placed, you can't get up from your chair. Your team's goal is to pass the basketball from one end of the room and into a laundry basket on the other side. If you drop the ball or it hits the ground for any reason, it has to go back to the beginning."

"Can I knock their ball out?" Pete calls out.

"Absolutely. As long as you can do it without getting up from your seat! So chair placement is crucial! Everyone get it?"

There are a few more questions, and then we're dismissed to choose our chair locations. I don't worry about the game and simply place my chair right next to Sarah's. "Hey, Sarah," I tell her right away, "I hope you know that I wanted you on our team."

She gives me a small smile. "Thanks, Vera."

"I hope you believe me. I don't know why Bolu didn't think to choose you."

"It's okay. Not everyone has to like me," Sarah says.

"That's not—"

"Getting ready to stop the other team's ball?" Vincent cuts in. "Good call, Vera!" And he plops his own chair down right in front of Annika's. "Your team's going down," he says, looking at both Annika and Sarah with a smirk.

When their team ends up winning, neither Annika nor Sarah

smirks back at Vincent. They are better people than I am. I definitely would have mocked him mercilessly if I was them.

Sarah ends up leaving early because she has a family thing the next morning—which makes me feel even worse that she came out to be with us even though she couldn't stay the whole time, and then she didn't even end up on our team. So at snack break, I find Bolu by the punch bowl. Pete's there, too, but I have no patience to try to get Bolu alone.

"Bolu! Seriously, why didn't you pick Sarah?"

Pete occupies himself with getting a cup of punch.

Bolu looks down at her feet, like she regrets it now. But she doesn't say anything.

Riven appears at my side. "Come on, you can tell us," she says, like she's been there all along. "We tell each other everything."

Bolu's lips pinch together. Then she says, "We don't, though, do we?"

"What do you mean?" I ask.

She looks up at both of us. "You guys have some big secret you're not telling us."

Pete frowns. "They do?" He sets his punch down on the table and turns so he's shoulder to shoulder with Bolu, and it suddenly feels like us versus them. Which is a terrible feeling.

"That's why they're always talking to Sarah and then hushing when we come close," Bolu says.

"Oh, didn't notice," Pete says. His obliviousness makes me want to pat him on the head.

"Is that what this is about?" I say instead. "You're upset that I've been telling Sarah things?"

"I'm not upset that you're talking to Sarah!" she says, though her refusal to pick Sarah earlier suggests otherwise. "I'm upset you're not talking to *me*! When I first met you all, you seemed like the type of friends who put each other first before everyone else, and I was so excited to be a part of that. But apparently that's not actually the case. Or maybe it's just not the case for me."

Pete steps forward. "Or me, apparently."

Riven meets my eye. We could deny everything. We could keep our secret. We could keep from being laughed at. We could keep hurting our friends.

"We were afraid you'd laugh at us," I admit.

"We wouldn't laugh at you," Bolu says.

"Speak for yourself," Pete says with a grin.

"Well, I wouldn't. Whatever it was. So that's no excuse."

I sigh. "You're right. We should have told you."

"And me, too," Pete chimes in.

"And you, too," I agree. It feels weird to tell them all about our notebook and our theories and stalking the Witches and the shadow monster right here in the middle of the church basement, though. "Why don't you all come over tomorrow morning, and we'll tell you?"

"Deal," Pete says.

"Bolu?" I turn to her.

Bolu lets her crossed arms drop. "Okay," she says.

I consider saying that she could have just told us all that rather than taking out her anger on Sarah. But for some reason, I don't think that would go over very well.

Later that evening, Riven sidles up to me and presses her shoulder into mine. "So, what are we going to tell them?" she asks.

I consider the options. Tell them the truth and get laughed at. Tell them something less than the truth and don't.

I'm about to suggest a lie—something close to the truth, but not quite there—when my gaze catches on Pete. He's staring off to our left; I follow his gaze, expecting him to be ogling Annika. But he's not looking at her; he's looking at . . . nothing. Just staring down at the empty space. Looking lost and alone, like he's only part of a whole.

Whatever's happening, it isn't only our problem. We're not the only ones feeling like pieces of ourselves are missing.

Waiting for the answer to her question, Riven follows my gaze. I can tell the moment she spots Pete, because the straight lines of her face soften into curves.

"Everything," I answer. "We tell them everything."

CHAPTER FIFTEEN

Riven, Pete, and Bolu show up at my house early the next morning. Mom and Dad have taken Isaac and Gertie to their Saturday morning judo lesson, so the house is unusually quiet. We sit at the kitchen table. Riven and I look at each other, unsure how to start.

"Would you agree with us that something is wrong?" I finally say.

Bolu frowns. "What do you mean by 'something'?"

It's my turn to frown. This is going to be even harder than I thought.

But then Pete chimes in. "She means the world feels wrong—like it was maybe supposed to end, but something artificial is keeping its heart beating."

We all fall silent.

Bolu still looks puzzled, and I want to add that to our list in our notebook: *Bolu doesn't understand. Pete understands maybe even better than we do.*

Instead, I pick up the notebook from the table and explain: "Right. The world feels wrong. But we don't know why. So we've been writing down some theories."

Pete takes the book from me and flips through it. He stops on the sketch of the white rose, and for a moment, I think he might actually cry, but then he flips a few more pages and reads through our scribbles. His eyebrows scrunch together. "The Witches?" he asks.

And that's when Riven and I really do tell them everything—about the graveyard sighting, about the shadow monster, about our disastrous spying expedition.

When we finish, I wait for the laughter. But they both just sit there in silence, contemplating.

Pete's forehead crinkles. "What about shadow magic?"

"Shadow magic?" Riven asks. She's clearly never heard of it, either.

"Yeah, like making shadows out of nothing. It's rare, I think, but my uncle has it."

My heart sinks. Has it simply been an aptitude all along? Did we really not think to look over the list of aptitudes? Are we on a wild goose chase?

"I don't know," Riven jumps in. "She made this shadowy wisp of a thing rise up from the ground. Is that what your uncle could do?"

"Like three-dimensional?" Pete shakes his head. "I've only seen him make shadows on the floor or wall."

I whip out my phone and search "shadow aptitude." Sure enough, multiple entries come up. I click on the first one and read it. "Shadow aptitude, or shadow magic, is the ability to create a shadow on a surface without needing something physical to block the light."

"This says the shadow has to be on a surface," I say. "So not three-dimensional."

Bolu clenches her jaw a few times as she thinks. "Well . . ." she says slowly, "could you have imagined that part?"

"I didn't—"

Riven puts her hand on my arm. "I know it's hard to believe," she says. "I didn't believe it at first, either."

"Gee, thanks, both of you!" I joke.

"Hey, you're the skeptic. You should understand not believing things," Riven jokes back.

"If I'm the skeptic, then if I do believe something, shouldn't that be even more reason to believe?"

"If that were true, I'd believe in your God," Riven points out.

"Look, there's a clear way to settle this," Pete jumps in.

"What's that?" Bolu asks.

"We all spy on the Witches."

"What? No way!" I say. "We were almost caught with just two of us. With four—"

"With four we'll have twice the brains. We'll be untouchable."

"That's an absurd argument," I say.

And yet, thirty minutes later, the four of us are marching down the street near Cecily's house. In my backpack is a hunk of wood we found in the garage that we're hoping to use as a step stool.

"This is getting heavy. You carry it." I pass the backpack off to Pete, who swings it on.

"We should go down the back alley instead of the main street," Riven suggests.

"See! We're already smarter with four!" Pete says.

I think about pointing out that Riven, whose idea it is, is one of the original two but decide against it.

As we head down the back alley, we all hush. The alley is quiet and empty. The snow is packed down from cars driving through, so it doesn't even crunch under our boots.

"I think this is it," Riven says, pointing to a garage. It's harder to tell from back here, since there aren't any house numbers, but there aren't that many garages in this alley, so she's got to be right.

Sure enough, as we creep around the side of the garage, there's the long, high window—though the garbage can we wrecked is gone.

"What if someone's home?" Bolu whispers, pointing to the house and all its windows looking out into the backyard. We freeze, studying the windows, watching for faces peering out at us or figures passing by. But there's nothing.

There's no noise coming from the garage, either. I gesture at Pete to get out the wood, which he does. He sets it carefully and quietly down on the snowy ground, and then everyone looks at me. Apparently I get the honors.

I step up onto the hunk of wood and peer into the garage window, ready to duck back down if someone is peering back at me. But there's no one inside. The dresser and chair and backdrop the Witches were using are all still set up in their little circle, and there are papers and notebooks here and there but no people.

"They're not here," I whisper to the others.

"Darn," Riven says.

Pete leans dejectedly against the side of the garage.

Bolu is still looking anxiously up at the house windows.

I step down off the wood, and Riven takes my place, peering into the window as if she doesn't believe me and has to see for herself.

"There are papers and stuff in there," she says, not as quietly as we have been.

"Papers?" Pete asks.

Riven explains how we saw them with a notebook and papers. "I bet there'd be answers on whatever's in there." She pokes her chin out at me, and it takes me only a moment to recognize the same look I give her whenever I want her to use her light magic.

"No way!" I say too loudly. "We are not breaking into Cecily's garage."

Pete's face lights up with delight. Bolu, on the other hand, looks horrified.

"That's a great idea," Pete says. "Vera, you can use your unlocking magic to get us in."

"We're not breaking and entering," Bolu says. "We could get arrested!" She looks genuinely afraid, and I suddenly remember photos of her cousin's bruised and bloodied face after he was arrested for what sounded like nothing.

Pete seems much less worried. I suspect he hasn't fully thought this through. "Only if we get caught," he says. "And can you really get in trouble for entering a garage if you don't touch or take anything?"

"And if they didn't want people investigating their stuff," Riven says before I can reply that yeah, it's still illegal, "maybe they shouldn't be conjuring monsters."

All three of them look expectantly at me. I'm not just a vote, I'm the only vote that matters. Without me, they can't get in—not without breaking a window or something, which I know they'd never do.

I know Bolu is expecting me to immediately say no, and especially with her and Pete here, I probably should say no. White Canadians like to think our country is above racism and police brutality, but of course we're not. However, might having me and Riven here with them—unfair as that is—balance things out? They'd be safe, right? And it's not like we'd be doing it for kicks; we're desperately trying to figure out why the universe's heart feels broken. Why our own hearts feel broken.

Taking the risk is clearly worth it to Pete, who feels the world's brokenness right along with us. Bolu, on the other hand, doesn't seem to feel the same way—doesn't have the same desperation for answers in her heart, pushing her forward.

Plus, for the first time since I opened the school door so Riven could retrieve her *Doctor Who* shirt, my aptitude could be truly useful. And Pete's right; breaking in to investigate a shadow monster does not feel wrong in the way that breaking in to steal something would be wrong. In fact, if this was a *Doctor Who* episode, we'd be the heroes. The Doctor is always unlocking doors with her sonic screwdriver to solve some sinister mystery.

A grin slips onto my face as I realize my aptitude is my own sonic screwdriver. I've never thought of it that way before.

"It's not like we're going to steal anything," I say. "We won't even touch anything." All we want are answers. Clues. All we want to do is stop whatever terribleness is happening. And we can't do that if we don't even know what is causing the terribleness in the first place.

Bolu crosses her arms but says nothing. She'll be okay, won't she?

I look around like I'm expecting someone else to speak up, to be my conscience. But of course, it's only the four of us.

While we stare each other down, Pete runs across the backyard and around the side of the house to check the front driveway. "No cars," he says once he returns. "I don't think anyone's home."

"It's like the universe set this up to make this happen," Riven says.

And it does sort of feel that way, like the universe itself wants answers. Like my aptitude is finally fulfilling its purpose. Still, that doesn't stop my heart from pounding right out of my chest as we walk up to the garage door in the backyard.

Bolu trails behind us, as if she fears what we're doing but fears being left out of some group activity even more. Which makes me feel terrible. I've got to get her out of this.

"Someone is going to need to keep watch out front," I say, trying to sound authoritative.

As usual, Riven understands me immediately. "Oh yes, that's crucial," she adds.

Bolu clearly sees right through us, but she gives us a look of gratitude anyway. "On it," she says. And then she speeds off toward the front of the house, distancing herself from our illegal behavior as much as possible.

Which only makes my heart pound harder. Deciding something is right doesn't make it any less scary.

"Maybe we shouldn't," I start to say. But as I do, I reach my hand up to the garage door handle, and I've barely touched the knob when I feel the moving of gears. The click. "Oh!" I test the knob, but I already know what's going to happen. The handle turns, and the door slides open.

"Guess they don't have an alarm system," Riven says, when we're greeted by silence.

I immediately experience one of those retroactive heart attacks where you're struck by how terribly things could have gone. "I didn't even think of that!" I say. "What would we have done?"

"We'd have run!" Riven says. "Now come on." She pushes past me and into the garage.

"Don't touch anything," Pete calls after her. Then he marches in after her, leaving me standing at the open door, alone.

My unlocking job is done. I look around the backyard, examining the house windows one more time. I could just wait outside until Riven is done, like last time. But the Doctor doesn't just open doors, she goes through them. So when Riven pops her head back out of the garage, says, "Come on, madam indecisive," and puts her arm through mine, I let her lead me into the garage.

The garage is dark and shadowy, but none of us make any move to turn on the light—even Riven, for whom it would be easiest. Cecily's family clearly doesn't use the garage for parking in; it's too full of stuff. There are bikes, a freezer, coolers, workout equipment, a shelf full of boxes labeled with things like *Christmas decorations* and *Mark's stuff.* To the left, where we saw the Witches do their magic, they've carved out a fairly large work space.

I walk a circle around the space. There are no signs of witchcraft (though admittedly, all I know about witchcraft I know from

Hollywood, and considering how much they get wrong about Christianity, they clearly can't be trusted on issues of religion). Still, there are no piles of bones, no circles of salt, no cauldrons, not even any candles or spices. Just notebooks and papers and pencils and a clipboard on the chair Cecily was in.

Pete is leaning over the dresser, looking at some of the papers.

"What's it say?" I let go of Riven's arm and wander over.

"Just numbers." I peer at the sheets he's studying, and sure enough, there are columns of dates and numbers.

"What do they mean?" I ask.

Pete shrugs.

"Move over," Riven says, knocking her hip into mine. I scoot over, and she pulls out her phone and holds it up.

"What are you doing?"

"Taking pictures. So we can look at this stuff again later. Because I don't want to be in here any longer than we have to. Do you?"

I shake my head. A quick in and out is definitely ideal. "Good idea." I pull out my own phone and head over to the backdrop to snap pictures of it. "You going to help?" I ask Pete.

He shakes his head. "The incriminating photos can stay in your possession, thank you very much."

So he *is* nervous, too. I simultaneously feel horrible for dragging him into this—even though the dragging basically happened the other way around—and relieved to know that I'm not the only one anxious about the illegal half of this whole breaking and entering thing.

I study the backdrop as I snap pictures of it—taking dozens because the lack of light makes most of them blurry. It's just a piece of wood with what looks like measurements drawn onto it. What are they measuring? The monster? None of it makes any sense.

"Is witchcraft about numbers? They didn't show that part in the movies."

"You've been watching a lot of witchcraft documentaries, have you?" Riven jokes.

"Oh, shut up and focus on your picture taking," I say.

"Maybe it's numerology," Riven suggests. "That's a thing, right?"

"No idea," Pete chimes in. I have no idea, either. But I lean forward to study the paper attached to the clipboard on the chair. There are five columns on the page, with dates under the first and various numbers under the others. Near the bottom of the page, a series of numbers are circled in pencil, with *Why?!?* scrawled beside them.

Pete sidles up beside me. "Study those later. Snap those pics and let's get out of here."

He's right. It already feels like we've been in here too long. So I take pictures of the paper and clipboard, then head toward the door, where Pete and Riven are already waiting.

"You going to lock it back up?" Pete asks once we step outside.

I scrunch up my nose. Last time I used my magic to lock something, I was wiped out for a solid day. And the nausea. I especially hate the nausea. "Let's just close it," I suggest. "We didn't touch anything. They'll just think they forgot to lock it."

Pete and Riven nod their agreement, so we leave the door and head around to the side of the garage to collect our wooden block.

We brush the snow off it, then stick it back in my backpack, which Pete puts back on. Then we head into the back alley.

My fingers itch to pull out my phone and start examining the pictures, but it makes more sense to wait until we're home, away from the scene of our crime. No, the scene of our investigation.

These numbers had better give us some answers. Or at least the information that lets us find the answers. It's impossible to solve a knights and knaves problem if none of the islanders says a thing.

We haven't gone more than one house when Pete stops walking. Riven and I stop, too, and turn back to look at him. "What is it?" I ask.

He looks puzzled. "Are we forgetting something?"

I look at Riven and then back at Cecily's family's garage. A wind ripples down the alley. I pull my coat tighter around my neck, then shrug.

"I don't think so," I say.

"Not that I can think of," Riven agrees.

Pete tilts his head to the side, then shrugs, too. "You're probably right," he says. "Don't know what I was thinking."

Riven and I simultaneously take two steps toward him, and then loop our arms through his. And then the three of us head home.

CHAPTER SIXTEEN

By the time we get home, my family is back from judo, and Dad invites Pete and Riven to stay for lunch. But then after lunch, Mom implies that it's family time and basically kicks Pete and Riven out. So despite a nagging feeling of discomfort and urgency that follows me around all day, the three of us don't get a chance to review and discuss the papers and numbers until that evening.

We share the pictures we all took and then start a group chat.

Pete: so…numerology?

Riven: From what I can tell from Googling it this afternoon, it seems to just be a belief that different numbers have different significance

Pete: so if 1 black cat crosses your path it's bad luck, but if 7 cross your path it's good luck, and if 19 cross your path you're probably going to die?

Riven: Yes, exactly that. You're 100% accurate.

Me: bahahhaak

Pete: is it used with witchcraft?

Riven: Yeah, I think so, maybe?

Me: Did you guys see the numbers circled on that clipboard picture?

Riven: No, let me look

I pull up one of the pictures I took of the clipboard, scanning down to the bottom of the page. The last several lines are all dated from this past week. I check the dates against the calendar on my phone. There are three from Sunday, three from Wednesday, and three from Friday. The numbers in the final, fifth column from Sunday and Wednesday are circled, with the word *Why?!?* scrawled beside them.

Pete: 111, 117, 121, 113, 118, 119?

I check the numbers Pete's recited with the circled ones in the picture.

Me: Yep, those are the ones

Riven: Ooh 111! I remember reading something about that when I was looking up numerology

Riven: Yeah here it is

Riven: 111 is supposed to remind you to rely on your inner wisdom

Riven: It's about bringing out the best in yourself

Me: That doesn't sound very sinister

Riven: Why would it be sinister?

Me: You know…witchcraft…

Riven: Witchcraft doesn't have to be sinister. Isn't one of the core tenets of Wicca "harm none"?

Me: Is it? Huh

Pete: so not all witches have pointy hats and black cats? lol

Me: What's with you and black cats today?

Pete: a black cat is my familiar

Me: Your familiar isn't a black cat. It's … a seahorse

Riven: Oh, yes, definitely a seahorse!

Pete: no way! if not a black cat, then definitely a t-rex!

Me: Can familiars be extinct animals?

Riven: Oh most def! Mine's totally a big-ol trilobite, and everyone's going to be like "WTF is that!" when it comes crawling up to me!

Me: lol

I look at the photo of the clipboard again. My eyes scan over the dates. What numbers did they record on the date Riven and I saw them create the shadowy wisp? I check the date in my calendar, then find it near the top of the page. Fifty-five, forty-four, forty-two. What do all these numbers mean?

We spend the next hour researching numerology and the meaning of numbers and how they relate to witchcraft, but nothing fits. Finally Riven suggests we go to a "metaphysical store" on Whyte Avenue called Modern Pagan and ask some (subtle) questions, which isn't a bad idea.

Riven: Should we go tomorrow?

Tomorrow is Sunday. It feels weird to think of going to church in the morning and then a witchcraft store in the afternoon—especially if there's stuff there for worshipping false gods or whatever. Even if the Witches don't practice that type of witchcraft, there'd probably be stuff there for people that do.

Me: How about Tuesday after school?

THE FORGOTTEN MEMORIES OF VERA GLASS

Riven: Works for me. Pete?

Pete: you guys go without me. mom would ground me forever if I went to a store called modern pagan

I hover over the keyboard, feeling a strange absence. It feels like there's someone else we should be asking, but this is it. There's only three of us.

Me: Okay. We'll report back

We log off not long after that, and that night, I fall asleep studying the sheet of numbers on my phone.

▲ ▲ ▲ ▲ ▲ ▲ ▲ ▲ ▲ ▲ ▲ ▲

The front window of Modern Pagan is set up simply, with only a couple of books, a necklace with a turquoise stone, and a small marble mortar and pestle. Still, I find myself pausing outside the place. This is not the type of store I ever thought I'd go in. I mean, even setting aside that I used to think witchcraft had something to do with the devil, the very first of the Ten Commandments is to not worship other gods. Which is what Riven says Wiccans do. By going in, is that what I'm doing?

Riven immediately picks up on my hesitation and pauses, too. She peers out at me from under the faux-fur-lined hood of her coat. "Do you want me to go in alone and report back to you?"

I shake my head. "No, that's okay. I'm sure God knows I'm not here to do any witchcraft or to search for non-God gods or whatever." I say it like a joke, but the words immediately resonate as true, giving me the courage to push forward, with Riven right behind me. A bell jingles above our heads as we enter the brightly lit store.

The clerk behind the counter is busy with a customer, so we

take a minute to look around. To the right is a glass shelf covered in gemstones of various sizes. To the left is a wooden shelf with bins full of various herbs, sort of like the bulk section in a grocery store. A sign says, "Save the planet. Bring your own reusable containers and have them weighed before and after."

I lean over to Riven. "Well, at least they're environmentally conscious," I say quietly.

"Oh, good," Riven says. "I'm definitely giving them a five-star Yelp review."

Before I can quip something back at her, the bell over the door behind us jingles. The woman who was at the counter has left. The clerk is free. As one, Riven and I head toward her.

The store clerk is about our age, though I don't recognize her. Which I suppose isn't surprising. If she lives around here, she'd be in a different school district; ours is south of here. She's got a frohawk, with the sides shaved short and the top thick with her natural curls, and is wearing a simple black T-shirt and jeans and a badge that says "My pronouns are she/her." "Can I help you?" she asks with a smile as we approach.

"We have some questions about numerology," Riven says.

"Oh, Tessa knows a lot more about that than I do," the girl says. "Let me see if she's free." She heads toward a door at the back of the store, leaving us to wait.

Near the counter is a display of gemstone necklaces. Riven picks up a black crystal necklace and turns it over to read the description on the back. "Do I have any obsessions that I need help breaking?"

I bring my hand to my face in mock consideration. After a moment, I say, "Turtles."

"Turtles?"

"Yes. You've mentioned them at least three times over the years we've been friends. That's truly excessive."

She nods gravely. "You are so right. I should definitely buy one of these to cure me of my turtle obsession." She puts down the black crystal and reaches for a pale pink stone, but before she can pull it off the stand, the clerk reappears through the back door of the store with a middle-aged white woman trailing after her.

The woman is wearing skinny jeans and a lacy black tank top, her shoulder-length hair is dyed bright pink, and her arms are completely covered in tattoos. Between her ears, her nose, and her eyebrow, I count nine piercings. She's not at all how I expected a witch to look.

"I'm Tessa," she says when she reaches the counter. "I'm doing a tarot reading shortly, but I'm happy to answer any questions before then."

Her tattoos are colored, and parts of the sleeves stand out as particularly vivid. A bright red rose at her elbow with vines wrapping down her forearm. A sharp green eye peering out from her other bicep. A tiny blue bird at her wrist.

She must spot me looking at them, because she says, "The color only lasts for a day or so, so I change up what I want to highlight each day."

I understand immediately. I've seen enough of my brother's (usually accidental) handiwork to recognize this aptitude. "You have color magic," I say.

She nods. "Best aptitude, in my opinion," she says. "I can make things whatever color I want, whenever I want."

Riven meets my eye and raises one eyebrow in a challenge. We're both feeling a little reckless, coming here.

"Color does you no good in darkness," I say as Riven throws her hand upward like we timed and rehearsed it. The store grows a few degrees brighter.

Tessa's laugh is an unexpectedly soft and tinkling thing. "Fair point. Plus they did use light recently to find the missing parts of the universe." She absentmindedly taps her fingers on her arm, right on the eyeball. "Still, I'd rather have my colors."

The missing parts of the universe? Something about that thought chills me. I'm going to need to remember to look that up later.

Tessa leans forward on the counter. "So what can I do for you? Coraline said you had questions about numerology?"

I glance around, realizing the other girl has disappeared.

"Yeah," Riven says, diving in. "We're pretty new to Wicca and numerology. We keep seeing certain numbers and we wondered if it has a meaning."

"Oh yes. That usually means the universe is sending you a message, and you should consider yourself very blessed. Here, let me get you a book on the meanings of various numbers." As she heads toward a bookshelf at the back of the store, Riven and I share a look. This is mostly just what we learned online and doesn't explain why the Witches are conjuring up shadow monsters or why they have sheets of numbers or why everything in the world feels wrong.

"Here you go," Tessa says when she returns. She hands us a paperback book with a brightly colored mandala on the front. "That'll tell you the meaning of most numbers you might see."

"If we're seeing a repeated number, should we try using that number in our spells and stuff?"

I'm glad Riven is asking the questions. I'm not sure I know enough about witchcraft to ask reasonable-sounding questions. In fact, the more I learn about witchcraft, the more I realize I'm wrong about it. For example, I can't spot a single Hollywood-esque cauldron or pointy black hat from where I'm standing in this store.

"Numerology is more about finding and interpreting your life path number, birth number, and name number, and determining what those mean for your life than about spells," Tessa explains. "But some people do incorporate the power of numbers in their spell work. For example, if you're dealing with the feminine, you might burn two candles instead of one on your altar."

We both nod, even though none of this is proving helpful at all and the mention of altars makes me uncomfortable.

"Does any of this have to do with shadows?" I blurt out.

"Ah, shadow numbers," Tessa says, rubbing her wrist right where the small blue bird sits. "The shadow traits of numbers are the dark side of every person—those negative traits that you need to come to terms with to gain a proper understanding of self. Shadow work is an important part of every witch's path to self-discovery."

Before she can say more, the bell over the door jingles, and a woman bundled in a long winter coat walks in. "Ah, my next client is here," Tessa says. "I'll have to excuse myself. But Coraline can help you find any other resources you might need."

I want to protest that we were just getting to the good stuff, but she's already striding off to greet the woman at the door.

Before we leave, we look over the books at the back of the store, but no books about shadow numbers or any kind of shadow magic jumps out at us. We end up buying the numerology book Tessa showed us, even though we suspect it won't tell us anything we can't find on the Internet.

"So do you believe in this numerology stuff?" Riven asks me on the bus ride home.

I consider for a moment. Then I say, "Okay, so you're on the island and you encounter three people. One says, 'My life path number is three.' Another says, 'My life path number is seven.' The third one says, 'My life path number is four.' Who's a knight and who's a knave?"

She cocks an eyebrow at me. "I have no idea."

"Exactly. It tells you nothing."

She laughs. "Maybe it would tell me something if I knew the meaning of numbers."

It's my turn to cock an eyebrow at her. "You think everyone born on the same day has the same destiny?"

She frowns. "No, I guess not. But then what's this shadow number stuff and what exactly are the Witches doing?"

My eyebrows knit together. I'd forgotten for a moment there that we were pursuing something that defies logic. Temporarily, anyway. "Maybe I'm wrong," I say as we get off the bus at our stop. "Maybe we'll research shadow numbers or traits or whatever and the answers will come to us and it will explain everything."

"Hopefully," Riven says.

CHAPTER SEVENTEEN

It doesn't explain everything. In fact, it doesn't explain even a little bit. "Okay, let's say that the Witches are somehow manifesting shadow traits into actual shadows—which is not a thing mentioned on any of these websites—then what in the world does that have to do with how terrible we've been feeling?" I'm leaning against the headboard of my bed, my legs folded into a peak under the blankets. Riven is leaning against my knees with her left arm, her phone in her right hand.

Riven sets down her phone and leans so her chin is resting on my knees. "I don't know. Maybe they're manifesting *our* shadow traits."

"I don't have any shadow traits. I'm perfect."

"Oh, right. That can't be the answer then." Riven picks her phone back up and returns to looking through the pictures we took of the Witches' notes. "I definitely don't have any shadow traits, either."

"You definitely have one big shadow trait," I say. "You're much *too* perfect. It's intimidating to the rest of the world."

"Hmm, yes, a very good point," Riven says. "I—wait. What is this?" She double-taps her phone to zoom in and then brings it just a few inches from her face.

"What's what?" My heart is suddenly racing. "Did you find something?" I sit up, causing Riven to topple into the space my knees are no longer occupying. She barely seems to notice; she props herself back up and peers at her phone again.

"Let me see!" I lean over, and she holds out her phone to me, but doesn't let go. "There," she says, pointing to the top right corner of her screen. The picture is of one of the number-covered papers, though it's zoomed in so much that I can't tell which one. In the top right corner, another paper sticks out from behind the first, and printed on it in grayscale block letters are the initials ARI.

"What am I looking at?" I ask.

"Isn't that the Aptitude Research Institute logo?" Riven asks, her voice practically humming with excitement.

"Yeah." The logo's a common visual in our house. It's on Mom and Dad's papers, on their briefcases, and even on some of their clothes. Dad has an ARI golf shirt, and they both have ARI hoodies. "So what?"

"So the ARI must be involved!"

"Involved in what?"

"In whatever's going on! That's why it feels too big for just a few teenage witches. It's not just them. It's a whole big conspiracy! Or maybe research gone wrong. Or an employee who's gone rogue. Maybe the Witches are actually the victims of some ARI experiments. I'm writing these things down." She reaches for the notebook and starts to scribble in it.

"I don't know, Riven," I say. When you've heard your parents complain about deadlines and paperwork and expense reports, it's hard to picture their workplace as the source of some big evil conspiracy.

"Look, I'm sure your parents aren't involved at all," Riven reassures me, as if that's the only reason I think her idea is ridiculous. "But just, you know, try to suss out whether they've heard of anything suspicious. Without being too conspicuous about it or anything. We don't want them to poke their heads in somewhere to investigate and become collateral damage."

Thinking of my parents as collateral damage would be upsetting if I didn't feel so sure that this has nothing to do with ARI and everything to do with the Witches. "Yeah, okay," I say anyway, because when Riven is this excited about something, I know she'll never drop it.

I chew on my thumbnail. When I look up, Riven is staring at me expectantly. She's wearing a T-shirt with a cutesy version of a *Legends of the Stone* mutant rabbit on it, and even it seems to be staring at me expectantly.

"What? I'm not going to do it right now! That'd be kind of conspicuous, don't you think?"

She nods reluctantly, her ponytail bobbing up and down. "Yeah, I guess that's true. So, what shall we do now, then?"

"*Doctor Who*?" I reach for my laptop, already knowing what Riven's answer will be.

"Let's watch a Jodie episode," Riven suggests. "I'm in the mood for some girl power."

"You're always in the mood for some girl power."

"Truth."

So we set the laptop up on a chair beside my bed. I settle back against the headboard, and Riven leans against my knees again. And for a little while I forget about all the weird things going on and about our investigation and I simply watch a *Doctor Who* episode with my best friend.

"I was reading online today about a concept called ghosting," Mom says with a forkful of carrots poised halfway to her mouth. "You wouldn't ghost anyone, would you, Vera? It seems incredibly rude."

We're at the dinner table Wednesday evening, eating pork, baby potatoes, and carrots made by Dad. Isaac is trying to break a world record for how many carrots he can fit in his mouth while Gertie has snuck a book to the table and isn't touching her food. She had a breakthrough with reading and suddenly is able to read pretty much anything. Now she always has her head buried in a book. I'm sure Mom and Dad have both noticed the book in Gertie's lap but are too enamored with her new love of reading to do anything about it.

Last week, I tried to sneak a book to the dinner table, but apparently it's not as cute when I do it.

"What's ghosting?" Dad asks.

Mom has to finish her mouthful of carrots before she can answer. "It's where you abruptly stop talking to someone without any explanation why."

"Oh, that's rude," Dad says.

"Right?!"

"Well, usually it's for a good reason," I explain.

"A good reason to disappear from someone's life without explanation? Promise me you won't ever do that to anyone, Vera. Promise me." Mom sounds sort of frantic.

Before I can say anything, Dad chimes in. "Vera, your mother asked you a question."

Which makes me angry. At least give me time to answer before assuming I'm not going to. "It wasn't a question," I say. "It was a demand." A plea is more like it, but I'm not admitting that.

"Vera!" Dad says.

"It's fine, Frank," Mom says.

"It's not fine. She shouldn't be talking to her parents like that."

And then they're at it again, arguing for the thousandth time. I'm sick of it.

"So, has ARI got any big, exciting projects going on right now?" I ask, breaking into their argument. It's the first distraction I can think of, and at least Riven won't be able to say I didn't try.

Dad's eyes light up for the first time all meal. "Well, Yixin has an interesting paper coming out. The solution to the universe's missing matter problem may help us solve some unanswered questions about aptitudes."

I sit up straight. "Missing matter?" This is the second time in as many days that someone has mentioned this. I know thinking a coincidence has meaning can be a logical fallacy, but still . . .

"Yes," Dad says, "it's—"

"Frank!" Mom butts in. "That's still confidential."

Dad sighs. "I was only going to tell her about the missing

matter solution, which is very public. And besides, as you know, the paper itself is in peer review."

"That's still not published. Our confidentiality—"

"Yeah, yeah, our confidentiality agreements . . ." And then they're off arguing again.

"It's okay. Forget I asked," I say, because I am so very tired of hearing about those agreements. "Let's just talk about the books we're reading or something." It's a topic that'll normally send each of them off on an excited rant, but today it's like they don't even hear me. Now they're arguing much too loudly about who a hypothetical judge would side with in interpreting their employment contract, while at least two of their three kids watch them, alarmed. (Isaac is oblivious.)

A lump forms in my throat. What if it *is* the ARI? What if ARI is doing something to them and it's turning them into supervillains. Or worse, what if it's their own work and they're turning themselves into supervillains? They both seem to know a lot about that article; maybe one of them was directly involved with the research.

But then they both notice that Isaac has dumped his milk out on his plate and is messily lapping it up like a kitten, and as they meet each other's eyes, clearly trying to collectively decide whether to scold him or just laugh, they're suddenly both just parents again, and Riven's idea goes back to sounding silly.

Except that evening, when we're all sitting around in the living room doing our own thing, I surreptitiously look up the missing matter problem on my phone. The science is complicated, and I definitely don't understand all of it, but I think I can make out enough to understand the basics. Essentially, while scientists believed a certain amount of normal matter, called baryons, existed in the universe, they had no way to measure or see a large chunk of it—until recently, that is. Someone came up with a way to use light to measure the missing parts, and they were able to confirm that the baryons are there in the exact quantities they expected.

Which, on the one hand, is sort of anticlimactic. There was no actual missing matter, just matter that couldn't be seen.

But on the other hand, I can't stop thinking about it—about this invisible matter. Scientists knew it was there; they could sense its absence, could calculate its weight. But they couldn't see it, couldn't fully understand it.

I, too, have an invisible weight that I can't see or understand, though mine is around my heart.

Could these things be related?

If the ARI is involved, it would have to be something to do with aptitudes. What did Dad say? That the missing matter solution may somehow answer some questions about aptitudes? What if they're trying to view aptitudes the same way scientists have managed to view the missing matter, and it's revealing a weight we weren't even aware of?

I glance over at my parents. My dad is showing Gertie pictures in a book about M. C. Escher. My mom is reading C. S. Lewis's *Mere Christianity* while Isaac happily sticks LEGO people in her hair. They're definitely not supervillains—at least not intentionally—but could they be doing something monumental without realizing it? Or might they know about something that someone else at ARI is doing? Like Dad's colleague with her new paper?

One thing's for sure: They are never going to tell me about it, at least not in detail. That dang confidentiality agreement. If I'm going to find out, I'm going to have to do it on my own.

A bit later, when I'm heading up to bed, I pass Mom's briefcase by the front door and stop to stare at it. "Good night, sweetheart," Mom says, making me jump a mile. I'm two stairs up, but she reaches up and puts a hand on my arm. "Whoa, are you okay? Bit jumpy!"

"Fine," I say. "I was just lost in thought."

"Well, don't forget to leave yourself some bread crumbs so you can find your way home," Mom says, and I smile and try to keep my gaze from drifting to her briefcase by the door.

When I get up to my room, I text Riven: What if we snuck into my parents' briefcases?

Instead of texting me back, she calls me. She skips right over hello and says, "Did you find something out?"

"No," I say. "Well, probably not." And then in a whisper, with my phone tucked between my ear and my shoulder as I put on my pajama pants, I tell her about the missing matter problem and what Dad said at dinner.

"I knew the ARI was involved," she says in a whisper, even though there's no need for her to whisper from her end.

"We don't know that," I say.

"But you suspect it. That's why you want to go through your parents' stuff."

"Hang on a minute," I tell her, then set the phone down while I put on the oversize T-shirt I use as a pajama top. When I pick the phone back up, I say, "I don't suspect anything. I'm just open to multiple possibilities." Especially ones that have to do with finding the source of an invisible weight.

"Right. Sure. So when are we going through their stuff?" She's stopped whispering.

I think it through. It has to be a time when Mom and Dad aren't home but their briefcases are. "How about on Saturday when they're at judo?"

Riven groans. "That's three whole days away. The ARI could end the entire world before then."

I plop down on my bed. "This has nothing to do with ending the world."

"You don't know that."

"You're right. I don't. I suppose we should say our goodbyes now, just in case. Goodbye, dear friend. It has been a real pleasure knowing you. I'll miss you when the universe disappears in a poof."

"Aw, you're going to make me cry. I'll miss you, too, you dork."

"Hey, you're the dork."

"Can we just agree that we're both dorks?"

"Granted. Love you, you dork."

"Love you too, dork."

"Good night."

"Good night."

CHAPTER EIGHTEEN

As the week goes on, I get more and more nervous about going through my parents' work stuff. It doesn't help that we have a math test on Thursday and a science test on Friday, so my nerves are already frayed. I've been so distracted by all this investigation stuff and by the empty feeling that seems to live in the pit of my stomach that I didn't start studying for either test as far in advance as usual. In fact, cramming about ionic compounds and the periodic table Thursday night takes me past midnight before I feel good and ready.

"How did it go?" Sarah asks me on Friday after the science test, as we're packing up our things.

"I bet you both bombed it," Vincent says from behind us.

"Come on, man. Why do you have to be such a dick all the time?" James jumps in.

"I'm not being a dick," Vincent says. "It's called joking. These two get it."

"Aren't jokes supposed to be funny?" I snap. "If you know science the way you know jokes, then you're the one who bombed that test."

Sarah snort-laughs.

Vincent scowls at me and stalks off. James gives an apologetic shrug, then shuffles after him.

"That was great," Sarah says. "So how *did* the test go for you?"

I'm never quite sure how to answer questions like that because I never feel great after a test, but I usually do better than I think. I settle for, "It was okay," which seems to be the right answer because Sarah agrees.

We talk about the test a bit, comparing answers as we head out into the hall. Then Sarah says, "Hey, do you want to come over tomorrow morning? My mom always makes this big feast like she's forgotten my brothers don't live with us anymore."

My stomach twists at the mention of tomorrow morning and what I'll be doing. "I'm sorry, but Riven and I have plans already." Plans to snoop through my parents' confidential and top-secret documents.

"Oh." Sarah's face falls for just a moment before she tightens it back into a polite smile. "You and Riven sure do a lot together."

"Well, yeah. She's my best friend."

"That's nice." Sarah looks down at her feet. "Really nice. Anyways, I should head off now. See you." She gives me a little wave and heads off down the hall.

"Sarah," I call after her, "I'd love to come over for breakfast another time."

She gives me a thumbs-up but doesn't look back.

At lunch, Riven and Pete and I talk about random crap. Riven and I haven't told Pete about the ARI logo. I know we're supposed to tell him everything now, but I asked Riven not to tell him anything, at least until we knew whether my parents were implicated. Not that I think they are. This whole ARI idea is probably silly. But still, it'd be nice to know for sure before we involve Pete.

Besides, Pete seems too busy being lost in thought all the time. Sometimes it feels like half of him is missing and he's disappeared too far inside himself to try to find it. Maybe this ARI research is a good thing, and they've discovered a way to find the missing pieces of Pete. The missing pieces of all of us.

"And that's why weasels are the worst," Riven says.

"Huh?" I say.

"Huh?" Pete echoes.

"Ugh, I take it back. You two are the worst. You're impossible to talk to lately."

"Sorry," Pete and I say at the same time.

"Let's just play cards," Riven suggests. So we do.

And then it's Saturday, and I'm greeting Riven at our door.

"Is that Riven?" Dad shouts from the kitchen. "Tell her I'm making apple pancakes."

Riven grins. "My favorite, Mr. Frank!" Riven shouts back.

Soon we're caught up in the hubbub of Saturday morning breakfast at my house, with Gertie having to be told a dozen times to put down her book and come to the table, and Isaac insisting he doesn't like apple pancakes though he's eaten them dozens of times, and Mom giving up on fighting with him and picking out all the apple pieces for him, and Dad narrowing his eyes at her, but the two of them not fighting because Riven is here. Which makes me extra grateful that she is.

And then they're all rushing off to judo, leaving us behind to "clean the kitchen, please." And then the house is quiet and it's just me and Riven and those two briefcases by the door.

"Well, should we hop to it?" Riven asks as soon as they've left.

I shake my head. "What if they come back because they forgot something?" It's not a stalling technique—at least, it's not only a stalling technique; they forget something and have to come back probably 10 percent of the time.

So we clean the kitchen instead, and when we're finished filling the dishwasher and enough time has passed that it's clear they're not coming back, Riven tosses the dish towel down on the counter, hooks her arm through mine, and marches me over to the brief-cases, where we stand staring at them. Neither of us makes a move toward them.

I'm not sure why I feel so reluctant to open them. I was comfortable breaking into a garage for the sake of an investigation. But that garage belonged to the Witches, who I don't care about, while these briefcases belong to my parents, who I do.

"We have to do it," Riven says finally.

"Do we?"

"Hey, it was your idea in the first place."

"Right." I twirl a curl around my finger. "What do the Witches have to do with all this anyways?" I step back and release the curl abruptly. "Actually, that's a good question."

Riven raises both eyebrows. "Did you just ask a question and then compliment yourself on it?"

"Look," I say, "I was just stalling. But my stalling brain made a point that we should actually think about. We know the Witches are doing something fishy, with their shadow monster and Cecily's disappearing. So shouldn't we be investigating them some more? Why the heck are we going down this ARI tangent?" I tighten my hands into fists and then release them.

"Uh, because we found a document with the ARI logo on it amidst the Witches' papers?" Riven says, like it's obvious.

I suppose it is obvious. I suppose my stalling brain is still stalling. But what if we do find out that the universe's problems are my parents' fault rather than the Witches'? Is that something I actually want to know?

I expect Riven to call me out on my stalling, but instead she pulls out her phone, unlocks it, and then pokes around on it for a bit. "Ah, here's one," she finally says. Then she turns to me. "You're on the island and you come across three people. The first says, 'Only one of us is a knave.' The second says, 'Only one of us is a knight.' The third says, 'We are all knaves.' Who's what?"

Somehow Riven always knows exactly what I need when I need it. "Okay, well, a knight could never say, 'We are all knaves,' so the third guy has to be a knave," I say. "Which means he's lying, which means there has to be at least one knight." I feel calmer already as I start to reason it through. "The other two contradict each other, which means they can't both be knights, which means one is a knight and one is a knave. Which means there are two knaves and one knight, which means the first is a liar and the second is telling the truth. So knave, knight, knave."

I step toward the briefcases. "All right, let's open them."

Riven grabs my arm. "Wait, that's all it took?

I turn to look at her. "I was only able to solve that problem because I had all the pieces of the puzzle. We're never going to figure out an answer unless we have all pieces. And maybe one of the pieces is in there." The fact is that we need answers. Weeks have gone by with no answers, only this emptiness inside me and no reason why. I need to know why. I need to figure out who's a knight and who's a knave and who's making the universe feel so wrong and why, even if I don't like the answer.

I give a little nod to Riven, and she throws her hand up and brightens the dim hallway.

Then she gives a little nod to me, and I step forward and put my hand on Mom's briefcase. I don't even have to touch the locks themselves, just the briefcase, and the locks pop open.

"Wow. Nice. You're getting better at that," Riven says. "Do this one, too."

So I pop open Dad's briefcase, too, and then I start going through Mom's and Riven starts going through Dad's.

Mom's briefcase is full of papers and a couple of textbooks— one on the science of light and another on aptitudes. I set the textbooks on the floor and reach for the stack of notebooks and loose papers.

I flip through the papers first. They're mostly scientific papers with titles like "Harnessing single-active plasmonic nanostructures for enhanced photocatalysis under visible light" or "The plasmonic nanostructures of energy-based aptitudes." Nothing that jumps out to me as sinister or as having anything to do with the missing matter problem, though admittedly I don't understand most of it.

I turn to the notebooks next, where I find pages of calculations and graphs drawn in pencil. Once again, most of it goes over my head, though like the papers, nothing jumps out at me as sinister or especially relevant.

"Oh!" Riven says from her spot on the floor a few feet away. "I think I found that paper your dad was talking about!"

"You did?" I lean over, and she throws her hand up to give us even more light as I look over her shoulder. The title of the small-printed research paper she's holding states, *Could the universe's missing matter solution also solve the aptitudinal dark matter versus normal matter question?* Under that are the names of a couple of researchers, including Yixin Chen. Neither of my parents are listed.

"Do you know what dark matter is?" Riven asks as she hands the paper to me.

"Sort of. I know that Vera Rubin, who I'm named after, discovered it." I try to recall what my parents explained to me about it years ago when they first told me stories of my namesake. "Something about galaxies rotating at a different rate than you'd think, meaning they're way heavier than they look."

"Oh, is that the missing matter they found?"

"No, I don't think so. Let me think." I try to remember what I read online, but my eyes keep wandering to the first few lines of the abstract at the top of the research paper. Which, it turns out, perfectly answers our question.

"Right, that was baryons," I say. "This paper confirms it was only normal matter they were able to identify with that complicated light technique they used. The dark matter that makes up 85 percent of the universe still can't be seen by light. Or something like that."

"So is that what the Witches are conjuring up, then? Dark matter?"

"No, I don't—" I pause, setting the paper down in my lap. My first thought was that if dark matter can't be seen by light, it shouldn't be visible as a shadow, either. But actually, I have no idea if that's true. And what if the Witches aren't doing any kind of mystical witchcraft at all? What if it's all science? That would make so much more sense. "Actually, maybe. I don't know. We're going to have to do more research."

Riven nods. "And read that to bits," she says, pointing to the research paper in my lap.

I nod. This paper does feel like the pivotal key that might tie everything together. Maybe my unlocking aptitude has finally opened something more than a lock.

I lean over and give Riven a side-arm hug that almost throws me off balance. She's a little farther away than I calculated in my head.

"Aww, what's that for?" she asks as she leans her head gently but awkwardly against mine.

"I never could have done this without you. Gotten the courage, I mean. I would have chickened out."

"I'm sure that's not true," she says, patting my shoulder. "But know what you do need me for?"

"What?"

"Remembering that you need to clean this all up before your family gets back home."

"Oh." I sit up abruptly. The floor is littered with texts and papers and notebooks we've taken from both briefcases. In the midst of Riven's pile of documents is a stainless-steel water bottle and what I hope is a clean pair of gray socks. "A very good point."

I fold up the research paper we've found and slip it into my left pocket, and then I return to the pile of stuff I extricated from my mom's briefcase. As I begin to slide things back into the main compartment, grateful that I didn't have to deal with a pair of my parents' socks, I spot a pocket I missed, just on the inside. I slide open the zipper and reach inside, finding a folded-up piece of paper. Just a single sheet, not like the small stack folded in my pocket.

The sheet is probably nothing important, but I find myself unfolding it anyway. The top right corner is stamped with the name and address of a doctor's office. At the bottom, a line catches my eye, but before I can read it properly, a click comes from my right. Riven is locking Dad's briefcase back up, no magic needed. Which means she's almost done. Which means she'll come over here next.

I never hide things from Riven, but this feels different. It's Mom's, and since it's from a doctor, it's private. I fold up the paper again and swiftly stick it in the right back pocket of my jeans. Seconds later, Riven is beside me and handing me the last of Mom's stuff, which I obediently slide inside.

I let Riven lock Mom's briefcase as I stand, the research report we've taken from my dad burning a hole in my front left pocket, and my mom's doctor's thing burning through the back right. Trying not to draw attention to either, I trot after Riven as she heads upstairs to my room, chattering away to me.

"Well that was productive," she says enthusiastically as she plops down on my bed. "We should probably make a copy of that research paper, don't you think? So we both have a copy to pore over?" Then she cocks her head. "You okay? Are you just going to hover there like a helicopter?"

I am still standing—hovering—just inside my bedroom door. "Um." Aside from that half hour where I didn't tell her about the graveyard shadow monster, I have no experience keeping secrets from Riven, and I'm clearly very bad at it. I need to do something about this paper in my back right pocket right away. "I—uh—I'm—I need to go pee."

"Then go pee, you dork."

"Right. Yes. I will do this thing."

I can hear Riven laughing as I leave the room. At least she doesn't seem to suspect anything. Bile rises in my throat at the thought that I'm hiding something from her. From my best friend. But I need to see this on my own.

In the bathroom, I lock the door behind me. Then I pull the paper out of my pocket and sit on the edge of the bathtub as I unfold it.

It's not anything sinister. It's not proof that my mom is some evil supervillain or involved in this whole dark matter issue in any way.

It's just a simple questionnaire, with questions like:

How often do you feel down, depressed, or hopeless?

How often do you have a poor appetite or feel like overeating?

How often do you feel tired or have little energy?

Mom has answered *at least half the time* to almost all the questions.

It's the final question that especially draws my attention, though. It reads, *Did anything particular trigger these feelings?*

In answer, Mom has written, *I don't know. I feel like I've lost something, like there's this empty hole in my heart. I can't explain it.*

Mom feels it, too. The loss. The inexplicable emptiness. The invisible darkness.

Is this why we're always fighting? Because we're both so weighted down by some invisible, unknowable force?

And if so, who can we blame for it? I tap my fingers on the edge of the bathtub. Are Mom and Dad's colleagues at the ARI at fault? Are the Witches? And now that I know about Mom, what do I do about it? Do I tell her? Do I admit that I broke into her briefcase and found this? Do I slip it back into her briefcase and say nothing? How do I decide?

I have no answers to any of these questions except the last one: I ask Riven. I don't know why I hid this from her in the first place. She's my best friend. I know she wouldn't do anything to hurt my mom or me. She loves us both. This might be my mom's secret, but it's too big for me to carry alone. I need Riven's help.

And besides, the fact that Mom feels these weird feelings too is a clue, isn't it? Maybe between that fact and the research paper and the ARI and the Witches, everything will tie together.

I don't fold the questionnaire back up. I hold it open in my hand as I unlock the bathroom and head back to my room. Head back to tell Riven.

When I get to my room, I start to talk as soon as I open the door. "Okay, so that research paper wasn't the only thing I found. I should have said something. I—"

I break off. And then I feel sort of silly. Because I don't know why I'm talking to an empty room. And also, I don't know why I'm crying.

CHAPTER NINETEEN

My bedroom is empty, just like I left it. The single blue wall stares mournfully back at me. For some reason, I grab my research notebook off my desk. On the first couple of pages are the notes I've been making about what I've found out about the Witches and that ARI logo on one of their papers. And then, nothing. Empty pages. Empty spaces. Emptiness.

None of it feels right. Everything feels wrong.

The research paper I just found after finally getting up the courage to search through my parents' briefcases is still in my pocket. I slip Mom's doctor's questionnaire in to join it. Neither of them feels important right now.

I sink down onto the bed, and just being there, alone, makes the tears fall faster. I don't know why.

Everything is wrong. Everything is wrong. The words repeat again and again in my head.

So even though it's the middle of the day, I climb under my blanket, and I cry myself to sleep.

CHAPTER TWENTY

I wake to Mom sitting down beside me on my bed. I sit up groggily. I consider telling her that I found her questionnaire, that she's not alone in whatever she's going through, that I feel it, too. That I feel it even stronger now, in this room on this bed. But when I open my mouth to speak, only a sob comes out.

Mom immediately wraps her arms around me and pulls me to her, and I cry into her shoulder while she strokes my hair.

She doesn't ask me what's wrong, which I'm grateful for, because how would I explain?

I don't know what's wrong. I only know that the emptiness inside me is growing like a fungus. Like a virus. Like a black hole.

The weight of it pulls me down, down, down, out of my mother's arms, and back under the covers.

I know I should read the research report I found. I know I should look up dark matter and invisible weights and complicated light measurements. But I can't even turn on the light in my room without getting out of bed and walking across the room to the switch—a thought that's inexplicably upsetting even though it's been true my entire life.

So instead, I stay in the fluctuating but persistent dark, drifting in and out of sleep, for the rest of the weekend.

On Monday morning, a small, quiet hope pulls me out of bed and gets me ready for school. It's the thought that maybe I've imagined it all. That nothing is wrong at all. That I'll get to school and everything will be right.

It's that thought that pushes me to pull on clothes, to turn down Mom's offer to let me stay home, to march step after step down the seven snowy blocks to school. It pushes me in through the school doors, to my locker, to gather my books for the day.

But then the thought—the hope—starts to slip away. Because I don't know where to go next. I feel like I should have somewhere to go in this in-between time before classes start, but I simply stand at my locker, with nothing to anchor me to reality. With the hope that was holding me together unraveling faster and faster. I'm about to fall apart in this crowded hallway.

And then someone is at my elbow. "Let's get out of here," Pete says. He apparently doesn't need my mom's intuition magic to see how close I am to breaking into a thousand pieces. He hands me back the coat I hung in my locker, closes the door, and then grabs my hand and pulls me down the hall.

Outside the school, we stand at a bus stop. It's cold, and the sun is only just starting to show on the horizon. Days are short this time of year. I put on the coat I'm still holding and zip it up to my chin, pull up my hood, and jam my hands in my pockets.

I follow Pete onto the first bus that arrives. In the distance I can hear the first bell ringing as the bus doors close. We ride the bus, standing, for only a few minutes to the transit center, where we hop on another bus and ride it for only a few minutes more.

I follow Pete off the bus and down a residential street. We walk in silence. I don't think either of us have said anything since we left the school—which is fine with me. I don't know what I would say.

And then Pete turns off the sidewalk to enter a gate, and suddenly I recognize where we are. We're at the cemetery on the route where we did our Halloween food drive. The cemetery where I first saw the Witches conjure a shadow monster.

I think at first that Pete has found something—that maybe he's going to show me something to do with the Witches or the shadow monster—but he just leads me down a path to a bench at the top of a short hillside covered in gravestones. He sits on the bench and gestures beside him, and I sit down, too.

In the small space of time it has taken us to get here, the sun has risen, though it doesn't seem that much lighter out. The sky is gray, like it's covered in one long expanse of cloud.

Our breath comes out in little white puffs as we sit in silence. The gravestones are sprinkled with snow; the boughs of the surrounding trees are heavy with white. It's not spooky like it was on Halloween. In fact, it's almost peaceful. The quiet rhythm of our breathing is like a lullaby for ghosts.

"I come here, sometimes," Pete says at last. "I don't know why. It's the only place things feel right." Then he mumbles an added, "At least, more so than in my dreams."

Pete and I have been best friends, just the two of us, since the beginning of junior high, and dating since the end of it. I slide closer to him and slip my hand into his pocket to find his own. "What happens in your dreams?" I ask, as I entwine my fingers with his.

Pete's hood is up like mine, so I can't see much of his shadowed face, but his eyes shut and stay that way for two long breaths before popping back open. I worry that he's going to shut me out like he sometimes does when he's not comfortable talking about his feelings, but then he says, "I'm in this cemetery. I walk down this hill to a gravestone near the bottom." We both gaze down the hill at the dozens of gravestones with their backs to us. "I'm always heading to a gravestone in particular, but it's never in the same place. Sometimes there. Or there." He points to different places on the hill with his other hand. "When I get to the stone and step around to see the front, there's no name. Just an empty gravestone."

I don't know why Pete's story gives me chills. Or why it makes me want to run down the hill and look at every gravestone until I find the ones that say—what? I don't know. I tighten my grip on his hand, and he tightens his grip right back. At least Pete's hand in mine is one thing I can count on. We've been dating for six months, though we're trying to keep things slow.

As we sit there, I finally pull the research paper I found in Dad's briefcase out of my pocket. Pete sits in silence beside me as I read it through slowly, trying to understand. He's used to me trying to research our way out of this. Of course, he doesn't believe half of the things I spout—like about the Witches especially, though he might be more willing to believe they're doing something with dark matter—but he'll tell me he believes I can solve it as often as he (lovingly) makes fun of me.

So much of the paper goes over my head, but from what I can make out, the authors theorize that they might be able to determine whether aptitudes rely on or interact with dark matter by using a similar test to the missing matter solution and extrapolating.

There's no mention of actual experiments, no mention of the Witches and whether dark matter can be manifested into some sort of shadow monster. It's all just theory. In other words, it might be a clue, but it's not an answer. I sigh and lean back against the cold bench. "What do you think is happening to us?"

Pete shrugs a half shrug, where his shoulders come up around his ears without coming back down. "I don't know. But whatever it is, it feels cruel."

"Cruel?"

"Yes, cruel. It's brutal to take something from someone without letting them know what's been lost. To be left to mourn . . . nothingness. How are you supposed to grieve?"

"Is that what you think happened? Something was taken?"

He shrugs. "Obviously I was a filthy rich vlogger who lost all his followers as a result of falling into this parallel universe. It's the only explanation why I'm not famous."

My laugh comes out in white puffs. "That would explain a lot."

"Right?!"

Then we both fall back into silence. The cold is starting to seep from the bench through my jeans, but I don't feel ready to leave this place. "What are we going to do, Pete?" I whisper.

For a moment, I think he doesn't hear me, but then he says, "Find the answer. Save the day. That's what you keep working on, right?" He gestures toward the paper in my hand.

"I'm trying." This dark matter stuff is complicated, but if the

Witches can make sense of it, I certainly can, too. Except . . . "What if I'm too late?" I whisper, slipping my hand back into his. "What if whatever's happening isn't reversible?" The emptiness in my stomach has the weight of a thousand stars. I haven't let myself consider that before.

"It has to be," Pete says. His voice is thick, like the white puffs have filled his throat instead of the air around us. He stares down toward the gray stones rising out of the earth, and I wonder how many times he's come here and sat on this bench, feeling the loss of who knows what.

He's right. It has to be reversible. It has to be solvable. And I'm going to figure out the answer. For Pete. For my parents. For myself.

"Let's go back to school," I say, releasing his hand and standing up. "I need answers. And I know where to get them."

♦ ♦ ♦ ♦ ♦ ♦ ♦ ♦ ♦ ♦ ♦ ♦ ♦

We make it back to school partway through second period, and though I want to march straight to science class and to the back of the room and demand that the Witches give me answers, I suspect Ms. Larson would then have me marching to the principal's office.

So instead, we loiter outside near the back entrance, hoping we're not spotted by any teachers before the lunch bell rings. "Want me to come with you when you confront them?" Pete asks.

I think it over, and then shake my head. "I feel like they'll be more likely to admit the truth to just one of us." I give him a peck on the cheek. "But maybe stick around nearby to step in if things get out of hand."

"Like if you end up trading your voice for legs?"

"Would you still love me if I didn't have a voice?"

He reaches out and pulls me closer by the loops of my jeans. "Would you still have lips for kissing?"

"Obviously. The Little Mermaid didn't lose her lips, weirdo."

He leans in and though his lips are cold as they meet mine, his breath is warm. He tastes like mint and blueberries. As he pulls away, he says, "Then yeah, it'd be fine."

"Wait, you'd be totally cool if I couldn't talk?"

"I mean, you'd make fun of me a lot less."

"Oh, I'd still find ways."

"That's why I said 'a lot less' instead of 'not at all.'"

At that, the lunch bell rings, and I give Pete a glare, then head inside and toward the cafeteria as he trails behind me. We have to walk all the way across the school to get to the cafeteria, so once we get there, the Witches are already there, settling into their usual place in the back corner.

I march straight up to them and demand that they give me answers. At least, that's what I do in my head. In real life, I stand in the entryway to the cafeteria, blocking traffic and staring awkwardly.

Pete grabs my arm and pulls me over to the nearby wall, out of the way. "What're you waiting for?"

I suddenly want to ask him to come with me. There are three of them and only one of me. It would be nice to have Pete right at my side.

But just because Pete makes me feel safe doesn't mean he'll make *them* feel safe. And it's a weird balance I need to find—making them feel threatened enough to talk but also safe enough to talk.

THE FORGOTTEN MEMORIES OF VERA GLASS

And also, Pete isn't great at this stuff. The investigating, the theorizing. Doing anything outside the head and heart he's gotten lost inside, somewhere deep down. It's enough of a fight for him to find his way out long enough to joke with me like he used to.

Which means the fight to find the truth is all on me, alone. Just like it always has been.

That thought opens a black hole in the pit of my stomach that threatens to grow and grow until it envelops not just me but this whole room. This whole city. The whole planet. "Nothing," I say. "I'm not waiting for anything." And then I'm doing it, for real this time. I'm marching across the room, alone, and then putting my fists down on their table, leaning in, and demanding, "Okay, Witches. It's time for you to tell the truth."

CHAPTER TWENTY-ONE

Three faces stare blankly back at me.

"The truth about what?" Isla asks.

Either they're all feigning ignorance or they have so many scientifically witchly projects going on that they don't know which one I'm talking about. "Whatever you're doing in Cecily's garage. With the dark matter shadow monster and . . ." I trail off. I have no idea what else they're doing there.

Isla's eyes widen with understanding, then narrow at me. "It was you! With the garbage can. That was you!" She turns to Cecily. "I told you it wasn't just some random homeless person."

Cecily cocks her head, her red hair tilting to the side. "Why were you spying on us?"

They're the ones who owe me an explanation and not the other way around, but I open my mouth and the words come tumbling out. "Because I saw you in the graveyard," I say, trying to find the words to explain. "And Cecily kept staring at our house. And there's this hole in my stomach that feels like emptiness, but also weighs me down like I'm carrying the whole universe around in my gut, and the hole keeps getting bigger and bigger and I miss . . . I don't know what. How can I not know what?"

I take a deep breath and lean in closer. "Something is wrong. And it has to be you guys who are causing it. Or the ARI who's using you to do it. It has to be. Maybe you don't even realize you're doing it, but you're breaking things. You're breaking me. You're breaking the entire world."

I expect them to be outraged at my accusation. Or maybe I expect that all three of them will dart from the table and take off running like they're bad guys who've just been caught red-handed in some action flick. What I don't expect is for Hayden to reach into her backpack, pull out a tissue, and hand it to me.

Which is when I realize I'm crying. Again.

Hayden slides over and makes room on the bench beside her. "Here," she says, and I hesitate for only a moment before sliding into the spot. I wipe my eyes and blow my nose.

"So, let me get this straight," Isla says. "You think somehow we're responsible for breaking the world." She scowls at me. She's clearly not over the whole me-spying-on-them thing.

"Look," I start to say, "I'm sorry I—"

"Why do you think the world is broken?" Cecily asks, cutting me off. She's staring at me intently.

I bite my lip, unsure how to explain something that's so far beyond words. I stare down at my hands, which clench the soggy Kleenex. "I don't know. Like I said, there's just this emptiness. Like pieces of my heart keep getting removed, but there are no scars, no surgical lines to explain how or why. I just feel sad. But I don't think I'm depressed. And no one has died. And yet . . ." I trail off.

There's a long pause that somehow feels quiet in the midst of this busy, chattery cafeteria. And then Cecily says, "And yet," as if she's agreeing with me.

I look up in time to catch Cecily and Hayden share a glance. Some unspoken agreement passes between them.

"We'll tell you everything we know if you tell us everything you know," Cecily says.

I blink. I wasn't expecting that. Not that I have anything to tell them; I've figured out nothing.

Isla opens her mouth as if she's going to protest, but then she looks from Cecily to Hayden and back again. They both look serious. And sad. She closes her mouth.

"Meet us on the front steps after school, and we'll head to Cecily's garage," Hayden suggests.

I can't think of what info they're hoping to get from me, unless they're going to make sure I haven't told anyone else what I've seen them do, then murder me. I glance back across the cafeteria, where Pete is leaning against a wall, trying to look casual.

"You can bring your boyfriend if you want," Cecily says.

I snap my head back. "I can?" This is all going so much more easily than I expected—you know, aside from the crying part and the fact that I haven't actually learned anything yet.

"I mean, I assume you trust him." She says this as a fact, not a question, like in her experience, boyfriends are always trustworthy and good—though I can't recall ever seeing her with anyone of any gender.

I look back at Pete. He is trying so hard to look nonchalant, staring at his phone as though some meme is especially riveting. Which would be convincing if his eyes didn't float up every ten seconds to check on me. If I were to give him the tiniest wave over, I know he'd be at my back in a flash.

"I do trust him."

Cecily gives this little nod-shrug that seems to say, *Right, that's what I said.* And miraculously, neither Hayden nor Isla objects. I guess I'm not going to have to face them entirely alone after all.

When I meet back up with Pete a short while later, he says, "Well?"

I don't know how to explain to him that the Witches seem sad and confused, not mastermindedly evil. Or that they seem to want answers as badly as I do. Perhaps the ARI is keeping them mostly in the dark.

Still, they're clearly involved somehow. Whether they're conjuring it through witchcraft or some sort of dark-matter-science trick taught to them by the ARI, their shadow monster thing is proof of that. And they have all but admitted that they've got some sort of secret. So instead I just say, "It's happening" in a hushed voice. "I'm going to get answers. And then I'm going to fix this." It's a promise I'm making to Pete, to the universe, to all that we've lost and can't seem to find. It's a promise I'm making to myself.

▲ ▲ ▲ ▲ ▲ ▲ ▲ ▲ ▲ ▲ ▲ ▲ ▲

After school, we meet the Witches at the front entrance. "You guys know Pete?" I ask.

"Your boyfriend of a million years? Sure," Isla says, giving Pete an appraising look.

I slip my hand into his. "We've only been dating for six months, actually."

Cecily's eyebrows raise. "Oh, really? I thought you guys started dating years ago."

I shake my head. It's a common misconception. Apparently a guy and a girl can't spend time together without everyone thinking they're *together*. Even our youth leaders thought we were dating long before we started seeing each other that way. In fact, when Pete first asked me out, I wasn't sure. It felt like we'd been brought together more by circumstance than by attraction. Even now, the feeling passes over me in a wave—the sense that it's only because our world is so small that we've become each other's everything.

As Pete squeezes my hand, though, it's like the spark that shoots up my arm spins me around 180 degrees and reminds me of the other side. Because if our world was bigger, maybe we'd never have found each other. Maybe we'd never have known how it felt to have our fingers lock perfectly together like two pieces of a puzzle.

If only I could shake the feeling that some of the puzzle pieces are missing.

"Well, are we going to go or what?" Isla crosses her arms. "Let's get this over with."

And so we go. We return to the garage I've already been to twice and Pete's been to once.

When Cecily says, "Please ignore the mess," as she opens the door, I don't tell her that we've already been inside and seen it all firsthand.

It's just like it was before, when Pete and I broke in. The place is full of stuff. Shelves piled with boxes. Old children's bikes. A rowing machine and a big blue partly deflated exercise ball.

When Cecily holds her palm out in front of her and the bare

bulbs in the ceiling spark to life, I have to bite back an urge to scream at her that she's doing it wrong. As if I know anything about light magic. As if it's reasonable for me to suddenly feel like I have a missing limb that surges with electricity. I push that thought—and the related phantom pains—away and continue to look around.

Near the door, the Witches have cleared an oval-shaped area. On one side of the oval is a dresser. On the other side is an old dining chair. At the tip is the white board drawn with lines.

Isla and Hayden both take off their coats and throw them on the rowing machine, then hop up onto the dresser. Piles of papers sit on either side of them. Cecily unzips her own coat and stands behind the chair, leaning on its back with her crossed arms. It's warm in here, despite the fact that it's snowy and cold outside. The garage must be heated.

Pete and I stand by the door, coats still on, ready for a quick escape, if needed.

I cross my own arms. Might as well skip the pleasantries. "So what's this big secret you're carrying on in here?" I say, jumping right in.

They all glance at one another, and then Cecily starts to explain. "We're trying to get an internship at ARI."

"Plural," Isla jumps in.

"What?" Cecily asks.

"Internships. Plural. With an *s*. An internship for each of us."

"Right. That's what I meant."

Isla puts her hand on her hip. "Because we're in this together."

"You bet we are. That's why I said internship singular in the first place. Because I think of us all as a unit."

"Aww, Ceci," Hayden says, and blows each of her friends a kiss.

Something about their friendship makes my stomach twist in longing. "Look, can we set aside the lovefest and go back to explaining what black magic you guys have been doing to secure those internships, plural?"

"Oh, we don't do black magic," Cecily says, dismissively. So if it's not about witchcraft, does that mean it's about black matter? Does it all come back to science?

"*You* don't do black magic," Hayden says. As she leans forward, for the first time I notice the pale pink gemstone dangling from her neck.

"I think she means you don't do the dark stuff," Isla says.

"Well, unless it's absolutely necessary. Like if an actor is dating someone who's totally wrong for her." She grins.

Pete takes a step forward. "Wait, so you guys are called the Witches, but you don't all practice witchcraft?"

Cecily shrugs. "Hayden's been practicing it for a long time, and she hasn't exactly been private about it. So when the three of us were grouped together for a project on the witches in *Macbeth* in eighth grade, people started calling us that and it stuck. People just assume we're all into it because we're so close."

"And you're not?" Pete asks.

Isla points her thumb at Hayden. "She's a full-fledged witch. I just dabble. And Ceci thinks it's all garbage."

"I don't think it's garbage," Cecily protests. "I'm just . . . skeptical."

I look from Hayden to Cecily. Neither of them seems bothered by their difference in opinion. I wonder what it would be like to have a best friend who didn't believe in the things that I did. Who, for example, didn't believe in God. At the thought, it's like a hole gapes open in the floor below my feet, threatening to pull me down, down, down. I grab Pete's arm to steady myself.

I can't let whatever darkness is trying to consume me win. I need to focus. I need to get some answers. I turn back to Cecily. "So you've been working with dark matter, right? To create some sort of dark matter shadow monster?"

"Shadow monster?" Hayden jumps in. Her light brown eyebrows furrow together. "You mean my shadow aptitude?"

"I thought shadow aptitude peeps could only create two-dimensional shadows," Pete points out.

"Well, yeah. That was the case for most of my life." Her shoulders slump. "But after my mom died a few years ago, my aptitude became a lot stronger." Isla puts her arm around Hayden's shoulders, and Hayden leans into her a bit but continues talking. "That's what started all this." She taps the pile of papers beside her. "Well, sort of. I mean, I started researching what makes aptitudes stronger. I don't know if you've looked into it at all, but it's actually pretty well-documented that grief and pain strengthens them. They're such strong emotions.

"And then . . . well, maybe you should tell this part." She looks at Cecily, who nods solemnly.

Cecily stares down at the clipboard on the chair. "A couple of months ago," she says quietly, "I started to feel . . . off. I couldn't explain it." She lifts her eyes to meet mine. "It felt like there was this empty hole in my stomach."

I inhale sharply, recognizing the words I used earlier in the cafeteria, but don't interrupt.

"I thought maybe I was struggling with depression or something, except there were things that just didn't make sense." She lowers her eyes again and fingers a pale blue beaded bracelet on her wrist. "And then Hayden noticed that my light aptitude was stronger and demanded to know why."

"Hey, I didn't demand!" Hayden protests.

"You definitely demanded," Isla says, though it's a tease, not an accusation.

"Look, I was curious. I had been reading for a couple of years about what makes aptitudes stronger, and Cecily didn't seem to fit into any of those categories. She hadn't lost anyone or gone through any major pain; she hadn't been practicing; she wasn't menstruating."

Cecily's eyes flick to Pete. "Hayden," she snarls, "you didn't need to mention that part."

Hayden just shrugs. "I mean, whether menstruation has any impact on aptitudes is pretty controversial anyways."

"Annnnnnyways, moving on," Cecily says quickly. "Hayden wondered if there might be some other cause for it that wasn't already documented. So we started doing a study. We thought it might have the added benefit of eventually getting us internships at ARI."

"Especially if we made some kind of breakthrough," Hayden adds.

"We've been measuring the strength of their aptitudes a few times a week," Isla chimes in. Her anger at me seems to have dissipated. "We'd do mine, too, but we couldn't think of any way to measure it. So we've just been doing theirs. And making notes of things like their moods and locations and whatever else we can think of."

"Like whether they're menstruating," I say, wryly.

Hayden grins. "Exactly."

"So, what'd you find?" I try not to sound too eager, but if they've found an explanation for the emptiness that weighs me down, I'm desperate to know.

Isla frowns. "Nothing. It all seemed to match with the research that was already out there. It was stronger over time, with practice. And strongest when Hayden was at her saddest."

"The anniversary of my mom's death," Hayden clarifies, and she leans into Isla again.

The image of the three of them around a grave, a human-size shadow rising between them, appears in my mind. "Was that Halloween?" I ask, already knowing the answer.

Hayden nods.

"So everything was as expected," Isla continues.

"Well, until a couple of weeks ago," Cecily says.

"What happened a couple of weeks ago?" Pete asks. He is clearly intrigued by the story, while I just want skip past it and jump to the answers.

Cecily and Hayden share a glance. "It happened again," Cecily says. "But to both me and Hayden this time. The weird sadness we couldn't explain. The emptiness in our stomachs. And both of our aptitudes got stronger without explanation."

I think of the paper we photographed with the numbers circled and the *Why?!?* scrawled beside them. "One hundred eleven, one hundred seventeen, one hundred twenty-one, one hundred thirteen, one hundred eighteen, one hundred nineteen," I mumble under my breath. I've looked the numbers up so often that I've memorized them.

"Huh?" Isla says. She clearly hasn't committed them to memory like I have.

I ignore her—ignore all of them—and pull out my phone,

bringing up the picture. Study the column of numbers. The numbers before the circled dates are smaller, in the forties and fifties. I should have noticed that before.

I shove my phone back in my pocket. "So what does this all have to do with dark matter?"

Cecily frowns. "Dark matter?"

Isla leans forward on the dresser, elbows on her knees. "You mean that stuff that makes up most of the universe but that we can't see?"

"Can't see except—" But then I break off. Because they've already explained that the shadow monster is exactly that: shadow. Just Hayden's plain old shadow aptitude.

And the ARI documents . . . "So, this ARI internship . . . it requires an application?"

As if she can read my mind, Hayden flips through the stack of papers that is half under her butt. "Yeah, they've got this whole"— she wrenches out a few papers with the ARI logo at the top—"list of things you have to attach, including a study. It can be any kind of science experiment type thing, but we thought actually working with aptitudes would give us the best shot. Except if we can't even figure out what's going on, so much for that idea."

"We thought maybe you'd have some answers," Cecily jumps in. She's fiddling with her bracelet again. "The way you were talking. About the terrible emptiness." And then she's staring at me, eyes filled with such hope. She wants me to have the answer, not for the sake of their study, but for the sake of her heart. "You think it has something to do with dark matter?"

"I . . . don't know." And with those words, I feel my own hope slipping away. Because they were supposed to be the ones with the answers. I reach for Pete's arm to steady myself. "I'm not sure it fits the way I thought."

I haven't considered every clue, though. And in a knights and knaves problem, if you're not considering every detail, you're doing it wrong. I turn back to Cecily. "Okay, but what about when you disappeared? What happened there?" My voice comes out too harsh, too demanding. I'm starting to feel frantic.

"When I disappeared? What do you mean?" Cecily looks genuinely confused.

"You were by my house. And then you were gone."

She shrugs. "Maybe when I went to visit my aunt? She lives right around the corner from you."

Around the corner. Exactly where I followed Cecily to before she disappeared. Could she just have gone into a house? Could it be that simple? Could everything I've been suspecting for the last couple of months be completely wrong?

I think through everything they've told me, then turn on Isla. "So, wait, you said you don't feel anything?"

She frowns. "I . . . don't think so?"

"Trust me, you'd know if you did," I say.

She looks down in her lap and says quietly, "We wondered if it might be something biological." She looks so sad at the thought that some experience of womanhood—no matter how unpleasant— might be out of reach to her.

"No," I say decisively. "Pete feels it, too."

"Does he?" She looks up, hopefully, but then her face falls as she looks around the room, perhaps realizing that she's the odd person out, the only person not experiencing whatever's going on.

You're lucky, I want to tell her. *To not have this darkness inside you, threatening to consume you, to tear you apart from the inside out.*

"So you don't have any answers?" Cecily asks—the exact words I want to say to them. It's not witchcraft, thankfully, but there's also nothing supporting my dark matter theory. I thought this confrontation would bring me closer to answers, but instead they feel farther away across the void.

I shake my head.

Hayden hops down off the dresser. "Well, can you at least give us more data? The date the feeling started. Where you were. If you noticed anything particular about your environment." She grabs a piece of paper and a pencil from the dresser and holds it out to me. "Here, if you give me your email address, I can send you a list of things that would be helpful to know."

I want to run out of this place crying, but instead I take the paper, put it down on the dresser beside Isla, and slowly write out my email address, focusing on each letter individually in an attempt to keep myself from falling apart.

Pete gives his, too, and then we're leaving, dragging our feet along the snowy sidewalk.

I was so sure the Witches had the answer; what does it mean if they don't? Does that mean there's no answer at all? Or is there an answer I just haven't found yet? And whatever *has* happened, am I running out of time to undo it? Have I lost everything? Or do I just have to keep looking?

Maybe it's all in our heads. Maybe Mom's idea of going to the doctor to talk about depression was the right one. Maybe we do all have seasonal affective disorder.

"What do you think is happening?" I ask Pete as we wait for the bus.

He only shrugs and leans his shoulder into mine. As always, he has no answers, only support. And I'm so very grateful for that support, but not for the first time, I wish I had someone to brainstorm with me. To bounce ideas off of. I wish the solution for this wasn't resting on my shoulders alone.

Pete and I ride the bus back to my house in silence. There was a time when we'd never be together in silence. Pete would always have a story to tell or a joke to make me roll my eyes. But over the last couple of months, we've spent more and more time in silent mourning for the nothingness that haunts us.

Pete slips his hand into mine and gives it a squeeze, and I squeeze his back, then bow my head in a silent prayer. *Please, God, I don't know if something's truly wrong or if this is all in my head. Help me to know which it is. Give me a sign. Give me something.*

A few minutes later, the bus is pulling up to the stop by my house. As Pete and I step off the bus onto the snow-covered pavement, I stop cold.

"What is it?" Pete asks.

"I don't know." I'm staring at the bus shelter. Its blue roof and four walls feel like they're trying to tell me something.

I pull away from Pete and step inside the shelter. One wall has an advertisement for a new housing complex. Another has a wooden bench. I step toward the bench, and the next thing I know, I'm kneeling in front of it, running my hands over its surface, scanning the graffiti carved into it and written onto it with a Sharpie.

I sense Pete step into the booth behind me.

"It's not here," I say. My voice is frantic.

"What isn't?"

"I don't know." And I don't. I don't know what I'm looking for. I just know that I'd recognize it if I saw it, and I don't see it.

Is this what mental illness looks like? Kneeling on the frozen ground, searching for things that can't be seen?

"Pete," I whisper, "what's wrong with me?" I rest my forehead on the bench.

Pete's footsteps crunch against the gravel as he takes two steps across the shelter and settles onto the bench.

"I don't know," he says. "But last week, I flipped through every page of our family albums. And when my dad came in to find me all choked up, with photo albums *everywhere*, he asked me what I was doing, and all I could say was, 'Looking for something.' "

I lift my head from the bench and study my boyfriend. His shoulders are sagging and the skin around his eyes is shadowed with exhaustion. I can picture him kneeling on the floor among those photo albums, the same way I'm kneeling on the floor of this random bus shelter.

Maybe we *should* both give up searching and go see a doctor or psychologist instead.

I want to climb onto the bench and squish up beside him and rest my head on his shoulder. But for reasons I can't explain, the thought of doing so feels like a violation of a sacred space—a space that doesn't belong to the two of us. We have plenty of spaces of our own, but this isn't one of them. I stand and hold my hand out to him. "Come on," I say, and then lead the way out of the bus shelter and back to my house.

Standing on the front porch, I pat my jeans pocket for my keys, but the pocket is empty. Before I can swing off my backpack to check its pouches, though, I feel it. The click of the lock.

I reach for the doorknob, and sure enough, the door easily swings open. I didn't used to be able to do that—to open locks without even touching them. With barely a thought.

"My aptitude's gotten stronger," I say in a hushed voice.

"Like the Witches," Pete says.

I nod, thinking of their pages and pages of carefully recorded numbers. Of their measurements. Of the proof that this isn't all just in our heads.

Something is definitely happening. It's not the Witches causing it or anything I've been able to figure out, but it's happening.

And I'm not the only one trying to figure it out. Really, the Witches have made way more progress than I have. There's someone else in my life who could probably make even more progress, who has the experience and knowledge to do so much more ably than me.

Maybe I don't have to carry this one on my shoulders alone after all. The weight of the emptiness is enough to carry.

CHAPTER TWENTY-TWO

"It's not depression." The words pop out of my mouth the moment my mom sticks her head in my bedroom to wish me good night. I've been sitting on my bed for an hour, staring blankly at my math textbook, thinking through how best to talk to her, but apparently the impulsive part of my brain got tired of waiting for the analytic part.

Mom closes her open mouth, which was probably going to say a simple *I'm going to bed; love you*, and her forehead creases down the middle. She pauses for only a moment before closing my door behind her, striding over, and settling beside me on the bed. She rests her hand on my blanket-covered knee. "Have you been feeling depressed, sweetheart?"

"No. I mean, yes, sorta, technically, but that's not what I'm talking about." I guess if I'm going to do this, I might as well dive right in. I push my textbook aside and reach under my pillow, where I've been keeping Mom's mental health questionnaire. I hold the folded paper out to her.

When she unfolds it, a million different emotions race across her face at once before it finally settles on motherly reassurance. "Oh, Vera, I'm sorry you had to see this." She doesn't ask how I got it in the first place; apparently, she's decided that's not the top priority in this conversation. "Please don't stress about it. This is not the first time in my life I've struggled with some symptoms of depression."

"It isn't?" She's never mentioned that. If she's had depression before, she should know what it feels like, so if she thinks whatever is happening is mental illness, wouldn't she know best? "When?"

"Once in the early years of my PhD. Another time when . . ." She tilts her head and gives me a reassuring smile. "Well, let's just say that growing and birthing a baby can wreak havoc on your body and hormones, sometimes. But Vera, it's nothing to worry about. Usually a few months on antidepressants clears my head right up again."

She runs her pinky finger up a line of her fuzzy, red-plaid pajama pants. "I know that's not the case with most people who battle depression. I've been lucky. I think my intuition magic helps me choose the right medication. Usually my doctor suggests one and usually I can tell right away whether I should go on it."

I lean forward. Maybe I'm reading too much into things, but that is a lot of times to say *usually*. "Usually . . . but not this time?"

She hesitates and then pats my knee again. "I'm telling you, Vera, there's nothing to worry about. My doctor and I are taking care of it."

Right. Because there's nothing more reassuring than someone telling you again and again that there's nothing to worry about.

She tenses her muscles like she's about to stand up, but then settles back onto the bed as though her intuition magic has told her this conversation is far from over. "Sorry. I shouldn't treat you like Isaac or Gertie, as though all you need is a mama's promise that everything will be all right." She reaches over and cups my chin with her right hand. "You're getting so grown up, and I know that inquisitive brain of yours is always thinking. Do you have any questions about any of this you want to ask me?"

I nod, unintentionally forcing her hand away from my face. "Just one main one. Don't you think—I mean . . . isn't it possible that this time your sadness has a different, external cause?"

She drops her right hand to her lap. "Oh, sweetie, depression always feels that way, at least for me. For those few months it's at its worst, it feels like this external shadow self is following me around everywhere, dragging me downward or fighting me for control of my body."

The thought of both our heavy sadnesses hovering over us like a shadow makes me want to signal to my phantom limb—the one I felt in Cecily's garage—to fill the room with light. Which is still nonsense, of course, but it only makes my sadness feel heavier.

"Doesn't this time feel different, though? Doesn't it feel . . . I don't know . . . bigger? Heavier? Emptier? Doesn't it feel like something is wrong?"

I expect her to shut me out like always and to tell me that no, it feels like every other time, and to book me an appointment with her doctor, but she simply pauses, considering.

"It's got to be something external," I say. "Why else would we all be feeling it?"

She narrows her eyes. "Wait. Who's 'we all'?"

And that's when I tell her everything.

Well, not everything. I don't tell her about using my unlocking aptitude to break into Cecily's garage, or about sneaking through the graveyard, or about thinking witchcraft was involved. But I do tell her about how she's not alone in whatever pit she's fallen into— that Pete and Cecily and Hayden and I are there, too. (And maybe Gertie, actually.) I tell her about the Witches' study, and how the abrupt, inexplicable strengthening of their aptitudes is evidence that something deeper is going on. I tell her about the hours and hours I've spent searching for answers all on my own.

I can tell Mom wants to ask a million questions, but her mom side wins out over her scientist side, and first she leans over, kisses me on my curly head, and says, "Oh, Vera, I'm so sorry you feel this, too. I mean, I guess I knew something was wrong when you couldn't get out of bed this whole weekend. I should have talked to you about it. I'm sorry I didn't."

I lean against her for a moment while I blink back my tears. Dang intuition magic always helping her know exactly what to say. Dang mom magic always making her hugs so perfect.

When we both straighten, Mom says, "It sounds like you've put a lot of time and thought into this. Do you have any hypotheses?"

I sigh. All my hypotheses have gone out the window. "For a while, I thought maybe it could have something to do with dark matter."

Instead of dismissing the idea, Mom cocks her head in thought. "That's an interesting thought."

"Is it?" I had started to think I had slipped down a very deep and very irrelevant rabbit hole with that theory.

"I have no idea if it has any merit, but it's certainly an interesting starting place. There's this theory out there that aptitudes interact in some way with dark matter, that influencing the gravitational pull of dark matter is what makes things like your unlocking magic work.

"Practically, astrophysicists are struggling to even prove that dark matter exists, but a colleague has a theory that—" She breaks off, because oh yeah, I didn't tell her about breaking into their briefcases, either, so she doesn't know that I've read the whole paper. "Well, it's worth investigating is what I'm saying. And we can think of other hypotheses, too. Do you think your friends would be willing to send their study results so far?"

And then she's off, planning away, making a list in her phone to look over the Witches' study and to contact this dark matter lab that's two kilometers underground in Ontario and to speak to her colleague and to look up some science thing that goes over my head.

And it's all such a relief. This is what I should have done in the first place. Rather than stalking the Witches, and believing in witchcraft, and trying to figure this all out on my own, I should have gone to my science PhD mother who does science research at a science institution.

My brilliant and capable mom has taken over, like I planned. It's no longer on me to fix whatever's broken in the world, to solve everything. Someone else's brain can pick away at the problem for a while.

When my mom finally leaves my room, I ask her to flick off the light, and I lie there on my bed for a while, staring up into the darkness. I still feel the heaviness of that darkness pressing on my chest. I still feel the emptiness, the sadness, the loneliness. But at least I'm not alone in fighting my way out of it anymore.

CHAPTER TWENTY-THREE

Last time Sarah invited me over, I was too tangled up in my investigation of witchcraft and dark matter and whatever else to find the time. But now, with a proper scientist taking over the problem, I have nothing to be caught up in anymore. So when Sarah asks me over for brunch on Saturday as we finish up our science lab on Thursday, I immediately say yes.

"Awesome!" Sarah's face lights up, and I wonder, not for the first time, whether she has many friends.

I suppose I can't talk. I have lots of friends through youth group, but I don't really hang out with anyone except Pete. Maybe Sarah and I need each other.

Despite the fact that I no longer have reason to obsess over theories during my every waking moment—or maybe because of it—the rest of the week goes quickly, and before I know it, I'm at Sarah's front door, ringing the doorbell. When the door opens a minute later, a middle-aged woman with graying hair and a big grin on her rounded face greets me. "You must be Vera!" she says with a twinkle in her eye. "Come in, come in. We're so happy you could join us this morning."

She ushers me inside, takes my coat, and gestures to where I can leave my boots. "Sarah!" she calls down the hallway. "Your friend is here."

When Sarah doesn't appear, she gives a little wave indicating I should follow her and then trots off down the hallway and up the stairs. The bottom half of the walls has wood paneling painted white. The top half has a burgundy wallpaper with a white floral pattern, and it boasts pictures of Sarah, her mom, and who must be her two older brothers. There's no dad in the pictures; I wonder if he and her mom are divorced.

Sarah pops out of a room to the left just as we pass a picture of her on horseback, decked out in full riding gear.

"I didn't know you rode horses," I say to her in greeting.

She's wearing one of the knit sweaters I've seen her in before at school—an oversize one in a simple gray, but with intricate criss-crossing cables.

"Yeah, I've been riding since I was maybe seven. Not competitively or anything, though. Just for fun."

"She's got a real way with horses," her mom says as she leads us into the kitchen. "She's a horse whisperer, that one."

"Mom!" Sarah blushes, but she looks proud, too.

"That's really cool. I've never even been within a few feet of a horse."

"Really? You should come riding with me some time!" Sarah continues to tell me about the ranch just outside the city where she rides and about her favorite horse, Licorice, as her mom puts us to work ladling pancake mix onto a skillet.

By the time we've made a big stack of pancakes, her mom has whipped up bacon, sausage, and scrambled eggs and also cut up a bunch of fruit.

"Sarah was right. This is quite the impressive feast," I say as the three of us settle in at the table. "Thank you, Mrs. Farrow."

"What a kind thing to say, Vera," Sarah's mom says. "Sarah, I like this girl already."

The window by the table shows a backyard piled with snow, but the sun hits the window just right, making this corner of the kitchen bright and cheery.

"Now, Vera," Sarah's mom continues, "we're not really the religious types, but I know Sarah's been going to your church's youth group. Do you usually say some kind of prayer before eating?"

"Um, yeah, we usually say grace," I say. "Just meaning we say a prayer of thanks for the food," I add, not wanting to assume that she knows what I mean.

"Well, then would you do us the honor of saying grace before we eat?"

I'm touched by her offer. Usually when I'm eating with non-Christians—and even some Christians—I have to bow my head myself and sneak in a silent prayer while people laugh and talk around me. Which is fine; I don't expect people to follow my own religious traditions. But still, this is nice.

"Thank you. I'd love to." I bow my head, close my eyes, and pray.

"Amen," Mrs. Farrow says when I finish, and Sarah echoes her.

"Amen," I agree.

Then we dive into the delicious feast.

After breakfast, we help Mrs. Farrow clean up, and then we head to Sarah's room to hang out for a bit. When we step into her room, the first thing I notice is the far wall. It's painted orange and filled with a shelving unit that's bursting with probably a hundred different colors of yarn. One shelf has jars with various knitting needles sticking out of them.

I stride straight for the shelves and grab a deep purple ball of yarn. "Hang on just a minute. You knit? Did you knit all those sweaters you wear?"

Sarah bites her bottom lip like she's worried I'm about to label her uncool, which couldn't be further from the truth. "Um, yeah, some of them. Not all of them."

"Did you knit that one?" I point at the gray, intricately cabled one she's wearing.

Her cheeks turn pink as she nods.

"Dude! That's so cool!"

As I put the yarn back, a framed photo of a middle-aged man catches my eye. He's got the same reddish-brown hair as Sarah's and about half as many freckles. He looks like he's trying to smile but is maybe one of those people who doesn't quite know how. I point to the picture. "Is that your dad?"

Sarah nods again. "He's my hero."

"Aww, that's sweet. Does he live here in Edmonton?"

"No, he died when I was ten."

"Oh! I'm sorry," I spit out. Her words were so matter-of-fact, but I can only imagine how heavy the emotion behind them must be.

"It's okay. I mean, it's not okay, obviously. But I'm coping with it okay now."

I'm realizing in this visit how little I know about Sarah. It's time for that to change. "I have an idea," I tell her. "We need to play a game." I look around for somewhere to sit. My gaze falls on her bed—the obvious choice—but for some reason a twinge in my stomach makes me plop down on the floor instead. "So we get to know more about each other."

I worry for a moment that I'm coming across as dismissive of her grief, but Sarah simply smiles and settles cross-legged onto the carpeted floor across from me. "What sort of game?"

"Let's call it . . . truth or dare, but without the dare. We ask each other questions and we have to answer with the truth."

"And if either of us doesn't want to answer?"

I think for a minute. "Then the game's over. You don't have to answer, but you don't get to ask the other person more questions, either."

"High stakes. I like it. I'm game."

I pull my mass of hair into a messy bun using the elastic I keep on my wrist. "Okay, you go first."

Sarah doesn't hesitate, just leans forward, puts her elbows on her knees and asks, "Do you ever question your faith?"

"Ooh, coming out of the gates with a hard hitter. This girl is not playing games, folks."

"Well? Do you?"

I give the question some thought. "I don't question whether God exists. I feel him there, you know?"

"But?"

"But . . . I do sometimes worry Christians do a less than stellar job at showing God's love."

She nods knowingly, which makes my heart ache. "That's not a deal breaker for you, though?" she asks.

"Hey, that's another question," I protest. "You're sneaking in another turn."

She throws up her hands. "Sorry. I'll save that one. It's your turn, then."

I want to start with something personal but fun. "Okay, this is probably the most clichéd question ever, but I have to ask: Do you have a crush on anyone?"

I can tell by the way her face immediately goes pink that her answer is yes.

"You have to tell me or our game is basically over before it started!"

"You'll keep it a secret?"

"Cross my heart," I say, drawing an X over my heart.

She leans forward and whispers, "I think James Pangilinan is kind of cute."

"James Pangilinan? From our science class?"

She nods.

I grin at her. "He is kind of cute. He's got terrible friends though," I add, thinking of his annoying lab partner, Vincent.

"Oh, golly, the worst," Sarah agrees, and then we both laugh.

And then it's Sarah's turn again, and I'm bracing myself for having to explain how I can feel uncomfortable about my church's stances on homosexuality and abortion and things like that and yet still love my church and the people in it and the safe place it gives me to be with God and feel at home in my faith.

But I'm saved from having to explain all that, because Sarah picks a different question: "Have you and Peter had sex?"

My eyes practically bug out of my head. "Wow, you're not holding back."

Her neck flushes a little red, but she doesn't back down. "Well, I've got to get the good ones in before one of us chickens out and refuses to answer and the game is over."

"Fair enough," I say. "And no, we haven't. We're going to wait until marriage."

Her eyebrows rise. "People still do that?"

"I don't know about people. But we do." We haven't actually talked much about sex yet, but the waiting is probably harder for Pete than it is for me. I love being near Pete, and I don't know what I'd do without him, but I don't think about sex all the time—or at all, really—like I'm told boys often do. But we've talked about it enough that I know Pete truly believes in waiting, so I know he'll never even suggest anything else.

"Wow. That's impressive. At least, I assume it is. No one's ever offered to have sex with me, so I don't actually know how hard it would be to resist."

"You just answered my next question," I say, and she laughs.

"Well, you get that one as a freebie, I guess."

The next questions we toss back and forth are easier. Her favorite color (orange), my oldest memory (eating a cookie while my parents raked leaves in the backyard), her favorite sibling (her oldest brother, David), my least favorite class at school (gym).

"Oh, I've got one," I say when it's my turn. "What's your aptitude?"

She bites her lip, hesitant for the first time in this game.

I lean in. "Ooh, is it something scandalous? Do you have attraction magic? Or some kind of new mutation, like asexual reproduction? Or—" I break off as I realize her face has gone sheet white.

"I'm not supposed to tell anyone," she whispers.

"Wait, *do* you have a mutation?" I'm whispering, too. I was joking when I suggested she might have a mutation, but now I'm thinking of that Russian boy who was captured and tested to death because of his mutation. "Never mind, you don't have to tell me."

"I swear it's not anything dangerous," she says, pleadingly, as though she thinks I'm worried she might suddenly destroy me with laser beam eyes.

"I won't tell anyone. I promise. I swear to God."

I just mean that I won't tell anyone that she has a mutation, but she must take it as a request to know more, because she says, "My grandma had memory magic, so my mom wondered at first if maybe I did, too, since I wasn't manifesting anything more physical. But then it became pretty clear pretty quickly that I couldn't remember things the way Grandma did."

I sit quietly as she speaks, unmoving. I'm afraid that she's telling me too much, but also I'm afraid that if I do much more than breathe, she'll stop talking. Aptitude mutations are fascinating.

"We eventually figured out that I could only make it work if I wrote things down. My thoughts are too scattered to be strong enough otherwise. I think because it's a mutation."

When she doesn't say anything further, I whisper, "Strong enough to do what?"

"To forget." And then it's like she's relieved to be telling someone about her aptitude for the first time in her life, because her explanation comes pouring out. She explains how whenever something bad happens, she can simply wipe it from her mind, forgetting about it entirely. "You promise you won't tell a soul?" she interrupts herself in the middle of it all.

I put my hand on my heart. "I swear it."

She nods, gets to her feet, and walks over to her bed, where she picks up a notebook from her bedside table. "If there's something I want to forget, I write it down in this notebook. And then *bam*, I forget that it ever happened."

My eyebrows rise. "That seems pretty powerful."

"Yeah, and it seems to be getting harder and harder to do. For the last year or so, it's wiped me out. The exhaustion takes a few hours to come on, but then I usually can't get out of bed for a good twenty-four hours after I do it."

"But your memory stays wiped? You really don't remember?"

She must sense my skeptical tone, because she says, "Look, I'll show you." She opens the notebook to a fresh page, sits down on her bed, and picks up a pen. "I'll forget . . . this conversation."

Before I can protest that I won't have any way of knowing whether she's actually forgotten it or is just pretending, she clicks her pen and begins to write.

I wait patiently until she's done. Until she's clicked her pen again, closed the book, and set it down on her bedside table.

Until she's looking at me and blinking, blinking, blinking. "What were we just talking about?" she asks.

And then I'm blinking myself, because what *were* we just talking about? "Oh!" It comes to me, and I grin at Sarah, who's sitting cross-legged across from me. "You just asked me my least favorite class—which is, obviously, gym class."

"Right. Obviously," Sarah agrees, cheerily.

"Which means it's my turn again. What's . . . um . . . your favorite band?"

She picks some obscure band I've never heard of, and then we play a while longer, until Sarah says she's feeling wiped out and ready for a nap, and I take that as my cue to thank her mom and head on home.

On the bus home, the emptiness that I feel like I've been holding back for hours comes flooding in, like I've opened the dam. *Mom's got it handled*, I remind myself. Then to distract myself from the loneliness I feel on this bus full of people, I think of other questions I could have asked Sarah—her worst memory, what makes her dad a hero, her aptitude. It's nice to think about these ordinary things, for once. It's nice to know that solving this great, sad mystery is out of my hands.

CHAPTER TWENTY-FOUR

Sarah looks tired Monday morning in our science class.

"Are you okay?" I ask her.

"Yeah, I just slept for like twenty-four hours straight on the weekend."

"Oh, wow! That's bananas."

She shrugs. "It happens to me sometimes. Just normally I remember—well, never mind."

Before I can ask her what she means, Vincent pipes up from behind us. "Hey, uggo, are you going to pass those papers back or what?"

Sarah whirls around. "What did you just call me?"

Vincent's boyish face turns slightly red, but his mouth hardens into a line. "I don't mean your face or anything. It's just those dumpy sweaters that—"

James smacks Vincent in the arm. "Shut up, dude."

"I don't think—"

"I said, shut up."

Sarah grabs the stack of papers off our desk that we're supposed to be handing back, takes one sheet for her and one for me, and then plops them down on their lab bench with a smack. The boys say nothing more.

"For the record," I say once she's facing the front again, "I love your sweaters." Today she's wearing a simple oversize burnt-orange one.

She doesn't say anything back, just buries her head in her worksheet.

After class, we head down the hallway toward the cafeteria together.

"Hey, sourface, wait up!" We both glance behind us to see Vincent scurrying after us.

"I don't want to talk to you!" Sarah picks up her pace, and I lengthen my stride to match hers.

"But I want to apologize."

"Keep your apology," Sarah snaps over her shoulder. Her voice doesn't have to travel far. He's broken into a run and has almost caught up to us. I look ahead, ignoring him.

"Look, I don't even want to apologize!" he says. "James made me. So come on. Wait up!"

I glance back just in time to see him grab for Sarah's backpack to slow her down. But she's only wearing it on one shoulder, so instead, he yanks it backward, snapping open one of the buttoned pockets and sending a small pouch flying. It lands on the hallway floor with a *thwack* and sends a handful of small, packaged tubes scattering across the floor.

Tampons.

I rush forward and try to sweep them up with one swoop, but they've scattered in too many directions.

A group of kids nearby starts to laugh.

"Is this yours?" says a boy's voice. I look up to see James holding his foot out to Sarah. Balancing on it is a white-and-yellow-wrapped tampon.

Sarah's face turns bright red. When she makes no move to take the tampon or even say anything at all, I step forward and snatch the tampon off James's foot.

"It's mine, actually," I say.

"No, it's not," says Vincent in his nasally voice. "It came out of Sarah's bag."

James glares at him as Sarah and I gather up the last of the tampons and stuff them into her pouch.

"What are you looking at me like that for?" Vincent says to James. "It's not like I—"

But we don't hear the rest of what he has to say, because we're already stalking off.

"Do you want to talk about it?" I ask Sarah once we're around the corner. We can still hear some students laughing behind us.

She shakes her head. "No. I just want to forget it ever happened. Vile Vincent."

Well, at least I know she's not too upset for catchy wordplay. "Vile Vincent indeed," I agree.

The next day, Sarah isn't at school. She must not be over whatever illness knocked her out over the weekend after all. I text her, but she doesn't reply.

She's back in class on Wednesday. "You feeling any better?" I ask her.

"I feel great," she says. "Never better."

One of the students in front of us passes back a stack of papers, and we each take one. Then I turn to hand the stack to the guys behind us. James Pangilinan takes the papers from me. Beside him is Paul Stevens.

"Hi, Vera," Paul says. He's white, and tall and thin, with blond hair and glasses. I don't know him well.

I blink at him. "Have you . . . have you always sat there?"

"Ouch!" He puts a hand to his heart. "You haven't noticed me right behind you these past few months?"

"I—no—I just . . ." I blink a couple more times. Of course I've noticed him there. He's been partners with James since the first day of class in September. "I mean, have you always had your stool that far to the left?" His stool is closer to the middle of the table than usual. That's what it is. That's what's bothering me.

He laughs. "Nah. I just feel particularly close to my boy James today."

He puts his arm around James's shoulders and starts singing "Kindred Spirits" from *Anne of Green Gables*.

James laughs and smacks his arm away. "Don't mind him," he says. "He's at least a better partner than . . ." He trails off, a confused crinkle forming between his smooth black eyebrows as he stares at the space just beyond where Paul is sitting.

"Oh, come on," Paul says. "Surely you can come up with at least one person in all of history that I'd be a better lab partner than."

"Like Darth Vader," Sarah says, chiming in.

James gives his head a little shake, and the crease between his eyebrows smooths away. "I don't know," he says. "Darth Vader was a pretty smart guy. He managed to design an entire Death Star with only one super-major, easily accessible, self-destructing flaw in it."

We all laugh at that, and then Ms. Larson starts her lecture and we have to get back to work.

Still, when I turn around, I can't shake the nagging feeling that something isn't quite right. As always.

Mom hasn't mentioned anything to me about her dark matter investigations since I first passed the idea on to her, and finally I can't take the waiting anymore. But when I ask her about it one evening after she's put Gertie and Isaac to bed, she tells me that I shouldn't worry and can trust things are going well, but that, as I know, she can't talk about it.

Which, no, I didn't know, actually. I didn't realize she would consider this to be an ARI thing and not an "us" thing. I didn't realize she would leave me out of it, like always.

Still, maybe it's for the best. It's not like I managed to make any progress on anything on my own. Perhaps the problem that weighs on us both is better off in the hands of people who know what they're doing. So instead of pouting and pressing for answers like I want to, I throw myself into everyday December life. Pete and I are both in the Christmas choir at church, and we have practice a couple of times a week, plus I have to fit in my Christmas shopping, plus I still have to babysit my siblings when they're not in after-school care.

Isaac has learned that Christmas colors are red and green, so we keep finding random things around the house turned one color or the other. When he turns my boots to a swirling red and green one morning, I don't even mind. It feels festive and it's not like it's permanent.

On Christmas Eve, after church, Pete and I stand in the snowy parking lot and exchange gifts. Big, heavy snowflakes float down around us, and people exchange hugs and "Merry Christmas!" greetings. It should feel perfect, but I can tell that we're both feeling the weight. The emptiness. The sense that Christmas just won't be the same this year—even though I can't think of anything that makes it different from any other year.

To distract us both from the darkness, I reach into my purse and pull out his gift. It's in a plain gold gift bag with silver tissue paper.

As Pete opens it, my chest tightens with the sudden fear that he'll think it's a pathetic gift.

"Did you make these?" he asks as he pulls out a big, filled Ziploc bag.

I nod nervously.

His face splits into a grin. "You found time to make cookies? You really do love me, don't you?"

My own grin mirrors his. Somehow, without me explaining, he understood that I had to stay up long past when everyone else in my family had gone to sleep, mixing and spooning onto trays and waiting for them in the oven.

"I do," I say. "I really do love you, Peter Davis."

Which prompts him to hand over the gift bag he's been carrying around with him that I've been pretending not to see. It's got a snowman on the front and a penguin on the back. I grab the white tissue paper that sticks out the top and take out what's inside.

It's a book called *Dark Matter and Other Secrets of the Universe.* I assume it's going to be coffee-table-lite-science, but flipping through reveals dense text and calculations and theories.

"The internet says it's the most detailed, up-to-date book on the subject, or whatever," Pete says. "So you can continue your research."

"Oh. But my mom—"

"I know, I know, she's taken over. As if that'll turn off your brain."

He's right. I've already found myself jumping from article to article on my phone at night, reading about dark matter and light aptitudes and missing pieces of the universe until I fall asleep. I'm sure the ARI is a million miles ahead of me, and I'm sure my research will help no one. But Mom won't talk to me about what they're doing, so how else am I supposed to keep the darkness—and dark matter—at bay?

There's a notebook, too. A plain black one.

"For recording stuff as you read," Pete says.

"How do you know me so well?" I ask him. Then I lean toward him. And when we kiss, the snow swirls around us like a universe of stars.

▲ ▲ ▲ ▲ ▲ ▲ ▲ ▲ ▲ ▲ ▲ ▲

Christmas morning, I wake to a text from Pete. *Merry Christmas. I love you* is all it says, but it makes me smile.

When I trudge downstairs, I find the rest of my family already up—my parents curled up on the couch with coffee, my siblings going through their stockings. "We thought we'd let you sleep in," Mom says with a yawn.

We've had Christmas with Mom's family already and Dad's family's isn't until tomorrow, so we spend the day at home, snacking on the appetizers Dad serves all day and gradually opening presents. It's a subdued day. Even Isaac and Gertie seem quieter than usual. It's like we're all waiting for someone to arrive and refusing to admit that they're never going to show up.

Still, despite that feeling, I start to settle into the cozy warmth of the day. Dad makes my favorite stuffed mushrooms. Christmas music plays softly in the background. And I get some nice presents from Mom and Dad—a video game I've been dying to play, a sweater, a pack of colorful gel pens.

In the afternoon, Dad hands me a small box. I open it and pull out a DVD.

"I've heard great things about that show," he says. "I think you'll like it. That's the first season of the reboot."

My first instinct is to make fun of him because no one uses DVDs anymore. But then I look down at the DVD in my hand. *Doctor Who*. I've never seen the show before—not even an episode—but the faces looking out at me feel familiar, like I've seen them a hundred times.

"Thanks, Dad," is all I say, and for some reason, it comes out in a whisper.

That night, in my room, I pop the first disc into my old-school laptop, turn out the light, and curl up on my bed. And maybe it's weird, maybe it's creepy, but for the entire forty-four-minute episode, I imagine someone is curled up on the other end of the bed, watching with me.

I imagine I am not alone.

▲ ▲ ▲ ▲ ▲ ▲ ▲ ▲ ▲ ▲ ▲ ▲ ▲

Sarah greets me at the door this time instead of her mom. "Hi!" Her face is all bright and cheery, and the red of her Christmas sweater is reflected in her cheeks.

It's a few days after Christmas—still during the holiday break—and she invited me over to hang out.

"Did you make this one?" I point to her sweater as she closes the door behind me.

She shakes her head. "Nah, I don't have patience for little details like this." She runs her finger over the line of reindeer heads across her chest.

"Well, it's cool," I say as I hang my coat in the closet.

"Thanks."

We stop in the kitchen to get a bowl of all-dressed chips before heading up to her room. We talk about Christmas gifts as we go.

"What did Pete give you for Christmas?" Sarah asks me as we enter her room.

"A book and a notebook." The text is proving to be extremely interesting but extremely dense. I can get through only a few pages at a time.

"Oh, I love a good notebook," Sarah says. "I need a new one soon."

"Yeah? Do you write?" I could picture Sarah as a budding novelist, writing stories in her cozy sweaters.

"Sort of." She glances toward the door, like she's afraid her mom might barge in on us at any minute, even though she's not even home. "I'm not supposed to talk about it."

I'm instantly intrigued. "You're not supposed to talk about your writing?"

She hesitates for a long moment, then says, "Can you keep a secret?"

"Of course," I say immediately.

"I don't mean like a basic sort of secret, like someone's crush, that you mostly keep but maybe tell a friend or two. I mean a real, genuine secret that you guard with your life. Can you keep one of those?"

I almost spout off *of course* again, but the solemnity of her question feels like it requires something more. I put my hand on my heart and say, "I swear to God."

She nods tersely and then taps a notebook on her bedside table. "Well, I write down things that happen to me, and then I . . . forget them."

"Forget them?"

She nods again. "I have forgetting magic. That's my aptitude."

My eyebrows knit together. "Forgetting magic?" I try to think through the list of aptitudes. "I haven't heard of that one."

"You wouldn't have." She bites her lip. "It's a mutation."

And then I understand her secrecy. As she explains to me how it took them a while to discover it, I keep thinking of that poor boy with the mutation, who died in Russia. Tomas Ivanovich Petrov.

"Doesn't sound very useful," I say in an attempt to lighten the mood once she finishes. "I want to remember things, not forget them. Like my keys."

She considers me. "There's nothing in your life you wish you could forget?"

I shrug. "I don't know. I'd have to think about it. Though now that I am thinking about it, there's an incident with a skirt on the front steps of the church that I wouldn't mind purging from my brain."

She laughs. "Well, that's how it works. I journal things, and then I forget that they ever happened."

I chew my lip, trying not to be skeptical. There's a ribbon bookmark in the notebook, about halfway through. Which means she's probably already filled half the thing. "That's a lot to want to forget," I say, pointing to the book.

"Oh, that's not even my only one. I have others, too." She kneels down beside her bed and starts reaching under it for something. "I've been doing this for years, though it's gotten harder over time. Completely wipes me out when I do it now."

While she searches under her bed and chatters away, I pick up her journal without even really thinking about it. Flip through the pages. There are pages and pages filled with neat, rounded printing.

Some names jump out at me as I turn the pages. Al. Simon. Bolu. Riven.

Sarah gets to her feet, a few notebooks of various shapes and sizes in her hand.

I wave the one in my hand at her. "Sarah, who are these people?" I don't recognize any of the names. You'd think I'd have met at least a couple of the people she's written about.

"Oh, you shouldn't read that. It's—" She breaks off as she looks up at my face. "Why are you crying?"

"Crying? I'm not—" But I break off, too, as I reach up and touch my face. My fingers come away wet. And then I feel them—the sobs that are fighting their way up from the pit of my stomach. The heaving shakes that are threatening to move my shoulders.

I look down at the journal. Something about this book is breaking me from the inside out.

I wipe at my face with my sleeve and shove the feelings away. If I tear in two now, I fear I might never find a way to put myself back together. I might crumple to the ground and stay there forever. And I'll never find answers from the floor.

"Sarah . . ." I say cautiously, "how, exactly, does your journaling work?"

She hesitates for only a moment before saying, "It's simple. Here, I can show you." She reaches for the journal.

An inexplicable wave of panic hits me. "No." I yank the book out of her reach.

She frowns, and I backpedal as quickly as I can. "I just mean, I don't need a demonstration. I believe you. You can just explain."

She nods. "That's probably for the best anyways. Like I said, actually doing it always wipes me right out."

"And what is it you do, exactly?"

"I just write about things that have happened to me that I want to forget. And then that's it, they're forgotten."

"How do you know you've forgotten them if you can't remember what they are?"

"Well, if it was something bad, I should be feeling sad about it, right? But I always feel happy after writing in there. Like a weight's been lifted."

I feel like whatever weight's been lifted from Sarah's shoulders has been deposited in my hands. Her journal is the heaviest thing I've ever held.

"Hey, Sarah, can I borrow this?" The words pop out of me before I can stop them. I know it's a weird request, but I have to ask.

"My journal? All my darkest secrets are in there."

"I know. I'll guard it with my life. I promise."

She chews on a thumbnail as she considers me. "No," she finally says. "And I'll take it back now."

So I do hand it back.

Later, though, once her mom is home from her nursing shift and we're all eating a snack of cookies and milk at the kitchen table, I excuse myself to go to the bathroom. Except instead of going there, I slip into Sarah's room. I find the journal by Sarah's bed. I slide it into my bag. And I take it home.

CHAPTER TWENTY-FIVE

There are stories about people named Al. Simon. Bolu. Riven. Rachel. Vincent.

I read about a crush Sarah had on Al and how heartbroken she was when he started dating another girl.

I read about a time Simon stole her Halloween costume at Value Village. About a time Bolu didn't choose Sarah for her team.

As I read through some of the stories, my heart breaks for Sarah. Her journal is full of times she was ignored, lied to, bullied, forgotten. At one story, my anger swells so big that I slam my fist into the bed. Apparently some girl named Angelica got half the school to dress up in ugly sweaters in mockery of Sarah's beautiful ones. I don't know how I missed that. I had no idea she went through that. I wish she'd told me. Maybe I could have done something.

Maybe I could do something now. I just need to figure out who this Angelica girl is.

I find the who's who book of student photos the school put out at the beginning of the year. It's alphabetical by last name, so I have to look through the entire grade to try to find her.

She's not there.

I try the other grades. She's not in those, either. It could be that she only came to our school after the book came out. But my heart is starting to pound in my chest.

On a whim, I find one of the other names in the journal. Something uncommon.

Bolu.

I search through the book for a Bolu. Once again, I search our grade, then the grades ahead. I look through my junior high yearbooks and search for her there in case she's younger. I can't find her anywhere.

I try Simon next. And yes, I find a couple of Simons in our year. But none of them are right. Because Sarah's written in parentheses, "At least, I think it was Simon. I have a hard time telling him apart from his twin brother." And none of the Simons I find are twins. In fact, I can only think of one set of twins in our grade, and they're both girls.

I flip a few more pages and read another journal entry. Apparently James, Sarah's current crush, had a crush on Rachel, one of the Witches. Except that doesn't make sense. The Witches are Cecily, Hayden, and Isla. Unless there was a fourth Witch that I've forgotten about, who's no longer part of their pack. I flip through the who's who book, studying the various Rachels that pop up, but I can't remember any of them ever being a Witch.

And then I try Riven. Or at least, I start to try Riven. I haven't even read her story yet, but just the thought of the name breaks down the walls I built earlier this afternoon to keep my emotions at bay. The next thing I know, I'm curled up on my bed, sobbing. Shoulders heaving. Snot dripping from my nose.

As I cry, my bedroom door creaks open, and little feet come plodding across the carpet. Gertie climbs onto the bed beside me, puts her small hand on my leg. She doesn't tell me not to cry. In fact, she doesn't say anything at all, just sits there with me in my inexplicable grief.

When my sobs finally abate, I turn to Gertie. "Sorry, was I too loud?"

She shakes her head. "Couldn't even hear you."

"Then how did you—" Then I break off. Intuition magic. I bet she has it, just like Mom.

Gertie hops off the bed, but before leaving, as if to answer my thought, she says, "You should read it."

"Read what?"

"Whatever was making you cry."

After she leaves, I open Sarah's journal again to the memory about Riven. I force myself to look past the simple word *Riven* that jumps out at me and instead read the words from the start.

I have to admit that I'm jealous of Vera's best friendship with Riven.

I stare at the words. The first time I looked at this page, I was too caught up in seeing the name Riven that I didn't even notice my own name.

My own name.

Except it can't be referring to me, because I don't know anyone named Riven. I keep reading.

Today I tried inviting Vera over for brunch, but she said she already has plans with Riven. She always has plans with Riven. I see them together everywhere.

I want a best friend like that. Someone I can share secrets with and eat with and hang out with after school and every weekend. Someone I can have inside jokes with and laugh with and cry with when I need to. Someone I could even trust to know about my mutation.

And I would like that person to be Vera. She's kind and thoughtful and I feel like we'd have a lot in common once we got to know each other.

But I'm never going to become friends with her if I'm always jealous of her other friends. I hate feeling jealous of Riven. I hate feeling sad that Vera turned me down because of plans with Riven. I want to forget this feeling. I want to forget about Riven.

I put down the journal without reading the rest. She wanted to forget about Riven, and clearly she did. Clearly I did, too.

Except this is ridiculous. It can't be real. She wrote this just to mess with me.

But then why didn't she want me to read it? Why did I have to steal it to read it?

My heart is racing.

I should tell Mom maybe. Except then she'll probably take this journal to the ARI and never let me see it again because of "confidentiality," and never talk to me about it, even though I'm in these pages. Even though this is about my life. So instead, I grab my phone and call Pete. "Hey." He answers on the first ring, like he's been waiting for me to call. Like he knows something's wrong.

"Do you know a Riven?" I spit the question out without saying hello first.

"A . . . Riven?"

"Yeah, a girl named Riven. Do you know her?"

"No. Should I?"

"What about a . . ." I flip through the pages of Sarah's journal. "Simon. Do you know a Simon?"

The line is quiet for a long time. At last, Pete says, "Vera, what's this about?" His voice is quiet, like he's a million miles away rather than just a dozen blocks over.

"I don't know." I twist a curl around my finger. "I don't know what's happening."

"Should I come over?"

"Yes," I say at first. And then, "No. Actually, don't. I have somewhere I need to go. Someone I need to see."

"Is everything okay?"

"Yes," I say. Which isn't entirely true. But I think things are going to be okay. I think I've finally stumbled upon some answers. And I think there's something that I can do about them. "I'll call you later."

▲ ▲ ▲ ▲ ▲ ▲ ▲ ▲ ▲ ▲ ▲ ▲ ▲

Half an hour later, I'm on Sarah's front step, pounding on her front door.

Her mom answers. "Vera? What can I do for you?" She looks surprised to see me, which makes sense, since I was just here a few hours ago. Her hair, which was loose when I was here earlier, is pulled back into a loose french braid.

"I, um, think I forgot something in Sarah's room."

She nods, accepting my explanation. "You can head on up. Sarah's up there."

I slip off my boots but am in too big of a hurry to take off my coat or mitts. I rush up the stairs to Sarah's room.

The door is open. Sarah is sitting on her bed, reading a book. She looks up when she sees me and smiles. "Hey, Vera. What are you doing here?" Her face looks cheery and relaxed.

I have no patience right now for small talk. I pull off my mitts and drop them on the floor. "Tell the truth, Sarah. What are you really doing?"

She stares blankly at me. "What are you talking about?"

"Let me put this another way." I pull the journal out of my purse. "I know what you're really doing."

She looks at the journal in my hands. "How did you—what did you—" She looks at her bedside table and the empty space where it used to be. When she turns back, the lines of her face have hardened into anger. "You took my diary? That was personal."

I push away the surge of guilt that passes through me. It can't be wrong to take something from a monster. My crime is so incredibly small next to hers. "Sarah! You're basically killing people!" Standing there looking at this freckled, reddish-brown-haired girl in her knit sweater, the words feel harsh, but I realize they're true. She's murdering people. Worse than that. She's unwriting them.

It occurs to me at that moment that maybe I should have called the police rather than coming here alone. But would they have believed me? They'd never have heard of forgetting magic, of course. It's not supposed to exist. So perhaps they would have thought her journal entries were just the made-up ramblings of some weird teen girl. They wouldn't have known, deep in the pit of their stomachs, that these aren't made-up people.

Even if Mom had vouched for me, would they believe her? And would she actually vouch for me? Or would she simply take my findings to the ARI and never talk to me about them again?

A wrinkle of confusion creases Sarah's forehead. "What are you talking about?"

"The people. You're murdering them. Don't you realize that? What you're doing, it's murder." I smack her journal loudly against my hand.

She looks blankly back at me, like she doesn't think of it that way at all. Like she feels no guilt.

And that's when it occurs to me: If I don't convince her that what she's doing is wrong, I could be the next person written out of existence. If she tried right now to write, I think I could stop her. I could tackle her, fight the pen out of her hand. I'm not that strong, but I'm strong enough to do that at least.

But what if she doesn't do it now? What if she waits until I leave and then sits down with her journal and pen and writes about this? Writes about how I stole and read her diary? I don't fully understand how the magic works, but it seems like it doesn't just erase her memory, it erases the entire person who made the incident happen. That's me. What if I'm walking home from her house and then suddenly I'm not anymore? What if suddenly I'm gone from the world?

My hands grow clammy at the thought.

"Sarah," I whisper, "what you're doing with your aptitude is wrong."

Her forehead wrinkle only furrows deeper. "With my aptitude? How can it be wrong to erase my own memories?"

"No, not that part. The other—" I break off. Maybe she doesn't

know. Relief floods through me at the thought. I study her confused, freckled face. Of course. She's not some villainous master-
mind who's deleting people from the earth. She's just a girl who
didn't realize her own power. I'll explain it and then she'll undo it
and all will be right in the world again.

I slip off my coat, set down my purse, and walk toward her,
settling myself on the edge of her bed. I place the journal down on
her lavender comforter between us and tap it, then hesitate, trying
to find the words to explain. "I . . . think your aptitude is so much
stronger than you realize."

She frowns. "What do you mean?"

"I mean that I don't think you're just erasing memories. I think
you're erasing people."

She shakes her head. "That doesn't make sense. My mom used
to read my entries sometimes, when I was younger, and she would
have noticed if that was happening."

I chew my lip. The Witches talked about how aptitudes become
stronger with practice and with pain. I think of all the journals
Sarah's filled, all the years of practice she's had. And every entry
is rooted in pain. "Well, maybe it started that way, with memories.
But the more you did it, the stronger it grew. And eventually, you
were doing a whole lot more.

"I'm telling you . . . you're not just erasing memories, you're
erasing people."

She narrows her eyes at me, like she doesn't believe me.

I thrust the journal at her. "Here, read one of your entries.
You'll see what I mean."

She shakes her head. "I can't."

My eyebrows furrow together. "Come on, you have to—"

"No, I mean, I physically can't. I've tried before. My eyes just sort of glaze over and I can't make myself read the words."

"That's weird. Okay. Um . . ." I tap my fingers on the notebook. I'm not giving up. "Oh! I'll read one to you then."

She hesitates for only a moment, then nods. "Okay."

I flip the book open to an entry somewhere in the middle and start to read. "Today, I went to Value Village to pick out a Halloween costume. I was—"

"It's not working."

"What do you mean?"

"I can't really focus on the words you're saying. You're like the adults in a Charlie Brown cartoon."

"Really? What the heck! Well, look, you're just going to have to trust me."

"Trust the person who stole my personal diary and read the whole thing?"

I nibble at a hangnail on my thumb. "Okay, when you put it that way, it doesn't look great. And I'm sorry. But you have to believe me. Look, when you write your entries, you're writing about things that have actually happened, right?"

"Sure. I mean, at least, I assume so. I don't actually remember them afterward. That's kind of the whole point."

"Right. So you'd think you'd be writing about real people. But Sarah, the people you've written about in here—they don't exist."

She frowns. "And you think I made them not exist?"

It sounds ridiculous, but I feel the truth of it from the tips of my fingers to the balls of my feet. "I do."

Perhaps Sarah feels the same truth, because she doesn't argue, just tips backward onto her bed so she's staring up at her ceiling.

She draws her knees to her chest. "Yeah, well," she says in a whisper, "maybe those people deserve to be gone. Maybe it's not my magic. Maybe it's justice."

"Justice? What are you talking about?"

She closes her eyes for a moment. When she opens them again, she doesn't meet my gaze. "Are they . . . are they really terrible? The things they've done to me?"

And just like that, the notebook in my hands becomes as heavy as Sisyphus's rock as I understand what it represents to Sarah. She has no idea what's written in it; she only knows that every entry represents something she'd rather not remember. And there are a lot of entries.

I'm not sure how to answer her. I certainly wouldn't want half the school making fun of something in my life that brings me joy. But at the same time, I bet the atrocities her brain has imagined are much worse. I reach out and put my hand on her ankle. "They're probably not as bad as you imagine. When you get the memories back, you'll see what I mean."

"When I get them back?"

"Yeah. You're going to undo them, right?" Of course she is. You can't find out that you've been making people disappear and then decide not to do anything about it.

Sarah bites her lip. "I don't think I can."

"What?!" Anger surges through me. "Of course you can! I know it's scary, but trust me, the memories aren't as bad as you think, and—"

"No, I mean . . ." She sits up. "I don't think I physically can." She takes the journal from me. It's still open to the page I tried to read to her. "I think—I think that reading the entries is how I would undo them. And you've seen how well that goes."

I bite my lip as I think. "Well, undoing magic is always harder than doing it, right? Maybe you just need to really, really focus."

"Vera, just doing the magic knocks me out for a day. What if undoing it kills me?"

"It's not going to kill you," I say quickly. "Have you ever heard of undoing magic killing someone?"

"Have you ever heard of magic making people disappear?"

"So you do believe me."

She shrugs noncommittally. "It doesn't matter whether I do. I can't read the words anyways."

I cross my arms in frustration. There has to be an answer. Except maybe there doesn't. If the first person said, "Both of us are knights," and the second person said, "Neither of us are knaves," there would be no solution. They could both be knights or both be knaves; there'd be no way to know.

A deep, hollow emptiness fills me to the core as I study the journal in Sarah's hands. The same emptiness I felt before, except now it has a name. Loss. Grief. Sorrow.

Which gives me a thought. Maybe in all her journaling, Sarah has lost things that matter to her, too. Maybe she's accidentally erased people or things she held in her heart.

"Sarah, how do you feel when you think of your journals? Sad? Afraid?"

She frowns. "You try having journals full of terrible things that happened to you that you can't remember and see how you feel."

"I don't mean that as a bad thing," I say quickly. "I just mean

maybe you can channel it. Pain's supposed to make aptitudes stronger, right? So maybe if you focus in on those feelings, you can undo
the magic."

"And you think that'll help?"

I nod.

"Okay," she says with a sigh. "I'll try. But no guarantees."

My heart thuds with excitement at her words. It has to work.
I'm sure it'll work. In a few minutes, this will all be solved, the
empty feeling in my gut will be gone, and the world will be back as
it should be.

I want to flip the pages of the book to the story about Riven,
to start with that one, but she's already staring down at the page
the book's open to, eyes narrowed, fists clenched, and I don't want
to interrupt.

After a minute or two, though, she interrupts herself. "It's not
working. I can't focus on the words."

"Try reading them aloud," I suggest.

She nods, then narrows her eyes again. The muscles in her jaw
clench. And then she opens her mouth and says, "Today . . ." Her
eyes flit up to mine in excitement. I grin at her. It's working!

She drops her gaze back to the page. "Today," she says clearly
and firmly as she reads, "I went to—"

And then she slumps forward, unconscious.

CHAPTER TWENTY-SIX

My first thought is that I've killed her.

I grab her wrist, feeling for a pulse.

I fumble around for a panicky moment, and then I feel it. *Thud. Thud. Thud.* Her blood is still pumping through her veins. Not dead. Thank goodness.

And she's still breathing, too. Her chest slowly rises and falls.

"Sarah?" I whisper. I lean down to try to look at her face, but her head is almost touching her bed. "Sarah!" I say a bit louder. She doesn't move.

I have no idea what I'm supposed to do. I still have her wrist in my hand, and I give it a little shake. The movement causes her body to tip to the side, so her head is resting on her arm.

It's like she's a doll, not a person. It's creepy. And frightening.

I hop off the bed and run to the bedroom door. "Mrs. Farrow?" I call. "Mrs. Farrow!" I run to the top of the stairs and call again. "Mrs. Farrow!"

She pops her head out of the kitchen. "Vera? Is everything okay?"

I shake my head frantically. "Sarah—she's fainted. Or something. Her heart's still beating, but she's unconscious."

I expect Mrs. Farrow to panic and run up the stairs, but instead she sighs. "Oh, that girl," she says. "I'll be right there." And then she disappears back into the kitchen, leaving me awkwardly standing at the top of the stairs. I hover there for a minute or two, wondering what in the world I'm supposed to do next, before Mrs. Farrow reappears and heads up the stairs and past me down the hall.

I follow her into the bedroom. Sarah is still hunched over like a limp puppet.

"Hmm, this one must have come on fast." Mrs. Farrow walks over to the bed, reaches down, and places a hand on Sarah's forehead. "Normally by the time she passes out, she's tucked herself up in bed with her pajamas on. Though maybe having you over distracted her from the warning signs."

"So . . . she's okay?"

She gently lifts Sarah's shoulders, laying her back on the bed. "Oh, she will be, sweetheart." She untangles Sarah's crossed legs and spreads them along the bed. Then Mrs. Farrow picks up the journal. She pauses with it in her hands, then looks at me. "She told you about her magic, didn't she?"

I can't see any reason to lie, so I nod.

She sighs. "I tell Sarah not to use her magic so much. I know some traumas might be better off forgotten, but the other things— the smaller things—they're what help us build resilience, you know? Those things might feel like the end of the world now, but someday she'd look back on them and realize how much they made her grow. But she insists on using her magic all the time, even though it makes her pass out. It usually knocks her out for about a day. She'll be up and about again by tomorrow evening. Here, come help me get her under the covers."

Together, we fumble with Sarah's limp body, pulling the covers out from under her, then draping them gently over her.

Should I explain to Mrs. Farrow that this time Sarah wasn't doing magic, she was undoing it? Should I explain everything? "Her magic seems pretty powerful," I say, tentatively.

She tucks the blanket around Sarah's shoulders. "More powerful than she realizes, I think," she says, and my breath catches in my throat. Maybe Mrs. Farrow already knows everything. But then she simply says, "When she erased her memory of her horse, that was heartbreaking."

"Licorice?" I ask, remembering the horse Sarah told me about.

Mrs. Farrow shakes her head. "We've only had Licorice for a couple of years. Before that, we had this beautiful chestnut mare named Sunshine. Sarah loved that horse. They were best friends for six years. But then one day, Sunny spooked and reared up, knocking Sarah off her back. She wasn't seriously hurt, but she felt betrayed, I think. So she took to her journal. She only meant to erase the memory, I think, but . . ." She swallows, hard. "The next time we went to the ranch, it was like Sarah couldn't even see Sunny. Her eyes glazed over her. When I mentioned Sunny, it was like she couldn't hear me. When Sunny came up to the fence, excited to see Sarah and to go for a ride, Sarah walked right past her. I thought maybe it would wear away with time, but it never changed. We ended up having to sell Sunshine and buy Licorice instead. Even today, she can't remember the horse she was best friends with for six years."

At least she didn't erase that horse entirely from existence, but still. Thinking of both horse and rider as Sarah walked past her dear Sunshine, unseeing, breaks my heart.

"Still, it's not all bad. At least she's able to remember her dad as a hero and not as . . ." She fiddles with the end of her braid. "Well, let's just say that I understand why she got so into using her aptitude in the first place." My eyes drift up to Sarah's picture of her trying-to-smile "hero" dad, who sits on her yarn shelf but who I haven't seen anywhere else in the house.

"Let's let her rest," Mrs. Farrow says as she pats Sarah's shoulder. "Come on, I'll walk you out."

Mrs. Farrow already looks burdened down by the complexity of her emotions. I don't want to burden her further by telling her that Sarah's magic has gotten even stronger and she's doing even more than erasing memories now. Besides, it's not really my story to tell.

I look at Sarah, lying there with her hair spread out on the pillow, eyes closed, chest rising and falling. "Can you ask her to call me tomorrow when she wakes up?" Hopefully she'll be okay. Hopefully she'll be okay, and we can try again.

"I will," her mother says with a small smile.

I eye the journal on Sarah's bedside table. I want to take it with me, but Sarah's mom is standing there watching me, ready to escort me back down to the front door. So instead, I simply scoop my purse and mitts off the floor and follow her down the hall, leaving the journal and Sarah behind.

"Do you need a ride home?" Mrs. Farrow asks me as I pull on my coat.

I shake my head. I'm not going home. I'm going to Pete's.

I told Sarah that I wouldn't tell a soul about her aptitude, but that was before I knew that it was erasing people. I guess that's one of the reasons the Bible says you shouldn't swear oaths in the first place; they can get complicated.

I swore that oath to protect Sarah. But now, there are a dozen other, unwritten people who need protecting. And besides, Pete is the other half of me, so if I make a promise, I make it on behalf of both of us, don't I? Plus, I trust Pete with my whole heart. I know he wouldn't do anything to put Sarah in danger.

Still, I throw up a quick prayer on my way to Pete's. No voice—loud, small, or internal—tells me it's wrong.

So when I get there, I tell Pete everything. As we sit on the couch in his basement, I tell him about the notebook. About the yearbook. About realizing that people are disappearing. About Sarah trying to undo the magic and passing out.

"Simon," is all Pete says when I finish.

"What?"

"You said one of the disappeared people was Simon."

"Do you know who that is?"

"No." He shakes his head sadly. "But maybe I should. It's been playing through my head, over and over, since you said it."

"Who was he?" I say, then correct myself. "*Is* he, I mean." Because it's not like he's dead. He's just . . . not currently in the world.

"I don't know." Pete runs his hand over his buzzed head. "A friend? A brother?"

I try to remember what Sarah's journal entry said about Simon. I wish I had the journal with me. "I think it said he has a twin."

At that, Pete's eyes meet mine. "A twin," he says softly. Tears immediately well up in his eyes, but he brushes them away with his sleeve. He swallows hard, like he's trying to hold back a sob.

I try to picture Pete with a twin. With a brother at all. How much would it change him to no longer be an only child? Would he feel less alone? More carefree? "Oh, Petey," I say, putting my arm around his shoulder.

Which is enough to break him. He leans into my shoulder and starts to sob. Tears for a brother he's never known but always felt. Tears for a loss he hasn't been able to put into words.

Somewhere deep down, I feel my own sense of loss. Of my apparent best friend. And of others. Because if Simon is missing from Pete's life, that means he's missing from mine, too. And I suspect he's not the only one.

This moment of grief and understanding, though—this is Pete's.

So I push my own feelings away and rest my head on his as he cries, his tears soaking my plain burgundy shirt.

After a little while, his tears ebb, and he sits up, grabs a Kleenex, and blows his nose. The sound is a foghorn, and as he meets my eyes, we both laugh as if he wasn't just weeping tracks of sorrow down my shirt.

He grabs another Kleenex and wipes his eyes, and then he takes my hand in both of his. "Do you want to talk about it?" he asks, solemnly.

I frown. "About what?"

"About that friend you've lost."

Something twists inside me. "She's not lost. They're not gone forever. We're going to fix this."

Pete cocks a skeptical eyebrow at me. His eyes are puffy and red-rimmed. "How? Sarah apparently can't do it."

"Can't do it *yet*." I pull my hand from his, stand up, and start to pace the room. "She just needs to make her magic stronger." I think through the options as I pace. "The Witches can help us with that, right? We'll borrow their research. And if we need to, we'll bring Mom in. And the ARI."

Pete looks uncertain, but I pat him on the shoulder. "When Sarah wakes up tomorrow, she'll call me, and we'll talk about trying again. You'll see."

Except Sarah doesn't call me on Sunday. She doesn't answer my texts or phone calls Sunday evening. And on Monday, she's not in school. Which I suppose shouldn't be surprising. If doing magic knocks her out for a day, it makes sense that undoing it would knock her out for a bit longer. *Impatience helps no one*, I remind myself over and over, trying to get my anxious mind to listen.

Pete doesn't come to school on Monday, either—he texted me that his parents let him stay home sick—and as I slip into a cafeteria table alone, the thoughts that I've been pushing away since I first read Sarah's diary start to trickle in.

What would it be like to have a best friend?

It's not like I've never had one before. When I was in kindergarten, Susan Kim and I refused to take a nap at naptime unless we had our mats beside each other. And in third grade, Eloise Parker declared a different person as her best friend every week, and even I had my turn. A couple turns, actually, throughout the year.

But something tells me those experiences are the flickering light of a candle compared to the shining light of a spotlight. A spotlight I've never experienced.

Except apparently I have. Did this Riven girl and I eat lunch together? Did we text each other between classes? Did I tell her everything and hear about her everything in return?

As I sit at my table, chewing my ham sandwich, I feel painfully alone.

How can I miss someone I don't even know? It's like I've found out that I was born with a third arm that they amputated, and suddenly I think I understand those phantom pains I've been feeling.

Except I'm getting that arm back. My apparent best friend isn't lost forever. Sarah will wake up and she'll try again—and again and again if she has to—and eventually it will work. Eventually, everyone will be out of that book and back into the world.

Maybe she's awake already and simply not calling me because she's mad at me for making her try when she wasn't ready. Maybe she's trying again right now without me. So I have nothing to worry about. Nothing to mourn. Just a ham sandwich to eat at this cafeteria table by myself, as I watch my phone like a hawk.

A body slips into the seat across from me. "Do you know if they've figured anything out?"

I look up. Cecily Murphy. Her auburn hair is pulled back in a tight ponytail, creating sharp angles in her face and darkness around her eyes.

Except it's not just the ponytail doing that, I realize. It's grief. Unexplained, inescapable grief.

I glance around the cafeteria, which is bustling and loud. "Let's go somewhere quiet," I suggest, and then gather up my things.

We head to the library, which is mostly empty, and find a quiet, abandoned table in the back corner. I slip into one chair, and Cecily takes the seat at the head of the table, rather than across from

me—we're so close our knees are almost touching. Like she understands this conversation needs to take place in whispers.

And then we just stare at each other. Cecily, waiting for me to
begin. Me, not knowing how or where. Because I can't exactly spit
out everything about Sarah. Who knows what Cecily would do with
that information? I barely know her. I can't trust that she wouldn't
put Sarah's life in danger, that she wouldn't unintentionally say
something that gets Sarah whisked away like that Russian kid.

But although I barely know Cecily, there is a cord that binds us
together. The loss of someone we loved once. The loss of someone
we can't remember.

The entries in Sarah's journal come back to me as I stare at
Cecily's hopeful, heartbroken face. Sarah "forgot" her crush
because he was dating Cecily. And she "forgot" one of the Witches,
also because of love. Which means Cecily has lost a boyfriend and
a best friend. All without understanding, without knowing why her
heart is shattered into a million pieces and held together only with
Scotch tape. She is me, just days ago.

So I have to tell her something. She passed her research on to
my mom, and I'm guessing she hasn't heard anything since, just
like me. Though right now I'm the one who knows more than my
mom does. I reach for a lie that will allow me to tell the truth.

"There is a person the ARI is studying. No one we would know,
I don't think. I found the papers in my parents' stuff. He has a
mutated aptitude. It . . . it lets him erase things. People."

I expect Cecily's eyes to go wide with understanding or maybe
do the opposite and narrow in disbelief. But instead she closes her
eyes for a moment, slips her hands between her knees, and slowly
breathes in and out. In and out. In and out.

When she opens her eyes again, she says, "What does that mean—that they're erased?"

"They disappear. And they're . . . forgotten. By everyone, it seems like."

She nods slowly, then bites her lip like she's fighting back tears. "I think I knew one of those people," she says, her voice barely more than a breath.

I nod, too. "You did. Two of them."

Her gaze jerks to mine at that. Perhaps I've overstepped. How would I know from reading confidential research papers that the people who disappeared knew Cecily? Maybe it doesn't make sense to my lie that I'd know such things.

But it feels so wrong for these people to have been forgotten. And it feels right for someone who loved them to remember at least their names.

So when Cecily whispers "Who?" with her eyes full of aching pleading, I tell her.

"The first was your boyfriend. His name was Al." With my terrible memory, I shouldn't remember most of the names in Sarah's journal. But it's like they've all been engraved in stone in my brain. Or like they've brought back to life a little piece of memory that had died.

"Al," Cecily repeats reverently. Her fingers go to the beaded bracelet on her wrist. It's light blue, like the endless sky on a cloudless summer day.

Just speaking and hearing the name Al makes my heart ache for reasons I can't explain, so I rush onward. "The other one was a Witch. Rachel."

Her auburn eyebrows crinkle together at that. "There were four of us?"

I shake my head. "I don't think so. I think it's like she never was." The theory comes to me for the first time, but it makes sense as I say it. It feels right.

Cecily considers this. "So if she never existed, when it came time to do our Witches project last year, we would have still needed a third. So there's a new Witch in her place."

I nod. "Yeah, she was replaced by—"

"No, don't tell me!" Cecily says abruptly.

"What? Why?"

She sits back in her chair. "I love them both so much. I don't want to find myself thinking one of them is some sort of replacement."

I nod. I'm sure she could figure it out if she thought about how she and Hayden have both been feeling loss, while Isla hasn't, but I guess it makes sense why she wants to avoid coming to that conclusion if she can.

Cecily swears and sucks in a breath as she takes in everything I've said. "Man, that aptitude's so powerful."

I sit in silence, giving her time to process. Not that a couple of minutes of silence are going to help that much. It's been two days, and I still feel like I've barely wrapped my mind around it.

Cecily fiddles with the beads on her bracelet. They clink together with quiet *click click clicks*. "It must be getting a lot stronger," she says thoughtfully.

"What makes you think so?"

She pulls the bracelet off her wrist and clenches it in her fist. "Al gave this to me. I don't know how I know that, I just do, somehow. Which means that a few months ago, the erasure was imperfect. It left pieces of them behind. But now . . . with Rachel . . . if it not only erased her but went back in time and changed things, made it as though she never existed . . . left nothing of her behind . . . that's so much stronger."

Her words are desperate, but they give me a strange sort of hope. Because if Sarah's aptitude is strengthening with each use, then surely her ability to undo it can be strengthened in the same way.

"The good news is that we're—I mean *they're* working to fix it. To undo the magic."

"Good," she says. "That's good." The bell rings then, signifying the end of the period, and Cecily pushes back her chair and stands.

"Cecily, you can't tell a soul about this," I say, suddenly realizing that maybe I should have made her promise this a lot earlier in the conversation. "The papers were all confidential. My parents would kill me if they found out I knew and told someone."

Cecily slips the bracelet back onto her wrist. After a moment, she says, "I promise. I won't tell anyone." Then she looks at me. "Do you think they'll manage it? Undoing it, I mean."

I stand, too. "They have to," I say firmly.

Cecily nods. "They have to," she agrees.

And we will. We will undo it. I just need Sarah to wake up and call me first.

CHAPTER TWENTY-SEVEN

Sarah doesn't call until Tuesday evening. My heart lurches as I see her name on the caller ID. It's happening. I'm finally going to get my best friend back—along with whatever else I've lost.

"Sarah!" I answer.

"Hey, Vera," she says quietly. She sounds tired.

"What happened to you? Why didn't you call me back?" There's a time and place for small talk, and this isn't it. Not when the lives of all those people in her journal are at stake. This time, *patience* helps no one.

"I only just woke up this afternoon."

"Wow!" Well, that's a bit of a setback. It's going to take us a long time to get through that notebook if she passes out for three days every time. But if that's what it takes, that's what it takes.

"Yeah. I woke up at the hospital. Mom took me when I didn't wake up when she thought I should."

"You're okay, though? When do you think you'll be up for trying again?"

"Vera, I'm not sure—"

"I know this first try was hard. But your aptitude has become stronger and stronger every time you use it; undoing it will probably follow the same pattern, right? It will get easier every time. We'll have you reading entire entries in no time!"

There's a long pause on the line. And then Sarah says, "I can't. The doctor told me I'm not to try something like that again. It's too hard on my body."

"You have to try again, though."

"I passed out for three days!"

I tighten my fist in frustration. "Yeah, and people don't exist because of you. Don't you think you should make that right, whatever the cost?"

"Vera, the doctor said it might kill me."

I draw in a sharp breath. "Kill you?"

"Yes. So I can't. I'm sorry."

I feel suddenly dizzy. I've been pacing in my room, and I reach for my bed to steady myself, then lower myself to a sitting position on the floor.

I wasn't expecting this. I thought it would be hard, sure. But impossible?

"Can't you at least try?" It comes out in a desperate whisper.

Sarah sighs. "If I die trying to bring one person back, you'll never be able to bring anyone back."

"If we never try to bring anyone back," I snap, "we get the same result."

"Except at least in that scenario, I'm still alive," she snaps back.

The line goes quiet, and for a moment I think she's hung up on me. But then she says, "I'm gonna go. I'm still really tired. I need more sleep." And then she's gone for real.

And so is my hope. Because really, I can't claim to know more than the doctor, who says Sarah could die. And I don't want Sarah to die.

Which means we're not getting them back. The people we've lost, they're gone for good.

I should call Pete and tell him the terrible news. Maybe we should go sit together in the graveyard and contemplate what we've lost.

But right now, the graveyard doesn't feel like the place I want to be. For reasons I can't explain, I want to be here, on my bed. I want to put on an episode of *Doctor Who*. I want to watch *Doctor Who* and I want to cry until no tears are left.

So that's what I do.

We are not actually out of options. I realize this in the middle of the night. I can tell Mom, and she can tell the ARI, and whatever research Mom's already got them doing, they can just direct that toward Sarah. I might not know more than a doctor, but aptitude researchers would. They can figure out how her aptitude works, and then figure out how to undo it. Sure, I probably won't get to know anything they're doing, but if it gets Riven back in my life and Simon back in Pete's, isn't that worth it?

I slide out of bed, bare feet on the cold ground. My parents have the thermostat programmed to drop down a few degrees while we sleep. I grab my gray hoodie off the floor and pull it on while I plod down the hall to my parents' room. Their bedroom door is open, and I can make out both of their sleeping, shadowy forms in the queen-size bed.

"Mom," I whisper into the darkness. "Mom."

The lump closest to me rolls in my direction. The other lump doesn't move. Thankfully, the dad-lump usually sleeps like a log. I don't know how much Mom has told Dad, and I'm not prepared for this conversation to be one against two.

"What is it, pumpkin?" Mom's whispered words are heavy with sleep. "Did you have a bad dream?"

It's been years since I last raced into their room in the middle of the night, running from the monster in my sleeping mind. I'm not sure whether it's endearing or insulting that she thinks that could be happening now, when I'm fifteen. Probably both. "No. I need to talk to you."

That's all it takes to get her to slip out of bed, grab her house-coat, and amble across the cold floor to me. My mom may not be perfect, but she always comes when I need her.

In silent unison, we make our way downstairs to the kitchen, where Mom puts on the kettle. Without asking me what I want, she makes me a hot chocolate with marshmallows and herself a chamomile tea with honey. Her intuition magic must still be asleep up in her warm bed because honestly, chamomile tea with honey sounds much more soothing right now.

Still, I take the hot chocolate without complaint. At least the warmth of the mug feels nice on my fingers.

The light switch is far away, and the thought of light magic makes my heart ache again, so I dismiss the idea of light. Mom does, too, apparently, because we face each other at the kitchen table, surrounded by darkness. I sit cross-legged on the hard chair, tucking my cold bare feet under my bum.

Mom says nothing, just waits for me to talk.

I go to take a sip of hot chocolate, but I can tell before the liquid even reaches my lips that it's going to burn my tongue. So instead, I set down the mug and say, "I've figured it out."

"Figured what out?" Her tone is polite, curious. She's still half asleep and is having trouble putting together the dots.

"About why we feel like we're missing parts of ourselves."

"Oh? You have a theory you would like me to investigate?" She takes a sip of her tea, then jerks back from the cup as she scalds her tongue.

"No, Mom, not a theory. The answer. We feel like we're missing pieces of ourselves because we are." And then I, once again, tell her everything. About Sarah's diary entries and how she's been erasing people by accident with her mutated aptitude and how she passed out for three days when she tried to undo it. "And the doctor says it might kill her if she tries again," I finish.

Mom has sat quietly through my explanation. I've assumed it's because she's so riveted, but as she studies me, I'm suddenly afraid that she thinks it's all nonsense.

But Mom just frowns and taps the arm of her mug. "And you think—you think I'm grieving the loss of one of these people?"

I nod slowly, willing her to believe me.

Mom looks down at her hands. The silence grows long. Her fingers twine together. Then she raises her eyes to meet mine. "Who?" she asks quietly.

I swallow a lump in my throat. "I . . . I don't know. We have names and that's about it." I pause, giving Mom a moment to process the unique grief of losing someone without knowing who. Of missing a piece to a puzzle but not knowing which one.

Tired of all the things I don't know, I spit out one of the things I do. "One girl who was erased—Riven—was my best friend. Apparently. *Is* my best friend. Because you can fix this, right? The ARI can study Sarah's brain and figure out how to bring them all back? Maybe it's something about dark matter after all, and it's reversible."

"Oh, Vera." Mom reaches across the table and rests her hand on mine. "I'm so sorry, but you can't tell anyone about this, ever. Promise me. You can't tell a soul."

"Why?"

"Don't you worry about that, sweetie. And I'll resolve everything that's been done so far. So there's nothing to worry about. Nothing at all." She stands, slides over, and wraps her arms around me in a hug that should be comforting but that mostly just blocks the tiny bit of light in this room from reaching me, plunging me into complete darkness.

"And we'll deal with the grief, okay?" she adds. "I'll book appointments for both of us with a therapist. I promise you we'll get through this. It's going to be all right."

And then she releases me and starts walking away. As if her meaningless reassurances are enough. As if a single hug from my mom is supposed to make everything better. As if I should accept everything she says at face value, always, and never ask any questions. As if I'm a naïve child, sitting here with my hot chocolate and marshmallows while my mommy sips grown-up tea and promises me a happily ever after, and that is enough.

It is not enough.

"Mom! Stop!" My shout echoes through our small, dark kitchen.

Mom whirls around. "What is it, Vera?" she asks, a touch of irritation in her voice.

"You have to stop doing this."

"Doing what?"

"Treating me like I'm a kid. You said yourself, the first time we talked about this, that you can't think of me as like Gertie and Isaac anymore. I've grown up. I have theories, and I've been researching all of this, and I figured out the stuff about Sarah, and I don't understand why we can't talk to the ARI, and I have questions, and you can't keep shutting me out like this."

Mom just stares at me as she stands there in the cold, dark kitchen with her navy-blue housecoat tied tight around her waist and her red plaid pajamas tucked into her socks. I know she loves me. I know she's trying to protect me, not hurt me. But without meaning to, she's doing the opposite.

"You and Dad never tell me anything," I continue. "You won't tell me about your research. You won't tell me about Dad's history with his aptitude. You expect me to just accept, based on his unexplained history, that my aptitude is evil and should never be used on other people's stuff, when actually it's way more nuanced than that, and sometimes unlocking magic can actually be useful, believe it or not.

"Mom, I don't need you to take this problem from me. I need you to help me with it. I need us to work together and figure it out."

The moonlight from the window illuminates my mom's blank

face. She fiddles with the belt on her housecoat for a moment as she studies me. And then she walks back over to the table and sits down. She reaches over and takes my hand. "I just want to keep you safe from pain. Your dad and I—we both do."

I shake my head at her. "Mom, the pain's already deep inside me. You know this because you feel it, too. We've lost people we can't remember. We've got these gaping holes inside us and nothing to fill them with. No memories, nothing. Our only option is to fix this."

That pain immediately writes itself across my mom's face—no, not writes itself, reveals itself. Like it's been there all along, but she's only now letting me see it. "Oh, Vera," she says, her voice breaking, "I so desperately wish we could."

And then she talks to me. Finally, truly talks to me.

She tells me how her colleagues are brilliant and capable and actively bringing about scientific progress. She tells me that she respects them and cares about them. "But I worry about some of them," she admits. "I worry about what they might do, what lines they might be willing to cross."

And then she tells me about the things her colleagues are striving for—from competitive grants, to scientific breakthroughs for the good of humanity, to dreams of a Nobel Prize. And she tells me about a conversation that happened after that boy, Tomas Ivanovich Petrov, was killed. "People started debating whether some sacrifices were worth it for the sake of progress. Whether sacrificing one innocent life for the sake of saving thousands, or even millions, might be a worthwhile cost sometimes. It was this emotionless, intellectual debate with some of them, this discussion of sacrifice. Not everyone, certainly, but some."

My eyes narrow. "And by 'sacrifice,' they mean *murder*."

"Well, I think they think of it as manslaughter at the very worst, not murder, since I don't think killing that poor boy was the point. But yes.

"When we think about stories of people like Tomas, we can't just say, 'Oh, that's Russia and would never happen here.' People who would sacrifice others in the interest of money or success or 'progress'—they are everywhere. Even here. We are not immune."

I frown. I am starting to see what she means. "Well, couldn't we go elsewhere then and—" I break off. "No, that wouldn't work. Her aptitude's too powerful. If the wrong person anywhere found out about it, they could force her at gunpoint to erase anyone they wanted." I think of poor Sarah, with her braces and her sweaters and her desperation to escape any bad experiences, stuck at the mercy of some scientist or terrorist or terrible politician. "Gosh, that would be brutal."

"Very brutal," Mom agrees. "And I'm not willing to risk Sarah's life or happiness like that. Are you?"

"Of course not," I say. The answer comes easily. I had already decided this, when Sarah told me that trying to undo her magic again might kill her, and it continues to be true. I sigh. "So we do nothing. And tell no one."

"We don't tell a single soul," Mom agrees, squeezing my hand. I squeeze hers back.

It's the same thing she demanded of me earlier in this conversation, but coming to the decision together after having talked it through makes the conclusion a little less devastating.

But only a little.

CHAPTER TWENTY-EIGHT

The graveyard is too bright. The sky is barren of clouds, and the sunlight bounces off the freshly fallen snow, making the whole place glitter with light.

"I should have brought my sunglasses," I grumble to Pete.

"Hold this," he says in reply. He hands me the bouquet he's holding, then sets to work brushing off our bench.

I glance down at the flowers I now grasp in my hands. A dozen white roses. A lump rises in my throat so big I feel as if I might choke.

It was Pete's idea to come here today. It's been two weeks since Sarah's failed attempt to undo her magic. Fourteen days of waking up each morning with our hearts split in two. Fourteen days of resignation weighing down every step.

There are still bits of snow on the bench that are stubborn and refusing to respond to the strokes of Pete's mitts, but I don't care. I sit down anyway, and Pete joins me, then takes the flowers back. They should smell of death and sadness, but instead their scent is sweet and perfumey. I'm glad to be rid of them.

We sit there in the silence for a while, shoulder to shoulder. Then Pete says, "You've got the list?"

I take off my mittens and pull a lined piece of paper out of my jeans pocket. On it is a list of names—twelve of them. One from every memory jotted down in Sarah's most recent diary. I looked through the diary to make sure we weren't missing anyone. I was surprised Sarah let me touch the thing again, but when I went to pick it up, her eyes were rimmed with guilt.

"Are you going to tell anyone?" she asked, worry lines etched across her forehead.

"No," I barked, much more harshly than I intended.

"If I could undo it, I would," she said, her eyes suddenly wet.

"I know," I said, more gently, taking the diary from her.

Now, I hold the list of names out in front of us. Some of the names make my gut twist just to look at them. Some of them conjure up nothing.

"What's the first name?" Pete asks as he pulls a single white rose out of the bouquet. This was all his idea. He wanted to hold our own little memorial. To say goodbye.

But how are we supposed to say goodbye to people we didn't even know?

"Al," I say. "Sarah had a crush on him, but he was dating Cecily. She saw them kiss in front of Cecily's house."

"Well, goodbye Al, loved by Cecily," Pete says, and he lays the rose down at our feet, where it blends in with the snow-covered path. Then he looks at me, expectantly. He gestures at the list, like he wants the next name.

"Is that it?"

"Is what it?"

"Is that all you're going to say?"

He shrugs. "What else is there to say?"

I shake my head. "I don't know." Something is bubbling up inside me, like a volcano. The heat rises up my throat. Because something tells me that I knew this boy, but I have no idea how. Was he a classmate? A friend? Family? He could be a cousin that I spent every weekend with since I was two years old, and I'd have no idea.

Pete bumps his shoulder into mine. "Vera? You okay?"

"Let's just . . . let's skip to one that I know." There's only one that fits that description. Riven. Sarah described her as my best friend, which is the only reason I know, at least in part, what I've lost.

Pete pulls out another white rose and hands it to me. I hold it in my mittened hands and take in a deep breath. "Riven," I say, then trail off. She was supposed to be my best friend, but I don't know anything about her. Did she have hobbies? What did she look like? Did she and Pete get along? What did we do together?

I don't know who her family is. Can't explain to them why they wake up each morning with a hole in their hearts. Maybe they don't even live around here. Riven was one of the later entries in the journal, which according to Cecily's theory means the erasure would have been stronger, more complete. Maybe they only moved here when Riven was born; when her entire existence was unwritten, that decision might have been undone.

What things am I missing from my life because she never existed?

I don't know when we met. Have we been best friends since we were five years old, or is she a new addition to my life?

I don't know anything.

"Riven," I try again, quietly, "I miss you." Because that part I do know. I feel it with every atom of my split-apart heart. My life isn't the same without her. "I miss you," I say again. My voice is a whisper that catches on the wind and floats off into the clear blue sky.

We sit in silence for a long moment, and then I look back down at the list. There are so many names. Are we really going to go through each one and feel ripped apart every time? To realize how little we know about each and every one?

"I wish I could have known them," I say, "just for a little while." I'm not sure if I'm talking about everyone or just the names that cause some flicker of emotion inside me. I suppose I'm happy not to know the girl who started that terrible, mocking ugly sweater contest. And for some reason I feel a small vindictive smugness about the guy named Vincent. But the others.

"Me, too." Pete tightens his grip on the flowers. "Should we pray for them?"

"Good idea," I say. Because God, at least, knows each of them in a way that we don't. Knows every forgotten detail about them. And there's comfort in that.

We bow our heads, and I start to choke out, "God, our father—" but then I break off. I lift my head. "Wait."

Pete looks up. "What is it?"

"Riven's parents might not live here."

He narrows just one eye in confusion. "You know who Riven's parents are?"

"No, I don't! I just had a thought. Well, it was Cecily's thought."

Pete looks at me, perplexed. "Okay . . ." He has no idea where I'm going with this.

But I am going somewhere with this. Because something has occurred to me. My thought about Riven's parents came from Cecily's theory that Sarah's magic had become stronger—strong enough to make it so that someone never existed. Strong enough to rewrite the past. It was just a theory, but really, Rachel's replacement with another Witch is proof that it's true.

I'm grinning. There are tears still running down my cheeks, but I'm grinning. "I know what we have to do." I stand abruptly and thrust the list of names at him. "You finish this. I have somewhere I need to be."

And at that, I take off at a run.

CHAPTER TWENTY-NINE

Sarah's mom answers the door.

"Hi, Mrs. Farrow. I'm here to see Sarah. Is she in?"

She invites me inside and tells me that Sarah's in her room and I can go on up.

I take my time removing my boots and coat this time. My idea is still solidifying in my head, and I take these final few moments to get the words right.

Up in her room, Sarah is lying on her bed on her stomach, reading a book. I tap on her open door.

She grins when she sees me. "Vera! What are you doing here?"

"I have an idea. A way you can bring all those people back without hurting yourself!"

"Really?" She pulls herself up so she's sitting on the edge of her bed.

"Yes. I've figured it out. You just need to write about your aptitude. In your diary, just like you wrote about those people." Science is great, but not every answer has to be scientific. Sometimes there's a practical solution.

She frowns. "Okay . . ." she says, clearly not getting it. "To make my magic disappear?"

"Not just disappear. Don't you see? Through your intense emotions and all your practice, you've reached a point where you don't just make people disappear, you make it so they never existed. And if your magic never existed, then you couldn't have written them out of existence in the first place. By unwriting your magic, you undo everything you did with it. Everything will go back the way it was!"

I expect Sarah's face to light up with excitement and realization. But she's still frowning. She brings her thumb to her mouth and chews on a hangnail as a furrow digs into her brow.

"What's wrong?"

She stops chewing. "Well, then I wouldn't have my magic anymore."

"Well, yeah, that's kind of the point. It's not like you're going to use it anymore!" I hesitate, studying her freckled face. "You're not going to use it anymore, right?"

She sits down on her bed. "I talked to Mom about it. There was definitely a time when my magic erased my memories and nothing else, because there are things that Mom remembers, and she wouldn't remember them if I'd erased them entirely.

"So I just need to relearn how to use my magic for that."

I stare at her in disbelief. "What are you going to do? Practice? Erase countless more people in the process?"

She gives me a sly grin. "Well, I was thinking I could practice with dictators, mass murderers, that sort of thing. People no one will miss."

I stare at her, blinking. "So you're going to play judge, jury, and executioner, all on your own?"

"Think it through, Vera. Imagine if I got rid of a murderer who'd killed twelve people. Like you said, it'd be like he never existed, right? So all twelve of those people would be alive again."

Sarah, you're a murderer who's killed twelve people, I want to say. But I don't think pointing that out would persuade her.

And maybe I'm the one who's wrong. Maybe I'm blinded by the tears that threaten to pool in my eyes every time I think of those I've lost. Maybe I can't think straight because of the heaviness of grief trying to drag me to the floor.

"I just want to make the world a better place," Sarah says. "I want my dad to be proud of me." When I look back up at Sarah, she's staring at that picture of her dad, which is surrounded by bright, happy colors of yarn. Unlike her dad, Sarah is smiling. There's no grief weighing down her shoulders, no sadness written in lines around her eyes.

Except.

In her lap, her fingers are clasped together so tightly that her knuckles are white. And that's when I realize something: Deep down inside, she is scared. She's terrified of my idea. Because if she erases her magic, she erases all its effects. Which means all her memories would come flooding back to her.

I turn my gaze to the photo. Her dad looks like a pretty ordinary guy, though I know that means nothing. What sort of bad memories has Sarah erased? Was he a violent abuser or just a self-absorbed screwup who never seemed like he cared? I don't know and neither does Sarah; if I were to ask her, she wouldn't be able to tell me.

And maybe she's right to be afraid. Maybe the weight of all those memories she's erased would break her.

Except as she starts to tell me about which terrible people she's been thinking of erasing, I know that's not true. She is strong enough. She could handle it. But she would never believe me if I told her that.

"What about the good memories?" I say abruptly, cutting into her description of some alleged serial killer in Texas who people are afraid will be found not guilty because the evidence isn't thorough enough. "Don't you want those back?"

Sarah's mouth quirks up at the corners, like she thinks I'm being silly. "I don't erase good memories, only bad."

"Sarah, when you unwrite entire people, you erase everything—good and bad. Don't you feel sad about that?"

An angry crease wrinkles her forehead. "Obviously I feel bad about it. I tried to undo it. And I would—"

"No, no. I don't mean, 'Do you feel guilty?' I mean, 'Do you miss them?'"

Her frustration shifts to confusion. "How do you miss someone who's never existed?"

So she doesn't feel it—the loss, the emptiness. When she first started erasing her memories, she really did erase only the bad. And even when her aptitude strengthened and she erased more memory than that, like with her horse, at least it still continued to exist in the world. But lately she's been erasing entire people from existence, and those people must not have meant much to her. That boy she had a crush on must have been no more than a crush from afar, an infatuation with someone she barely knew. She doesn't understand how her magic doesn't just erase people, it rips a hole in the world, in the hearts of everyone who loved them.

I don't think I could convince her that she's strong enough to handle the bad, but maybe she could understand how hard it is to lose the good. She needs to understand.

Maybe if she erased just one more person. Someone who meant something to her. Maybe if she felt this ache, she'd understand that magic like this can't continue to exist, can't continue to create these holes in the universe. Maybe if she felt the heart-splitting pain of losing her best friend.

I step closer to her. "Sarah, who's your closest friend?"

She hesitates for a moment, her freckled cheeks turning pink. Then she says quietly, "You."

I stop short at that—partly with surprise, partly because it changes everything. Except does it? If I was willing to risk someone else's life, I should be willing to risk my own. Really, this is better. If I had convinced her to risk erasing some innocent person, wouldn't that make me no better than those scientists who killed that boy?

I think of Sarah's journal entry about how she wanted to be my best friend. I think about how eager she has always been to hang out with me and about how I've never seen her with any other friends. I think about how we've genuinely had fun together, during science lab, at her house, at youth group.

I have to believe this will work, that once Sarah feels the pain of loss, she'll do anything to undo it. This has to work. It has to.

I swallow hard, then firm up my shoulders. "Erase me," I spit out before I can change my mind.

"What? I'm not going to—"

"Listen, it's the only way you can understand the real impact of your magic and why it needs to be undone. You need to feel the impact of losing someone you can't remember. It's hard, Sarah. Harder than you probably think.

"All our time working on our science labs together, that'll be gone. When we sat on your floor and played truth or truth, gone. Breakfast with me and your mom, gone. You won't remember any of it. But you'll feel it. You'll feel the loss of it."

She frowns. "I thought you can't remember the people who are erased."

"I can't! But I feel the place they used to be. It's like your magic removes the person from space and time but leaves behind a person-shaped hole."

She raises both eyebrows. "I didn't know that," she says quietly.

My heart skips a beat. Maybe I won't need to go to any extremes. Maybe just explaining it has been enough. "Do you see why you can't continue to have your magic? Do you see why it has to be undone?"

She looks down at her hands, then back to me. "I'm sorry, Vera. I'm really and truly sorry for the pain I've caused you. But don't you think your pain is worth erasing a few serial killers from existence?"

The bile in my stomach threatens to rise up my throat. Because part of me thinks she might be right. But if she's right, that means I'm never getting back my best friend. And Pete is never getting back his twin brother. And holes will continue to be made in the universe.

And that can't be right. Can it?

At the same time that flicker of doubt shoots through my mind, Sarah's gaze shoots again to the picture of her dad. Just for a moment. Just long enough to remind me that it's not about serial killers, not really. It's about Sarah being too afraid to face the hard things. It's about journal after journal filled from start to finish and shoved under her bed. It's about her fear of the dark making all of us miss out on the light.

"I still don't think you understand," I say. "Well, maybe you understand in theory, but you don't feel it. You need to feel it." I grab her diary from her bedside table and thrust it at her. "Go on. Erase me. Do it."

She puts up her hands, refusing to take the book. "I'm not going to do it. No matter how many times you ask."

I'm not asking, I'm demanding, but there's no reason for her to listen to me. At least, no reason yet. I drop the book in her lap. "If you don't do it, I'll tell the whole world about your aptitude. I'll post about it online everywhere I can think of, and the next thing you know, you'll be stolen away by some terrorist organization or another to force you to erase the people they want erased, by threat of torture."

She straightens her shoulders. "You wouldn't do that."

I straighten my own shoulders to match. "I would."

She taps her fingers on her diary. The sound fills the quiet room. *Tap. Tap-tap. Tap-tap.* "And what if it doesn't work? What if I erase you and still don't see a reason to erase my magic entirely?"

"That's a risk I'm willing to take."

"So you're willing to risk your own life for the chance to save twelve others?"

Not just any twelve lives. My best friend. My boyfriend's brother. And others who I'm sure mean something to me, I just don't know in what way. The people I long for with all my heart.

My palms are starting to sweat with nervousness, but I nod. What will it be like to be gone? Will I go to heaven, like I've died, or will my soul be snuffed out of existence just like my body?

She studies me. Then she says, "Okay."

I blink at her. "Okay? As in, you'll do it?"

She nods and picks up a pen from her bedside table.

I swallow. I have to admit, I sort of thought she'd back down. I thought she'd give in and undo her magic entirely. Bring everyone back.

Tears spring to my eyes, and as she balances the diary on her knees and starts to write, I want to swat the pen from her hand. I want to tackle her and force her to stop.

Instead, I dig my nails into the palms of my hands and focus on my breathing. Because one of two things is true: Either Sarah is a psychopath, or when she feels the emptiness of loss, she'll do anything to undo it. And thinking of Sarah's love of horses, her crush on James, her closeness with her mom, the way she knits her own sweaters, her willingness to play truth or truth . . . well, I don't think she's a psychopath.

So I have to believe this plan will work.

Which means instead of tackling her to the floor, I lean against the nearby wall and wait. The wall holds me up, which is good, because I'm not sure my legs are capable of the job any longer. They tremble and shake as Sarah writes and writes, stopping only to tuck her hair behind her ear.

When she finally finishes, she stands and hands the book to me.

I take it from her with shaky hands. My breathing is rushed. When I disappear, will the book fall through my hands and hit the floor with a thud? How long will it take me to disappear? Will I even have time to read what she's written?

I try to slow my breathing as I start to read, forcing my eyes to focus on the words. She's written about how good it feels to forget the bad things, but how she didn't mean to erase the people and how her magic is powerful and—I break off reading and look up at her. "Wait, Sarah, this isn't about me. This is about your aptitude."

Her cheeks flush pink again and she looks down. "You're right," she says in a hushed voice. "Some good things should never be erased." And then she crumples to the floor.

CHAPTER THIRTY

I do not like hospitals. We had to spend a fair bit of time in one a few years ago, when my grandma passed away, and they feel like sickness and death. And there's that overbearing scent of sanitization lingering everywhere.

I have to make a conscious effort not to plug my nose as Pete and I approach the information desk where a security guard sits, typing on a computer. Her hair is pulled back in a tight bun. She looks up from her typing as we reach her desk. "How can I help you?"

"We're here to see Sarah Farrow," I tell her. "F-a-r-r-o-w."

She taps the letters and then clicks on a few things. "Ah, here we go. She's in room B2104." She gives us a series of directions in lefts and rights that I can't keep track of. I'm too busy trying not to crinkle my nose at the smell. She must notice my eyes glaze over, because then she gestures at a sign behind us and simplifies it to, "Just follow these signs to the elevator. Go up to the second floor, then follow signs to section B21."

We thank her, and as she hands us our visitor stickers, she recites a list of rules. "Visiting hours are from eleven to seven. No more than two visitors at a time. No need to sign out or anything when you leave."

"Yes, ma'am," Pete tells her. I nod my agreement.

Then Pete and I head toward the elevators. They're down a long hall, back in the direction we came from, and we walk in silence. Our steps are out of sync with each other, and Pete keeps stepping on the lines. "You're going to break your mother's spine," I say.

"What?"

"You know, 'Step on a line, break your mother's spine.'"

He stares at me blankly. Apparently he didn't have that childhood rhyme.

"Never mind," I say, and we continue walking in silence.

As we round a corner and head toward the elevators, an arm slips through mine. "What'd she say?"

"You were right," I say. "No more than two visitors allowed at a time."

Riven grins, yanks the visitor sticker off my shirt, and sticks it on her own chest. "Good thing we're not big rule followers," she says. "Right, team?"

"Well, maybe we can just go in two at a time," Simon says from behind us.

"I'm sure as long as we're quiet, no one will even notice," Bolu suggests as she punches the button for the elevator.

A moment later, the elevator pings, the doors open, and the five of us pile in.

We follow signs to section B21, just like the security guard said. Every time we pass a nurse or doctor or someone who looks like they belong, my heart races with nervousness that they're going to kick us all out, but no one even gives us a second glance. I guess we all look like we know where we're going.

When we reach room B2104, I head in first, with the other four trailing me in a line. There are four beds in the room, but I spot Sarah right away in the first bed to the right. The bed is raised so she's in a half-sitting-up position, but her eyes are closed and her skin looks pale. You can't even see her freckles in this dim fluorescent light.

"She looks dead," Pete whispers to us. "Is she dead?"

Her eyes fly open. "I can hear you," she says.

Pete gives a little high-pitched shriek and jumps backward, and the rest of us laugh. Even Sarah.

"Shhh," Bolu hushes us with a grin. "You're all going to get us kicked out of here."

"We're only supposed to visit you two at a time," I explain to Sarah.

She nods. "I don't think they're very big sticklers on the rules—as long as we're not disruptive."

"Yeah, Pete, stop being so disruptive." Riven elbows him, and he sticks his tongue out at her like he's Isaac or Gertie.

Bolu pushes through the rest of us and plops down in the chair beside the bed, leaning in toward Sarah. Bolu was uncertain about Sarah as a member of our group at first, but ever since this whole clique of girls at school made fun of Sarah's sweaters, Bolu has been fiercely protective of her. Though Bolu credits something else for the change.

"Are you sure you're okay with me inviting Sarah to youth

group?" I asked her one day. She's so possessive of our group that I worried it might bother her.

But she simply said, "Vera, if the Witches can add a fourth witch when there were only three witches in *Macbeth*, we can certainly add a new person to our own group." I hadn't noticed that about the Witches before, but when I watched for them, I realized she was right. They must have recently added this girl Isla into their group as a fourth Witch.

"So, Sarah, what happened?" Bolu asks now. She's wearing this chic, rose-colored, intricately cabled sweater that she's worn at least once a week since Sarah knitted it for her. "Your mom said you were in a coma for five days!"

She shrugs. "I have no idea. The doctors can't find anything wrong with me. They've done a lot of tests. But I just passed out and didn't wake back up again until yesterday."

"Maybe she swooned when Al walked in the room," Riven whispers to me so the others can't hear. I roll my eyes. Riven has this theory that Sarah has a crush on my brother Al, though I think she's got her eye on James in our science class.

"Did you try to reverse a ton of magic or something?" Pete asks. "Did that once when I was a kid. Simon dared me to basically make my food a salt lick and then eat it, and I tried to be all clever and undo it right before I popped it into my mouth. I passed out instead. Conked my head right on the floor."

"That explains a lot," I say.

"Hey!"

When people stop laughing, Sarah shakes her head. "Nah, I didn't undo any magic."

Riven and Bolu and I share a glance because we know something the boys don't. We found out recently, when Sarah had us girls over for brunch, and the four of us sat on her bedroom floor and played a game of truth or truth. When I asked Sarah what her aptitude was, she admitted that as far as she knows, she doesn't have one.

"What do you mean?" Riven asked her. "Everyone has one."

Sarah just shook her head. "If I have one, it's never showed itself."

Now Simon steps forward and rests one hand on the foot of the bed. "Well, we're glad you're awake and seem to be okay."

It must be the sincerity in his voice that makes Sarah tear up. If there's one thing Simon is good at, it's sincerity. When Sarah told us one time that sometimes she doesn't feel strong enough to handle her complicated, overwhelming feelings of both love and hatred for her dad who died five years ago, it was Simon who reached across the table and told her that while he knew she was strong enough, we were all here to support her at times she felt like she wasn't.

"Thank you, Simon," Sarah says now, and I know, like me, she feels lucky he's in our lives.

"Is there anything we can get for you?" I jump in before things get too mushy.

Sarah's eyes light up. "Actually," she says in a hushed voice, "I'm dying for some pizza. The food here is . . . not so great."

I'm pretty sure there's a pizza place down in the cafeteria. "I'm on it," I say.

"I'll go with you," Riven announces, and the two of us head off.

In the hallway, two girls who look just a couple of years older than us are being wheeled on gurneys one after another down the hall.

"What do you think that's about?" I ask Riven after they disappear around a corner.

"Maybe one's donating a kidney to the other and they're heading for the operating room," Riven suggests.

"Awwwww."

"Would you give me your kidney if I needed it?"

I link my arm with Riven's as we head down the hall. "Riv, if I thought I might lose you, I'd give up anything to save you. My kidney, my arm, my nose."

"Oh, good, I'd love to have your nose. It's so small and perfect."

"Well, it's yours if you need it. I'd even give up traveling through time and space to save you. And world peace. And love."

"Love? What's this about love?" Pete pops up beside me.

"You decided to come with us?" Riven asks.

"Nah, just needed to find the bathroom," Pete says. "Apparently it's this way."

"Ah."

"You can't fool me into a subject change, though. Why're you guys talking about love?"

"We wouldn't tell you even if we were talking about love," I joke. "You're terrible at keeping secrets."

"If I was so terrible at secrets, I'd have told you already that I'm thinking of asking Annika out."

"Again?" Riven asks. "Oh, Pete, don't become one of those stalker guys who can't take no for an answer."

Pete puts his hand over his heart. "I won't. I promise. It's only the second time. And I swear, if she says no, it'll be the last." His gaze drops to his feet and his voice quiets. "But I kinda think she might say yes."

For the briefest of moments, my heart feels like it's been ripped out of my chest. It's like a gasp of air, a sharp stab, a break of a bone.

And then, the feeling is gone just as quickly. I smile at Pete. "Well, I hope she says yes."

"Thank you," he says. And then, "Oh, here's my stop."

He veers off down a hall to the right, toward a BATHROOM sign. Just before he reaches the restroom, though, he turns around and our eyes meet. All he's doing is going to the bathroom, but for some reason I can't explain, it feels like we're saying goodbye.

But then his eyebrows rise, cheery and unburdened, and he grins at me, his bright eyes twinkling. And I wonder, for a moment, if I'm reading everything wrong, and this "goodbye" actually means "hello." Which, I know, is a completely nonsensical thought.

Riven tugs at my arm. "Hey, you okay?"

I look at her, and when I look back, Pete is gone. The moment is gone. This mystery is not something I need to figure out right now.

"Yeah," I say. "Yeah, I'm fine. Let's go get that pizza."

Riven takes an oversize step forward.

"What are you—" Then I realize. She's avoided stepping on a line.

"Gotta keep my mother's spine in tip-top shape," she says with a grin. And so we work our way down the hall, arm in arm, avoiding any lines.

"Hey, would you really give up all those things for me?" Riven asks at the end of the hall as we wait for the elevator.

"You're my best friend," I say. "I'd give up my life for you." The elevator pings. "Oh, except for the time and space one. If the Doctor showed up in his TARDIS to take me off to travel through time and space, I wouldn't give that up for anything. Not even you."

Riven laughs. "Well, good. Because I hope what you'd really do is convince the Doctor to come pick me up as well. Then we could travel through time and space together!"

"Together!" I agree. And as the elevator door closes and the little box we're in starts to move, I can almost imagine that's just what we're doing.

ACKNOWLEDGMENTS

Publishing a book is so much more of a group effort than I realized before becoming an author. While my stories' plots, characters, and words might originate from me, I'm blessed with an entire legion of souls who help me transform them from a seed of an idea to this book in your hands (or your technological gizmo), and I'm eternally grateful for them all.

There is, of course, the Abrams publishing team, full of wonderful folks who are brilliant at their jobs. Thank you to managing editor Amy Vreeland, art director Hana Nakamura, cover designer Maggie Edkins, copyeditor Shasta Clinch, and proofreader Penelope Cray. And especially thanks to my editor, Maggie Lehrman, who is an expert at providing critiques that make me excited to get to work.

An infinite number of thank-yous to my agent, Lauren Abramo, and the rest of the team at Dystel, Goderich & Bourret. Not only does Lauren always have my back, but she is also one of the wisest people I know. I feel so lucky to have such an incredible source of insight and knowledge only an email away.

Thank you so much as well to authenticity reader Blossom Thom and sensitivity editor Talia Johnson. I am so grateful for your honest and insightful comments that helped me improve not only this book and the characters in it, but my writing in general.

And then there are the people who pour their hearts into helping me polish my writing even though they receive nothing in return except my gratitude and love: Kristine Kim, thank you for letting me spoil every bit of Vera's story as I brainstormed and plotted, for giving Vera a title, and for your (distanced) company and support every single day. Mom, thank you for always being my first reader and for your never-ending enthusiasm for my characters. Katelyn Larson, Marley Teter, and Emily Bain Murphy, thank you for always being such brilliant, insightful beta readers. I can always trust you to "get" my books—but more importantly, I can always trust you to "get" *me*!

Finally, there are the people who, along with those already mentioned above, help me survive each day in this hard and strange world.

Thank you to my family—to Mom, Dad, Em, Dan, Dewi, Avery, Anyu, Will, and, of course, Cosmo and Dingo. Thank you to the Moses family, the Slofstra family, and the Priemaza and Baher families. I love you all.

And thank you to all of my found family. My dear friends, Laura Geddes and Erin Dawson. My house church group (including a special shout-out to the real Bolu). My "nieces" and "nephews": Laura, James, Maxx, and Zane. My YAwriters family: Chelsea Sedoti, Josh Hlibichuk, Morgan Messing, Rachel Foster, Jo Farrow, Greg Andree, Tasha Christensen, Leann Orris, Annie Cosby, Katie Doyle, Jess Flint, Phil Stamper, and others already mentioned. And many others.

Thank you to all my author friends, who help me navigate not only this publishing world, but life in general, including Jilly Gagnon, Isabel Van Wyk, Kristen Orlando, and so many others.

Last but definitely not least, thank you to my superhero of a husband, Lorne. I truly do not know how I would get through life without you. I love you and I'm so glad we're a team.

ABOUT THE AUTHOR

Anna Priemaza is an author, lawyer, and university instructor in Edmonton, Alberta, where she lives with her husband. She can never quite remember how old she is, as she knits like an old lady, practices law like an adult, fangirls over YouTubers like a teen, and dreams like a child.